Also by Anthony Doerr

The Shell Collector
About Grace
Four Seasons in Rome

Memory Wall

Stories

ANTHONY DOERR

Scribner

New York   London   Toronto   Sydney

Scribner
A Division of Simon & Schuster, Inc.
1230 Avenue of the Americas
New York, NY 10020

First Scribner hardcover edition July 2010

SCRIBNER and design are registered trademarks of The Gale Group, Inc., used under license by Simon & Schuster, Inc., the publisher of this work.

For information about special discounts for bulk purchases, please contact Simon & Schuster Special Sales at 1-866-506-1949 or business@simonandschuster.com.

The Simon & Schuster Speakers Bureau can bring authors to your live event. For more information or to book an event, contact the Simon & Schuster Speakers Bureau at 1-866-248-3049 or visit our website at www.simonspeakers.com.

Designed by Carla Jayne Jones

Manufactured in the United States of America

1   3   5   7   9   10   8   6   4   2

Library of Congress Control Number: 2009052245

ISBN 978-1-4391-8280-2
ISBN 978-1-4391-8285-7 (ebook)

Some of the stories in this collection have appeared elsewhere, in slightly different form: "Memory Wall" and "Afterworld" in *McSweeney's;* "Procreate, Generate" in *Granta;* "Village 113" in *Tin House* and *The O. Henry Prize Stories 2008;* and "The River Nemunas" in *Tin House.*

For Shauna

Contents

You have to begin to lose your memory, if only in bits and pieces, to realize that memory is what makes our lives. Life without memory is no life at all, just as an intelligence without the possibility of expression is not really an intelligence. Our memory is our coherence, our reason, our feeling, even our action. Without it, we are nothing.

—LUIS BUÑUEL, MY LAST SIGH

Memory Wall

TALL MAN IN THE YARD

Seventy-four-year-old Alma Konachek lives in Vredehoek, a suburb above Cape Town: a place of warm rains, big-windowed lofts, and silent, predatory automobiles. Behind her garden, Table Mountain rises huge, green, and corrugated; beyond her kitchen balcony, a thousand city lights wink and gutter behind sheets of fog like candleflames.

One night in November, at three in the morning, Alma wakes to hear the rape gate across her front door rattle open and someone enter her house. Her arms jerk; she spills a glass of water across the nightstand. A floorboard in the living room shrieks. She hears what might be breathing. Water drips onto the floor.

Alma manages a whisper. "Hello?"

A shadow flows across the hall. She hears the scrape of a shoe on the staircase, then nothing. Night air blows into the room—it smells of frangipani and charcoal. Alma presses a fist over her heart.

Beyond the balcony windows, moonlit pieces of clouds drift over the city. Spilled water creeps toward her bedroom door.

"Who's there? Is someone there?"

The grandfather clock in the living room pounds through the seconds. Alma's pulse booms in her ears. Her bedroom seems to be rotating very slowly.

"Harold?" Alma remembers that Harold is dead but she cannot help herself. "Harold?"

Another footstep from the second floor, another protest from a floorboard. What might be a minute passes. Maybe she hears someone descend the staircase. It takes her another full minute to summon the courage to shuffle into the living room.

Her front door is wide open. The traffic light at the top of the street flashes yellow, yellow, yellow. The leaves are hushed, the houses dark. She heaves the rape gate shut, slams the door, sets the bolt, and peers out the window lattice. Within twenty seconds she is at the hall table, fumbling with a pen.

A man, she writes. *Tall man in the yard.*

Memory Wall

Alma stands barefoot and wigless in the upstairs bedroom with a flashlight. The clock down in the living room ticks and ticks, winding up the night. A moment ago Alma was, she is certain, doing something very important. Something life-and-death. But now she cannot remember what it was.

The one window is ajar. The guest bed is neatly made, the coverlet smooth. On the nightstand sits a machine the size of a microwave oven, marked *Property of Cape Town Memory Research Center.* Three cables spiraling off it connect to something that looks vaguely like a bicycle helmet.

The wall in front of Alma is smothered with scraps of paper. Diagrams, maps, ragged sheets swarming with scribbles. Shining among the papers are hundreds of plastic cartridges, each the size of a matchbook, engraved with a four-digit number and pinned to the wall through a single hole.

The beam of Alma's flashlight settles on a color photograph of a man walking out of the sea. She fingers its edges. The man's pants are rolled to the knees; his expression is part grimace, part grin. Cold water. Across the photo, in handwriting she knows to be hers, is the name *Harold*. She knows this man. She can close her eyes and recall the pink flesh of his gums, the folds in his throat, his big-knuckled hands. He was her husband.

Around the photo, the scraps of paper and plastic cartridges build outward in crowded, overlapping layers, anchored with pushpins and chewing gum and penny nails. She sees to-do lists, jottings, drawings of what might be prehistoric beasts or monsters. She reads: *You can trust Pheko.* And *Taking Polly's Coca-Cola.* A flyer says: *Porter Properties.* There are stranger phrases: *dinocephalians, late Permian, massive vertebrate graveyard.* Some sheets of paper are blank; others reveal a flurry of cross-outs and erasures. On a half-page ripped from a brochure, one phrase is shakily and repeatedly underlined: *Memories are located not inside the cells but in the extracellular space.*

Some of the cartridges have her handwriting on them, too, printed below the numbers. *Museum. Funeral. Party at Hattie's.*

Alma blinks. She has no memory of writing on little cartridges or tearing out pages of books and tacking things to the wall.

She sits on the floor in her nightgown, legs straight out. A gust rushes through the window and the scraps of paper come alive, dancing, tugging at their pins. Loose pages eddy across the carpet. The cartridges rattle lightly.

Near the center of the wall, her flashlight beam again finds the photograph of a man walking out of the sea. Part grimace, part grin. That's Harold, she thinks. He was my husband. He died. Years ago. Of course.

Out the window, beyond the crowns of the palms, beyond the city lights, the ocean is washed in moonlight, then shadow. Moonlight, then shadow. A helicopter ticks past. The palms flutter.

Alma looks down. There is slip of paper in her hand. *A man,* it says. *Tall man in the yard.*

DR. AMNESTY

Pheko is driving the Mercedes. Apartment towers reflect the morning sun. Sedans purr at stoplights. Six different times Alma squints out at the signs whisking past and asks him where they are going.

"We're driving to see the doctor, Mrs. Alma."

The doctor? Alma rubs her eyes, unsure. She tries to fill her lungs. She fidgets with her wig. The tires squeal as the Mercedes climbs the ramps of a parking garage.

Dr. Amnesty's staircase is stainless steel and bordered with ferns. Here's the bulletproof door, the street address stenciled in the corner. It's familiar to Alma in the way a house from childhood would be familiar. As if she has doubled in size in the meantime.

They are buzzed into a waiting room. Pheko drums his fingertips on his knee. Four chairs down, two well-dressed women sit beside a fish tank, one a few decades younger than the other. Both have fat pearls studded through each earlobe. Alma thinks: Pheko is the only black person in the building.

For a moment she cannot remember what she is doing here. But this leather on the chair, the blue gravel in the saltwater aquarium—it is the memory clinic. Of course. Dr. Amnesty. In Green Point.

After a few minutes Alma is escorted to a padded chair overlaid with crinkly paper. It's all familiar now: the cardboard pouch of rubber gloves, the plastic plate for her earrings, two electrodes beneath her blouse. They lift off her wig, rub a cold gel onto her scalp. The television panel shows sand dunes, then dandelions, then bamboo.

Amnesty. A ridiculous surname. What does it mean? A pardon? A reprieve? But more permanent than a reprieve, isn't it? Amnesty is for wrongdoings. For someone who has done something wrong. She will ask Pheko to look it up when they get home. Or maybe she will remember to look it up herself.

The nurse is talking.

"And the remote stimulator is working well? Do you feel any improvements?"

"Improvements?" She thinks so. Things do seem to be improving. "Things are sharper," Alma says. She believes this is the sort of thing she is supposed to say. New pathways are being forged. She is remembering how to remember. This is what they want to hear.

The nurse murmurs. Feet whisper across the floor. Invisible machinery hums. Alma can feel, numbly, the rubber caps being twisted out of the ports in her skull and four screws being threaded simultaneously into place. There is a note in her hand: *Pheko is in the waiting room. Pheko will drive Mrs. Alma home after her session.* Of course.

A door with a small, circular window in it opens. A pale man in green scrubs sweeps past, smelling of chewing gum. Alma thinks: There are other padded chairs in this place, other rooms like this one, with other machines prying the lids off other addled brains. Ferreting inside them for memories, engraving those memories into little square cartridges. Attempting to fight off oblivion.

Her head is locked into place. Aluminum blinds clack against the window. In the lulls between breaths, she can hear traffic sighing past.

The helmet comes down.

Three Years Before, Briefly

"Memories aren't stored as changes to molecules inside brain cells," Dr. Amnesty told Alma during her first appointment, three years ago. She had been on his waiting list for ten months. Dr. Amnesty had straw-colored hair, nearly translucent skin, and invisible eyebrows. He spoke English as if each word were a tiny egg he had to deliver carefully through his teeth.

"This is what they thought forever but they were wrong. The truth is that the substrate of old memories is located not inside the cells but in the extracellular space. Here at the clinic we target those spaces, stain them, and inscribe them into electronic models. In the hopes of teaching damaged neurons to make proper replacements. Forging new pathways. Re-remembering.

"Do you understand?"

Alma didn't. Not really. For months, ever since Harold's death, she had been forgetting things: forgetting to pay Pheko, forgetting to eat breakfast, forgetting what the numbers in her checkbook meant. She'd go to the garden with the pruners and arrive there a minute later without them. She'd find her hairdryer in a kitchen cupboard, car keys in the tea tin. She'd rummage through her mind for a noun and come up empty-handed: Casserole? Carpet? Cashmere?

Two doctors had already diagnosed the dementia. Alma would have preferred amnesia: a quicker, less cruel erasure. This was a corrosion, a slow leak. Seven decades of stories, five decades of marriage, four decades of working for Porter Properties, too many houses and buyers and sellers to count—spatulas and salad forks, novels and recipes, nightmares and daydreams, hellos and goodbyes. Could it all really be wiped away?

"We don't offer a cure," Dr. Amnesty was saying, "but we might be able to slow it down. We might be able to give you some memories back."

He set the tips of his index fingers against his nose and formed a steeple. Alma sensed a pronouncement coming.

"It tends to unravel very quickly, without these treatments," he said. "Every day it will become harder for you to be in the world."

Water in a vase, chewing away at the stems of roses. Rust colonizing the tumblers in a lock. Sugar eating at the dentin of teeth, a river eroding its banks. Alma could think of a thousand metaphors, and all of them were inadequate.

She was a widow. No children, no pets. She had her Mercedes, a million and a half rand in savings, Harold's pension, and the house in Vredehoek. Dr. Amnesty's procedure offered a measure of hope. She signed up.

The operation was a fog. When she woke, she had a headache and her hair was gone. With her fingers she probed the four rubber caps secured into her skull.

A week later Pheko drove her back to the clinic. One of Dr. Amnesty's nurses escorted her to a leather chair that looked something like the ones in dental offices. The helmet was merely a vibration at the top of her scalp. They would be reclaiming memories, they said; they could not predict if the memories would be good ones or bad ones. It was painless. Alma felt as though spiders were stringing webs though her head.

Two hours later Dr. Amnesty sent her home from that first session with a remote memory stimulator and nine little cartridges in a paperboard box. Each cartridge was stamped from the same beige polymer, with a four-digit number engraved into the top. She eyed the remote player for two days before taking it up to the upstairs bedroom one windy noon when Pheko was out buying groceries.

She plugged it in and inserted a cartridge at random. A low shudder rose through the vertebrae of her neck, and then the room fell away in layers. The walls dissolved. Through rifts in the ceiling, the sky rippled like a flag. Then Alma's vision snuffed out, as if the fabric of her house had been yanked downward through a drain, and a prior world rematerialized.

She was in a museum: high ceiling, poor lighting, a smell like old magazines. The South African Museum. Harold was beside her, leaning over a glass-fronted display, excited, his eyes shining—look at him! So young! His khakis were too short, black socks showed above his shoes. How long had she known him? Maybe six months?

She had worn the wrong shoes: tight, too rigid. The weather had been perfect that day and Alma would have preferred to sit in the Company Gardens under the trees with this tall new boyfriend. But the museum was what Harold wanted and she wanted to be with him. Soon they were in a fossil room, a couple dozen skeletons on podiums, some as big as rhinos, some with yardlong fangs, all with massive, eyeless skulls.

"One hundred and eighty million years older than the dinosaurs, hey?" Harold whispered.

Nearby, schoolgirls chewed gum. Alma watched the tallest of them spit slowly into a porcelain drinking fountain, then suck the spit back into her mouth. A sign labeled the fountain *For Use by White Persons* in careful calligraphy. Alma felt as if her feet were being crushed in vises.

"Just another minute," Harold said.

Seventy-one-year-old Alma watched everything through twenty-four-year-old Alma. She *was* twenty-four-year-old Alma! Her palms were damp and her feet were aching and she was on a date with a living Harold! A young, skinny Harold! He raved about the skeletons; they looked like animals mixed with animals, he said. Reptile heads on dog bodies. Eagle heads on hippo bodies. "I never get tired of seeing them," young Harold was telling young Alma, a boyish luster in his face. Two hundred and fifty million years ago, he said, these creatures died in the mud, their bones compressed slowly into stone. Now someone had hacked them out; now they were reassembled in the light.

"These were our ancestors, too," Harold whispered. Alma could hardly bear to look at them: They were eyeless, fleshless, murderous; they seemed engineered only to tear one another apart. She wanted to take this tall boy out to the gardens and sit hip-to-hip with him on a bench and take off her shoes. But Harold pulled her along. "Here's the gorgonopsian. A gorgon. Big as a tiger. Two, three hundred kilograms. From the Permian. That's only the second complete skeleton ever found. Not so far from where I grew up, you know." He squeezed Alma's hand.

Alma felt dizzy. The monster had short, powerful legs, fist-size eyeholes, and a mouth full of fangs. "Says they hunted in packs," whispered Harold. "Imagine running into six of those in the bush?" In the memory twenty-four-year-old Alma shuddered.

"We think we're supposed to be here," he continued, "but it's all just dumb luck, isn't it?" He turned to her, about to explain, and as he did shadows rushed in from the edges like ink, flowering over the entire scene, blotting the vaulted ceiling, and the schoolgirl who'd been spitting into the fountain, and finally young Harold himself in his too small khakis. The remote device whined; the cartridge ejected; the memory crumpled in on itself.

Alma blinked and found herself clutching the footboard of her guest bed, out of breath, three miles and five decades away. She unscrewed the headgear. Out the window a thrush sang *chee-chweeeoo*. Pain swung through the roots of Alma's teeth. "My god," she said.

THE ACCOUNTANT

That was three years ago. Now a half dozen doctors in Cape Town are harvesting memories from wealthy people and printing them on cartridges, and occasionally the cartridges are traded on the streets. Old-timers in nursing homes, it's been reported, are using memory machines like drugs, feeding the same ratty cartridges into their remote machines: wedding night, spring afternoon, bike-ride-along-the-cape. The little plastic squares smooth and shiny from the insistence of old fingers.

Pheko drives Alma home from the clinic with fifteen new cartridges in a paperboard box. She does not want to nap. She does not want the triangles of toast Pheko sets on a tray beside her chair. She wants only to sit in the upstairs bedroom, hunched mute and sagging in her armchair with the headgear of the remote device screwed into the ports in her head and occasional strands of drool leaking out of her mouth. Living less in this world than in some synthesized Technicolor past where forgotten moments come trundling up through cables.

Every half hour or so, Pheko wipes her chin and slips one of the new cartridges into the machine. He enters the code and watches her eyes roll back. There are almost a thousand cartridges pinned to the wall in front of her; hundreds more lie in piles across the carpet.

Around four the accountant's BMW pulls up to the house. He enters without knocking, calls "Pheko" up the stairs. When Pheko comes down the accountant already has his briefcase open on the kitchen table and is writing something in a file folder. He's wearing loafers without socks and a peacock-blue sweater that looks abundantly soft. His pen is silver. He says hello without looking up.

Pheko greets him and puts on the coffeepot and stands away from the countertop, hands behind his back. Trying not to bend his neck in a show of sycophancy. The accountant's pen whispers across the paper. Out the window mauve-colored clouds reef over the Atlantic.

When the coffee is ready Pheko fills a mug and sets it beside the man's briefcase. He continues to stand. The accountant writes for another minute. His breath whistles through his nose. Finally he looks up and says, "Is she upstairs?"

Pheko nods.

"Right. Look. Pheko. I got a call from that . . . physician today." He gives Pheko a pained look and taps his pen against the table. Tap. Tap. Tap. "Three years. And not a lot of progress. Doc says we merely caught it too late. He says maybe we forestalled some of the decay, but now it's over. The boulder's too big to put brakes on it now, he said."

Upstairs Alma is quiet. Pheko looks at his shoetops. In his

mind he sees a boulder crashing through trees. He sees his five-year-old son, Temba, at Miss Amanda's school, ten miles away. What is Temba doing at this instant? Eating, perhaps. Playing soccer. Wearing his eyeglasses.

"Mrs. Konachek requires twenty-four-hour care," the accountant says. "It's long overdue. You had to see this coming, Pheko."

Pheko clears his throat. "I take care of her. I come here seven days a week. Sunup to sundown. Many times I stay later. I cook, clean, do the shopping. She's no trouble."

The accountant raises his eyebrows. "She's plenty of trouble, Pheko, you know that. And you do a fine job. Fine job. But our time's up. You saw her at the boma last month. Doc says she'll forget how to eat. She'll forget how to smile, how to speak, how to go to the toilet. Eventually she'll probably forget how to swallow. Fucking terrible fate if you ask me. Who deserves that?"

The wind in the palms in the garden makes a sound like rain. There is a creak from upstairs. Pheko fights to keep his hands motionless behind his back. He thinks: If only Mr. Konachek were here. He'd walk in from his study in a dusty canvas shirt, safety goggles pushed up over his forehead, his face looking like it had been boiled. He'd drink straight from the coffeepot and hang his big arm around Pheko's shoulders and say, "You can't fire Pheko! Pheko's been with us for fifteen years! He has a little boy now! Come on now, hey?" Winks all around. Maybe a clap on the accountant's back.

But the study is dark. Harold Konachek has been dead for more than four years. Mrs. Alma is upstairs, hooked into her machine. The accountant slips his pen into a pocket and buckles the latches on his briefcase.

"I could stay in the house, with my son," tries Pheko. "We

could sleep here." Even to his own ears, the plea sounds small and hopeless.

The accountant stands and flicks something invisible off the sleeve of his sweater. "The house goes on the market tomorrow," he says. "I'll deliver Mrs. Konachek to Suffolk Home next week. No need to pack things up while she's still here; it'll only frighten her. You can stay on till next Monday."

Then he takes his briefcase and leaves. Pheko listens to his car glide away. Alma starts calling from upstairs. The accountant's coffee mug steams untouched.

TREASURE ISLAND

At sunset Pheko poaches a chicken breast and lays a stack of green beans beside it. Out the window flotillas of rainclouds gather over the Atlantic. Alma stares into her plate as if at some incomprehensible puzzle. Pheko says, "Doctor find some good ones this morning, Mrs. Alma?"

"Good ones?" She blinks. The grandfather clock in the living room ticks. The room flickers with a rich, silvery light. Pheko is a pair of eyeballs, a smell like soap.

"Old ones," Alma says.

He helps her into her nightgown and squirts a cylinder of toothpaste onto her toothbrush. Then her pills. Two white. Two gold. Alma clambers into bed muttering questions.

Wind-borne rain starts a gentle patter on the windows. "Okay, Mrs. Alma," Pheko says. He pulls the quilt up to her throat. "I got to go home." His hand is on the lamp. His telephone is vibrating in his pocket.

"Harold," Alma says. "Read to me."

"I'm Pheko, Mrs. Alma."

Alma shakes her head. "Goddammit."

"You've torn your book all apart, Mrs. Alma."

"I have? I have not. Someone else did that."

A breath. A sigh. On the dresser, three lustrous wigs sit atop featureless porcelain heads. "Ten minutes," Pheko says. Alma lays back, bald, glazed, a withered child. Pheko sits in the bedside chair and takes *Treasure Island* off the nightstand. Pages fall out when he opens it.

He reads the first paragraphs from memory. *I remember him as if it were yesterday, as he came plodding to the inn door, his sea chest following behind him in a hand-barrow; a tall, strong, heavy, nut-brown man . . .*

One more page and Alma is asleep.

B478A

Pheko catches the 9:20 Golden Arrow to Khayelitsha. He is a little man in black trousers and a red cable-knit sweater. In the bus seat, his shoes barely touch the floor. Gated compounds and walls of bougainvillea and little bistros lit with colored bulbs slide past. At Hanny Street the bus pauses outside Virgin Active Fitness, where three indoor pools smolder with aquamarine light, a last few swimmers toiling through the lanes, an elephantine waterslide disgorging water in the corner.

The bus fills with township girls: office cleaners, waitresses, laundresses, women who go by one name in Cape Town and another in the townships, housekeepers called Sylvia or Alice about to become mothers called Malili or Momtolo.

Drizzle streaks the windows. Voices murmur in Xhosa, Sotho, Tswana. The gaps between streetlights lengthen; soon Pheko can see only the upflung penumbras of billboard spotlights here and there in the dark. *Drink Opa. Report Cable Thieves. Wear a Condom.*

Khayelitsha is thirty square miles of shanties made of aluminum and cinder blocks and sackcloth and car doors. At the century's turn it was home to half a million people—now it's four times bigger. War refugees, water refugees, HIV refugees. Unemployment might be as high as sixty percent. A thousand haphazard light towers stand over the shacks like limbless trees. Women carry babies or plastic bags or vegetables or ten-gallon water jugs along the roadsides. Men wobble past on bicycles. Dogs wander.

Pheko gets off at Site C and hurries along a line of shanties in the rain. Windchimes tinkle. A goat picks its way through puddles. Torpid men perch on fenders of gutted taxis or upended fruit crates or beneath ragged tarps. Someone a few alleys over lights a firework and it blooms and fades over the rooftops.

B478A is a pale green shed with a sandy floor and a light blue door. Three treadless tires hold the roof in place. Bars seal off the two windows. Temba is inside, still awake, animated, whispering, nearly jumping up and down in place. He wears a T-shirt several sizes too large; his little eyeglasses bounce on his nose.

"Paps," he says, "Paps, you're twenty-one minutes late! Paps, Boginkosi caught three cats today, can you believe it? Paps, can you make paraffin from plastic bags?"

Pheko sits on the bed and waits for his vision to adjust to the dimness. The walls are papered with faded supermarket circulars. Dish soap for R1.99. Juice two for one. Yesterday's laundry hangs from the ceiling. A rust-red stove stands propped on bricks in the corner. Two metal-and-plastic folding chairs complete the furniture.

Outside the rain sifts down through the vapor lights and makes a slow, lulling clatter on the roof. Insects creep in, seeking refuge; gnats and millipedes and big, glistening flies. Twin veins of ants flow across the floor and braid into channels under the stove. Moths flutter at the window screens. Pheko hears the accountant's voice in his ear: *You had to see this coming.* He sees his silver pen flashing in the light of Alma's kitchen.

"Did you eat, Temba?"

"I don't remember."

"You don't remember?"

"No, I ate! I ate! Miss Amanda had samp and beans."

"And did you wear your glasses today?"

"I wore them."

"Temba."

"I *wore* them, Paps. See?" He points with two fingers to his face.

Pheko slips off his shoes. "Okay, little lamb. I believe you. Now choose a hand." He holds out two fists. Temba stands barefoot in his overlarge jersey, blinking his brown eyes behind his glasses.

Eventually he chooses left. Pheko shakes his head and smiles and reveals an empty palm.

"Nothing."

"Next time," says Pheko. Temba coughs, wipes his nose. He seems to swallow back a familiar disappointment.

"Now take off your glasses and give me one of your barnacle attacks," says Pheko, and Temba stows his glasses atop the stove and leaps onto his father, wrapping his legs around Pheko's ribs. They roll across the bed. Temba squeezes his father around the neck and back.

Pheko rears up, makes exaggerated strides around the little shed while the boy clings to him. "Paps," Temba says, talking into his father's chest. "What was in the other hand? What did you have this time?"

"Can't tell you," says Pheko. He pretends to try to shake off the boy's grip. "You got to guess right next time."

Pheko stomps around the house. The boy hangs on. His forehead is a stone against Pheko's sternum. His hair smells like dust, pencil shavings, and smoke. Rain murmurs against the roof.

TALL MAN IN THE YARD

Monday night Roger Tshoni brings the quiet little memory-tapper named Luvo with him up into the posh suburb of Vredehoek and breaks, for the twelfth time, into Alma Konachek's house. Roger has white hair and a white beard and a nose like a large brown gourd. His teeth are orange. He gives off a reek of cheap tobacco. The band of his straw hat has *Ma Horse* printed three times around the circumference.

Each time Roger has picked the lock on the rape gate, Alma has woken up. He thinks it might have to do with an alarm but he has not seen any alarms inside the house. Roger has given up trying to hide anyway. Tonight he hardly bothers to keep quiet. He waits in the doorway, counting to fifteen, then leads the boy inside.

Sometimes she threatens to call the police. Sometimes she calls him Harold. Sometimes something worse: boy. Or kaffir. Or darkie. As in, Get to work, boy. Or: Goddammit, boy. Sometimes she stares right through him with her empty eyes as if he were made of smoke. If he frightens her he simply walks away and smokes a cigarette in the garden and breaks back in through the kitchen door.

Tonight Roger and Luvo stand in the living room a moment, both of them wet with rain, looking out at the city through the glass balcony doors, a few red lights blinking among ten thousand amber ones. They wipe their shoes; they listen as Alma mutters to herself in the bedroom down the hall. The ocean beyond the waterfront is an invisible blackness in the rain.

"Like an owl, this lady," whispers Roger.

The boy named Luvo takes off his wool cap and scratches between the four ports installed in his head and climbs the stairs. Roger crosses into the kitchen, takes three eggs from the refrigerator, and sets them in a pot to boil. Before long Alma comes shambling out from the bedroom, barefoot, bald, no bigger than a girl.

Roger's hands whisper across his shirtfront, find an unlit cigarette tucked into his hatband, and return to his pockets. It's his hands, he has learned, more than anything else, that terrify her. Long hands. Brown hands.

"You're—" hisses Alma.

"Roger. You call me Harold sometimes."

She drags a wrist across her nose. "I have a gun."

"You don't. You couldn't shoot me anyway. Come, sit." Alma looks at him, confounded. But after a moment she sits. The blue ring of flame on her cooktop casts the only light. Down in the city the pinpoints of automobile lights dilate and dissolve as they travel between raindrops on the windowglass.

The house feels close around Roger tonight, with its ratcheting grandfather clock and spotless sofas and the big display cabinet in the study. He wants desperately to light his cigarette.

"You got some new cartridges today from your doctor, didn't you, Alma? I saw that little houseboy of yours drive you down to Green Point."

Alma keeps silent. The eggs rattle in their pot. She looks as if time has stopped inside her: rope-veined, birdlike, expressionless. A single blue artery pulses crosswise above her right ear. The four rubber caps are seated tightly against her scalp.

She frowns slightly. "Who are you?"

Roger doesn't answer. He shuts off the burner and lifts out the three steaming eggs with a slotted spoon.

"I am Alma," Alma says.

"I know it," Roger says.

"I know what you're doing."

"Do you?" He places the eggs on a dishtowel in front of her. A dozen times now over the past month they've done this, sat at her kitchen table in the middle of the night, Roger and Alma, tall black man, elderly white woman, the lights of Trafalgar Park and the railway yards and the waterfront strewn below. A tableau not quite of this world. What does it mean, Roger wonders distantly, that the countless failures of his life have funneled him into this exact circumstance?

"Eat up now," he says.

Alma gives him a dubious look. But moments later she takes an egg and cracks it on the surface of the table and begins to peel it.

THE ORDER OF THINGS

Things don't run in order. There is no A to B to C to D. All the cartridges are the same size, the same redundant beige. Yet some take place decades ago and others take place last year. They vary in intensity, too: Some pull Luvo into them and hold him for fifteen or twenty seconds; others wrench him into Alma's past and keep him there for half an hour. Moments stretch; months vanish during a breath. He comes up gasping, as if he has been submerged underwater; he feels catapulted back into his own mind.

Sometimes, when Luvo comes back into himself, Roger is standing beside him, an unlit cigarette fixed in the vertex of his lips, staring into Alma's cryptic wall of papers and postcards and cartridges as if waiting for some essential explanation to rise up out of it.

Other times the house is noiseless, and there's only the wind sighing through the open window, and the papers fluttering on the wall, and a hundred questions winding through Luvo's head.

Luvo believes he is somewhere around fifteen years old. He has very few memories of his own: none of his parents, no sense of who might have installed four ports in his skull and set him adrift among the ten thousand orphans of Cape Town. No memories of how or why. He knows how to read; he can speak English and Xhosa; he knows Cape Town summers are hot and windy and winters are cool and blue. But he cannot say how he might have learned such things.

His recent history is one of pain: headaches, backaches, bone aches. Twinges fire deep inside his neck; migraines blow in like storms. The holes in his scalp itch and leak a clear fluid; they are not nearly as symmetrical as the ports he has seen on Alma Konachek's head.

Roger says he found Luvo in the Company Gardens, though Luvo has no memory of this. Lately he sleeps in Roger's apartment. A dozen times now, the older man has kicked Luvo awake in the middle of the night; he hustles Luvo into a taxi and they climb from the waterfront into Vredehoek and Roger picks two locks and lets them into the elegant white house on the hill.

Luvo is working from left to right across the upstairs bedroom, from the stairwell toward the window. By now, over a dozen nights, he has eavesdropped on perhaps five hundred of Alma's memories. There are hundreds more cartridges to go, some standing in towers on the carpet, far more pinned to the wall. The numbers engraved into their ends correspond with no chronology Luvo can discover.

But he feels as if he is working gradually, clumsily, toward the center of something. Or, if not toward, then away, as if he is stepping inch by inch away from a painting made of thousands of tiny dots. Any day now the picture will resolve itself; any day now some fundamental truth of Alma's life will come into focus.

Already he knows plenty. He knows that Alma as a girl was obsessed with islands: mutineers, shipwrecks, the last members of tribes, castaways fixing their eyes on empty horizons. He knows that she and Harold worked in the same property office for decades, and that she has owned three silver Mercedes sedans, each one for twelve years. He knows Alma designed this house with an architect from Johannesburg, chose paint colors and doorknobs and faucets from catalogs, hung prints with a level and a tape measure. He knows she and Harold went to concerts, bought clothes at Gardens Centre, traveled to a city called Venice. He knows that the day after Harold retired he bought a used Land Cruiser and a nine-millimeter Crusader handgun and started driving out on fossil-hunting trips into a huge, arid region east of Cape Town called the Great Karoo.

He also knows Alma is not especially kind to her houseman Pheko. He knows that Pheko has a little son named Temba, and that Alma's husband paid for an eye operation the boy needed when he was born, and that Alma got very angry about this when she found out.

On cartridge 5015 a seven-year-old Alma demands that her nanny hand over a newly opened bottle of Coca-Cola. When the nanny hesitates, grimacing, Alma threatens to have her fired. The nanny hands over the bottle. A moment later Alma's mother appears, furious, dragging Alma into the corner of a bedroom. "Never, ever drink from anything one of the servants has put her lips on first!" Alma's mother shouts. Her face contorts; her little teeth flash. Luvo can feel his stomach twist.

On cartridge 9136 seventy-year-old Alma attends her husband's funeral service. A few dozen white-skinned people stand beneath chandeliers, engulfing roasted apricot halves. Alma's meticulous little houseman Pheko picks his way through them wearing a white shirt and black tie. He has a toddler in eyeglasses with him; the child winds himself around the man's left leg like a vine. Pheko presents Alma with a jar of honey, a single blue bow tied around the lid.

"I'm sorry," he says, and he looks it. Alma holds up the honey. The lights of a chandelier are momentarily trapped inside. "You didn't need to come," she says, and sets the jar down on a table.

Luvo can smell the nauseating thickness of perfume in the funeral home, can see the anxiety in Pheko's eyes, can feel Alma's unsteadiness in his own legs. Then he is snatched out of the scene, as if by invisible cords, and he becomes himself again, shivering lightly, a low ache draining through his jaw, sitting on the edge of the bed in Alma's guest room.

Soon it's the hour before dawn. The rain has let up. Roger is standing beside him, exhaling cigarette smoke out the open bedroom window, gazing down into the backyard garden.

"Anything?"

Luvo shakes his head. His brain feels heavy, explosive. The lifespan for a memory-tapper, Luvo has heard, is one or two years. Infections, convulsions, seizures. Some days he can feel blood vessels warping around the columns installed in his brain, can feel the neurons tearing and biting as they try to weave through the obstructions.

Roger looks gray, almost sick. He runs a shaky hand across the front pockets of his shirt.

"Nothing in the desert? Nothing in a Land Cruiser with her husband? You're sure?"

Again Luvo shakes his head. He asks, "Is she sleeping?"

"Finally."

They file downstairs. Memories twist slowly through Luvo's thoughts: Alma as a six-year-old, a dining room, linen tablecloths, the laughter of grown-ups, the soft hush of servants in white shirts bringing in food. Alma sheathing the body of an earthworm over the point of a fishhook. A faintly glowing churchyard, and Alma's mother's bony fingers wrapped around a steering wheel. Bulldozers and rattling buses and gaps in the security fences around the suburbs where she grew up. Buying a backlot brandy called white lightning from Xhosa kids half her age.

By the time he reaches the living room, Luvo is close to fainting. The two armchairs and the lamp and the glass balcony doors and the massive grandfather clock with its scrollwork and brass pendulum and heavy mahogany feet all seem to pulse in the dimness. His headache is advancing, irrepressible; it is an orange flame licking at the edges of everything. Each beat of his heart sends his brain reverberating off the walls of his skull. Any moment his field of vision will ignite.

Roger tugs the boy's wool cap over his head for him, loops a long arm under his armpit, and helps Luvo out the door as the first strands of daylight break over Table Mountain.

TUESDAY MORNING

Pheko arrives just after dawn to the faint odor of tobacco in the house. Three fewer eggs in the refrigerator. He stands a minute, puzzling over it. Nothing else seems disturbed. Alma sleeps a deep sleep.

The estate agent is coming this morning. Pheko vacuums,

washes the balcony windows, polishes the countertops until they shine a foot deep. Pure white light, rinsed by last night's rain, pours through the windows. The ocean is a gleaming plate of pewter.

At ten Pheko drinks a cup of coffee in the kitchen. Two tea towels, crisp and white, are folded over the oven handle. The floors are scrubbed, the dishwasher empty, the grandfather clock wound. Everything in its place.

It occurs to Pheko that he could steal things. He could take the kitchen television and some of Harold's books and Alma's music player. Jewelry. Coats. The matching pea-green bicycles in the garage—how many times has Alma ridden hers? Once? Who even knows those bicycles are here? Pheko could call a taxi right now and load it with suitcases and take them into Khayelitsha and before nightfall a hundred things Alma didn't know she had could be turned into cash.

Who would know? Not the accountant. Not Alma. Only Pheko. Only God.

Alma wakes at ten thirty, groggy, muddled. He dresses her, escorts her to the breakfast table. She sits in her chair, tea untouched, hands quivering, strands of her wig stuck in her eyelashes. "I used to come here," Alma mutters. "Before."

"You don't want your tea, Mrs. Alma?"

Alma gives him a bewildered look.

Upstairs the memory wall ruffles in the wind. The estate agent's sedan glides into the driveway at 11:00, precisely on time.

THE SOUTH AFRICAN MUSEUM

Luvo wakes in the afternoon in Roger's one-room apartment in the Cape Flats. Beside him is a table and two chairs. Pans in a cupboard, a paraffin stove, a row of books on a shelf. Not much more than a prison cell. Roger's one window reveals the bottom corner of a billboard, perhaps twenty feet away. On the billboard a white woman in a whiter bikini reclines on a beach holding a bottle of Crown Beer. From where he lies Luvo can see the lower half of her legs, her ankles crossed, the pale bottoms of her bare feet flecked with sand.

Through the walls and ceiling ride the racket of the Cape Flats, laughter, babies, squabbles, sex, the rumbles of engines and fans. Six or seven times, in the month or so Luvo can remember sleeping here, he has heard the drumbeat of gunfire. Women with glossy nails and chokers around their throats drift through the open hallways; every evening someone comes past the door whispering, "Mandrax, Mandrax."

Roger is out. Probably following around Alma. Luvo sits at the table and eats a stack of saltines and reads one of Roger's books. It is an adventure novel about men in the Arctic. The adventurers are out of food and hunting seals and the ice is thin and it seems any moment someone will break through and fall into freezing water.

After an hour or so Roger is still not back. Luvo takes two coins from a drawer and scrubs his face and hands in the sink and runs a wet paper towel over the toe of each sneaker. He fixes his watchcap over the ports in his head and rides a bus to the Company Gardens.

He enters the South African Museum around 4 p.m. and steps past the distrustful looks of two warders and into the paleontology gallery. Hundreds of fossils are locked in glass cases, specimens from all over southern Africa: shells and worms and nautiluses and seed ferns and trilobites, and minerals, too; yellow-green crystals and gleaming clusters of quartz; mosquitoes in drops of amber; scheelite, wulfenite.

In the reflections in the glass it is as if Luvo can see the papers and cartridges pinned to Alma's wall floating in the dimness above the stones. Bones, teeth, footprints, fishes, the warped ribs of ancient reptiles—in Alma's memories Luvo has watched Harold return from the Karoo boiling with ardor, enthusing about dolerite and siltstone, bonebeds and trackways. The big man would chisel away at rocks in the garage, show Alma whole amphibians, a footlong dragonfly embedded in limestone, little worm tracks in hardened mud. He'd come into the kitchen, flushed, animated, smelling of dust and heat and rocks, safety goggles pushed up over his forehead, waving a walking stick he'd picked up somewhere, nearly as tall as he was, made of ebony, wrapped with red beads on the handle and with an elephant carved on the top.

The whole thing infuriated Alma: the safari-tourist's walking stick, the goggles, Harold's boyish avidity. Forty-five years of marriage, Alma would announce, and now he had decided to become a lunatic rockhound? What about their friends, what about going for walks together, what about joining the Mediterranean Cruise Club? Retirees, Alma would yell, were supposed to move *toward* comforts, not away from them.

Here is what Luvo knows: Inside Roger's frayed, beaten wallet is a four-year-old newspaper obituary. The headline reads *Real Estate Ace Turned Dinosaur Hunter.* Below it is a grainy black-and-white of Harold Konachek.

Luvo has asked to see the obituary enough times that he has memorized it. A sixty-eight-year-old Cape Town retiree, driving with his wife on backveld roads in the Karoo, had stopped to look for fossils at a roadcut when he had a fatal heart attack. According to the man's wife, just before he died he had made a significant find, a rare Permian fossil. Extensive searches in the area turned up nothing.

Roger, with his straw hat and white beard and tombstone teeth, has told Luvo he went out to the desert with dozens of other fossil hunters, even with a group from the university. He says several paleontologists went to Alma's house and asked her what she'd seen. "She said she couldn't remember. Said the Karoo was huge and all the hills looked the same."

Interest slackened. People assumed the fossil was unrecoverable. Then, several years later, Roger saw Alma Konachek leaving a memory clinic in Green Point with her houseboy. And he started following them around town.

"*Gorgonops longifrons,*" Roger told Luvo a month ago, on the first night he brought the boy to Alma's house. Luvo has engraved the name into his memory.

"A big, nasty predator from the Permian. If it's a complete skeleton, it's worth forty or fifty million rand. World's gone crazy for this stuff. Movie stars, financiers. Last year a triceratops skull sold to some Chinaman at an auction for thirty-four million American dollars."

Luvo looks up from the display case. Footfalls echo through the gallery. Knots of tourists mill here and there. The gorgon skeleton the museum has on a granite pedestal is the same one Harold showed Alma fifty years before. Its head is flat-sided; its jaw brims with teeth. Its claws look capable of great violence.

The plaque below the gorgon reads *Great Karoo, Upper Permian, 260 million years ago.* Luvo stands in front of the skeleton a long time. He hears Harold's voice, whispering to Alma through the dark hallways of her memory: *These were our ancestors, too.*

Luvo thinks: We are all intermediaries. He thinks: So this is what Roger is after. This incomprehensibly old thing.

WEDNESDAY NIGHT, THURSDAY NIGHT

When Luvo wakes, Roger is standing over him. It's after midnight and he is back inside Roger's apartment. The shock of coming into his own, tampered head is searing. Roger squats on his haunches, inhales from a cigarette, and glances at his watch with a displeased expression.

"You went out."

"I went to the museum. I fell asleep."

"Am I going to have to start locking you in?"

"Locking me in?"

Roger sits on the chair above Luvo, sets his hat on table, and looks at his half-smoked cigarette with a displeased expression.

"Someone put a realty sign in front of her house today."

Luvo presses his fingertips into his temples.

"They're selling the old lady's house."

"Why?"

"Why? 'Cause she's lost her mind."

Spotlights shine on the tanned legs of the Crown Beer woman. Below her leaves blot and unblot the cadmium-colored lights of the Cape Flats. Dim figures move now and then through the trees. The neighborhood seethes. The tip of Roger's cigarette flares and fades.

"So we're done? We're done going over there?"

Roger looks at him. "Done? No. Not yet. We've got to hurry up." Again he glances at his wristwatch.

An hour later they're back inside Alma Konachek's house. Luvo sits on the bed in Alma's upstairs bedroom and studies the wall in front of him and tries to concentrate. In the center, a young man walks out of the sea, trousers rolled to his knees. Around the man orbit lines from books, postcards, photos, misspelled names, grocery lists underscored with a dozen hesitant pencil strokes. Trips. Company parties. *Treasure Island.*

Each cartridge on Alma's wall becomes a little brazier, burning in the darkness. Luvo wanders between them, gradually exploring the labyrinth of her history. Maybe, he thinks, at the beginning, before the disease had done its worst, the wall offered Alma a measure of control over what was happening to her. Maybe she could hang a cartridge on a nail and find it a day or two later and feel her brain successfully recall the same memory again—a new pathway forged through the dusklight.

When it worked, it must have been like descending into a pitch-black cellar for a jar of preserves, and finding the jar waiting there, cool and heavy, so she could bring it up the bowed and dusty stairs into the light of the kitchen. For a while it must have worked for Alma, anyway; it must have helped her believe she could fend off her inevitable erasure.

It has not worked as well for Roger and Luvo. Luvo does not know how to turn the wall to his ends; it will only show him Alma's life as it wishes. The cartridges veer toward and away from his goal without ever quite reaching it; he founders inside a past and a mind over which he has no control.

On cartridge 6786 Harold tells Alma he is reclaiming something vital, finally trying to learn about the places he'd grown up, grappling with his own infinitesimal place in time. He was learning to see, he said, what once was: storms, monsters, fifty million years of Permian protomammals. Here he was, sixty-some years old, still limber enough to wander around in the richest fossil beds outside of Antarctica. To walk among the stones, to use his eyes and fingers, to find the impressions of animals that had lived such an incomprehensibly long time ago! It was enough, he told Alma, to make him want to kneel down.

"Kneel down?" Alma rages. "Kneel *down*? To who? To what?"

"Please," Harold asks Alma on cartridge 1204. "I'm still the same man I've always been. Let me have this."

"You're out of your tree," Alma tells him.

On cartridge after cartridge Luvo feels himself drawn to Harold: the man's wide, red face, a soft curiosity glowing in his eyes. Even his silly ebony walking stick and big pieces of rocks in the garage are endearing. On the cartridges in which Harold appears, Luvo can feel himself beneath Alma, around her, and he wants to linger where she wants to leave; he wants to learn from Harold, see what the man is dragging out of the back of his Land Cruiser and scraping at with dental tools in the study. He wants to go out to the Karoo with him to prowl riverbeds and mountain passes and roadcuts—and is disappointed when he cannot.

And all those books in that white man's study! As many books as Luvo can remember seeing in his life. Luvo is even beginning to learn the names of the fossils in Harold's display cabinet downstairs: sea snail, tusk shell, ammonite. He wants to spread them across the desk when he and Roger arrive; he wants to run his fingers over them.

On cartridge 6567, Alma weeps. Harold is off somewhere, hunting fossils probably, and it is a long, gray evening in the house with no concerts, no invitations, nobody ringing on the telephone, and Alma eats roasted potatoes alone at the table with a detective show mumbling on the kitchen television. The faces on the screen blur and stray, and the city lights out the balcony windows look to Luvo like the portholes of a distant cruiseliner, golden and warm and far away. Alma thinks of her girlhood, how she used to stare at photographs of islands. She thinks of Billy Bones, Long John Silver, a castaway on a desert beach.

The device whines; the cartridge ejects. Luvo closes his eyes. The plates of his skull throb; he can feel the threads of the helmet shifting against the tissues of his brain.

From downstairs comes Roger's low voice, talking to Alma.

Friday Morning

An infection creeps through Site C, waylaying children shanty by shanty. One hour radio commentators say it's passed through saliva; the next they say it's commuted through the air. No, township dogs carry it; no, it's the drinking water; no, it's a conspiracy of Western pharmaceutical companies. It could be meningitis, another flu pandemic, some new child-plague. No one seems to know anything. There is talk of public antibiotic dispensaries. There is talk of quarantine.

Friday morning Pheko wakes at four thirty as always and takes the enameled washbasin to the spigot six sheds away. He lays out his razor and soap and washcloth on a towel and squats on his heels, shaving alone and without a mirror in the cool darkness. The sodium lights are off, and a few stars show here and there between clouds. Two house crows watch him in silence from a neighbor's eave.

When he's done he scrubs his arms and face and empties the washbasin into the street. At five Pheko carries Temba down the lane to Miss Amanda's and knocks lightly before entering. Amanda pushes herself up on her elbows from the bed and gives him a groggy smile. He sets still-sleeping Temba on her couch and the boy's eyeglasses on the table beside him.

On the walk to the Site C station Pheko sees a line of schoolgirls in navy-and-white uniforms, queuing to climb onto a white bus. Each wears a paper mask over her nose and mouth.

He climbs the ramp and waits. Down in the grassy field below them forgotten concrete culverts lie here and there like fallen pillars from some foregone civilization, spray-painted with signs: *Exacta* and *Fuck* and *Blind 43. Rich Get Richer. Jamakota dies please help.*

Trains shuttle to and fro like rattling beasts. Pheko thinks, Three more days.

CARTRIDGE 4510

Alma seems more tired than ever. Pheko helps her climb out of bed at 11:30. A clear liquid seeps from her left eye. She stares into nothingness.

This morning she lets Pheko dress her but will not eat. Twice an agent comes to show the house and Pheko has to shuttle Alma out to the yard and sit with her in the lounge chairs, holding her hand, while a young couple tools through the rooms and admires the views and leaves tracks across the carpets.

Around two Pheko sighs, gives up. He sits Alma on the upstairs bed and screws her into the remote device and lets her watch cartridge 4510, the one he keeps in the drawer beside the dishwasher so he can find it when he needs it. When she needs it.

Alma's neck sags; her knees drift apart. Pheko goes downstairs to eat a slice of bread. Wind begins thrashing through the palms in the garden. "Southeaster coming," says the kitchen television. Then ads flicker past. A tall white woman runs through an airport. A yardlong sandwich scrolls across the screen. Pheko closes his eyes and imagines the wind reaching Khayelitsha, boxes cartwheeling past spaza shops, plastic bags slithering across roads, slapping into fences. People at the station will be pulling their collars over their mouths against the dust.

After a few more minutes, he can hear Alma calling. He walks upstairs, sits her back down, and pushes in the same cartridge again.

CHEFE CARPENTER

Friday Roger shepherds Luvo up a sidewalk in front of a different house than Alma Konachek's, on the opposite side of the city. The house is wrapped by a twelve-foot stucco wall with broken bottles embedded in the top. Nine or ten eucalyptus trees stand waving above it.

Roger carries a plastic sack in one hand with something heavy inside. At a gate he looks up at a security camera in a tinted bubble and holds up the sack. After perhaps ten minutes a woman shows them through without a word. Two perfumed collies trot behind her.

The house is small and walled with glass. The woman seats them in an open room with a large fireplace. Above the fireplace is a fossil of what looks like a smashed, winged crocodile spiraling out of a piece of polished slate. All around the room, Luvo realizes, are dozens more fossils, hung from pillars, on pedestals, arrayed in a backlit case. Some of them are massive. He can see a coiled shell as big as a manhole cover, and a cross-section of petrified wood mounted on a door, and what looks like an elephant tusk cradled in golden braces.

A moment later a man comes in and leans over the collies and scratches them behind the ears. Roger and Luvo stand. The man is barefoot and wears slacks rolled up to the ankles and a soft-looking shirt that is unbuttoned. A great upfold of fat is piled up against the back of his skull and a single gold bracelet is looped around his right wrist. His fingernails gleam as if polished. He looks up from the dogs and sits in a leather armchair and yawns hugely.

"Hello," he says, and nods at them both.

"This is Chefe Carpenter," Roger says, though it's not clear if he is saying this to Luvo or not. Nobody shakes hands. Roger and Luvo sit.

"Your son?"

Roger shakes his head. The woman reappears with a black mug and Chefe takes it and does not offer Luvo or Roger anything. Chefe drinks the contents of the mug in three swallows, then sets the mug down and grimaces and cracks some bones in his back and rolls his neck and finally says, "You have something?"

To Luvo's surprise Roger produces from the plastic sack a fossil Luvo recognizes. Roger has taken it from Harold's cabinet. This one contains the impressions of a seed fern, three fronds pressed almost parallel into it, nearly white against the darker stone. Looking at it in Roger's hands makes Luvo want to run his hands across the leaves.

Chefe Carpenter looks at it for perhaps four or five seconds but does not get up from his armchair or reach out to take it.

"I can give you five hundred rand."

Roger lets out a forced, unctuous laugh.

"Come now," Chefe says. "In the sunroom right now I have a hundred of these. What can I sell these for? What else do you have?"

"Nothing right now."

"But where is this big one you're working on?"

"It's coming."

Chefe reaches down for his mug and peers inside and sets it back on the floor. "You owe money, don't you? Men are coming to collect money from you, aren't they?" He glances over with a soft look at Luvo, then looks back. "You have a long way to go to repay your debt, don't you?"

Roger says, "I'm working on the big one."

"Five hundred rand," Chefe says.

Roger gives a defeated nod. "Now," Chefe says, and stands up, and his big, shiny face brightens, as if a cloud has moved away from the sun. "Shall I show the boy the collection?"

UPSTAIRS

There are blanks on Alma's wall, Luvo is learning, omissions and gaps. Even if he reorganized her whole project, arranged her life in a chronological line, first memory to last, Alma's history running in a little beige file down the stairs and around the living room, what would he learn? There'd still be breaks in time, failure in his understanding, months beyond his reach. Who is to say a cartridge even exists that contains the moments before Harold's death?

Friday night he decides to abandon his left-to-right method. Whatever order once existed in the arrangement of these cartridges has since been shuffled out of it. It's a museum arranged by a madwoman. He starts watching any cartridge that for some unnameable reason stands out to him from the disarray pinned to the wall. On one cartridge nine- or ten-year-old Alma lies back in a bed full of pillows while her father reads her a chapter from *Treasure Island*; on another a doctor tells a much older Alma that she probably will not be able to have children. On a third Alma has written *Harold and Pheko*. Luvo

35

runs it through the remote device twice. In the memory Alma asks Pheko to move several crates of books into Harold's study and arrange them alphabetically on his shelves. "By author," she says.

Pheko is very young; he must be newly hired. He looks as if he is barely older than Luvo is now. He wears an ironed white shirt and his eyes seem to fill with dread as he concentrates on her instructions.

"Yes, madam," he says several times. Alma disappears. When she returns, what might be an hour later, Harold in tow, Pheko has put practically every book on the shelves in Harold's office upside-down. Alma walks very close to the shelves. She tilts a couple of titles toward her, then sets them back down. "Well, these aren't in any kind of order at all," she says.

Confusion ripples through Pheko's face. Harold laughs.

Alma looks back to the bookshelves. "The boy can't read," she says.

Luvo cannot turn Alma's head to look at Pheko; Pheko is a ghost, a smudge outside her field of vision. But he can hear Harold behind her, his voice still smiling. He says, "Not to worry, Pheko. Everything can be learned. You'll do fine here."

The memory dims; Luvo unscrews the headgear and hangs the little beige cartridge back on the nail from which he plucked it. Out in the garden the palms clatter in the wind. Soon the house will be sold, Luvo thinks, and the cartridges will be returned to the doctor's office, or sent along with Alma to whatever place they're consigning her to, and this strange assortment of papers will be folded into a trash bag. The books and appliances and furniture will be sold off. Pheko will be sent home to his son.

Luvo shivers. He thinks of Harold's fossils downstairs, waiting in their cabinet. He can hear Chefe Carpenter's voice as he showed Luvo several smooth, heavy teeth that he said belonged to a mosasaur, hacked out of a chalk pit in Holland. "Science," Chefe had said, "is always concerned with context. But what about beauty? What about love? What about feeling a deep humility at our place in time? Where's the room for that?"

"You find what you're looking for," Chefe had said to them before they left, "you know where to bring it."

Hope, belief. Failure or success. As soon as they stepped outside Chefe's gate, Roger had lit a cigarette and started taking shaky, hungry pulls.

Luvo stands in Alma's upstairs bedroom in the middle of the night and hears Harold Konachek whispering as if from the grave: *We all swirl slowly down into the muck. We all go back to the mud. Until we rise again in ribbons of light.*

This wind, Luvo realizes, right now careering around Alma's garden, has come to Cape Town every November that he can remember, and every November Alma can remember, and it will come next November, too, and the next, and on and on, for centuries to come, until everyone they have ever known and everyone they ever will know is gone.

Downstairs

Three eggs steam on a towel in front of Alma. She cracks one open. Out the window the sky and ocean are very dark. The tall man with the huge hands is waving his fingers around in her kitchen. "Running out of time," he says. "You and me together, old lady."

He begins stalking the kitchen, pacing back and forth. The balcony rails moan in the wind, or else it's the wind moaning, or the wind and railing together, her ears unable to unbraid the two. The tall man raises a hand to the cigarette in his hatband and puts it between his lips, unlit. "You probably think you're a hero," he says. "Up there waving your sword against a big old army."

Roger waves an imaginary sword, slashing it through the air. Alma tries to ignore him, tries to focus on the warm egg in her fingers. She wishes she had some salt but does not see a shaker anywhere.

"But you losing. You losing bad. You losing and you going to end up just like all them other old, rich junkies—you going to blitz out, zone out, drift away, feed yourself a steady stream of those memories. Until there's nothing left of you at all. Aren't you? You're just a tube now, hey, Alma? Just a bleeding tube. Put something in the top and it drops right out the bottom."

In Alma's hand is an egg she has evidently just peeled. She eats it slowly. In the face of the man in front of her something suppressed is flickering and showing itself, an anger, a lifelong contempt. Without turning her head she has the sense that out there in the darkness beyond her kitchen windows something terrible is advancing toward her.

"And what about the houseboy?" the tall man is saying. She wishes he would stop talking. "From one angle it probably has the look of sacrifice. Oh, a good boy, fit, speaks English, disease-free, got himself a little piccanin, rides ten miles each way on the bus from the townships to the suburbs to make tea, water the garden, comb out her wigs. Fill the refrigerator. Clip her fingernails. Fold her old-lady underthings. Apartheid's over and he's doing women's work. A saint. A servant. Am I right?"

Two more eggs sit in front of Alma. Her heart is opening and closing very quickly in her chest. The tall black man is wearing his hat indoors. A sentence from *Treasure Island* comes back to her, as if from nowhere: *Their eyes burned in their heads; their feet grew speedier and lighter; their whole soul was bound up in that fortune, that whole lifetime of extravagance and pleasure, that lay waiting there for each of them.*

Roger is tapping his temple with one finger. His eyes are whirlpools into which she must not look. I am not here, Alma thinks.

"But from another angle what does it look like?" the man is saying. "Houseboy lets himself in the gate, through the door, watches you dodder about, moves beyond the edges of your memory. Lined up for his inheritance, surely. Fingers in the till. He eats the sausages, too, doesn't he? Probably pays the bills. He knows the kind of money you're spending with that doctor."

"Stop talking," says Alma. She thinks, I am not here. I am not anywhere.

"I did it to the boy," he says. "I can tell you, you don't even know what I'm saying. I found him in the Company Gardens and who was he? Just an orphan. I paid for the operation. I fed him, I took care of him. I brought him back. I keep him healthy, don't I? I let him wander around."

The headlights of a passing car swing through the yard, drain through the trees. Alma's fear rises into her throat. The headlights fade. The wind flies over the house.

"Stop talking right now," she says.

"You eat now," says Roger. "You eat and I'll stop talking and the boy upstairs will find what I'm looking for and then you can go die in peace."

She blinks. For a moment the man in her kitchen has transformed into a demon: imperious, towering; he peers down at her from beneath a limestone brow. He is waving his terrible hands.

"We all have a gorgon in here," the demon says. He points to his chest.

"I know who you are." She says this quietly and with great intensity. "I see you for what you are."

"I bet you do," says Roger.

NIGHTMARE

In a nightmare Alma finds herself in the fossil exhibit she went to with Harold fifty years before. All the gallery's overhead lights have been switched off. The only illumination comes from sweeping, powder-blue beams that slice through the room, catching each skeleton in turn and leaving it again in darkness, as if strange beacons are revolving in the lawns outside the high windows.

The gorgon Harold was so excited about is no longer there. The iron brace that supported the skeleton remains, and a silhouette of dust marks where it stood. But the gorgon is gone.

Alma's heart quickens; her breath catches. Her hands are at her sides, but in the dream she can feel herself clawing at her own throat.

A column of blue light, swinging through the arcade of museum windows, shows cobwebs, shows the skeletal monsters in their various postures, shows the empty pedestal, shows Alma. Shadows rear up and are sucked back into darkness. The roof above her makes oceanic groans. The purpose of her errand veers past her, there, then gone.

Then she sees. In the window looms a demon. Nostrils, a jaw, a face chalked white with dry skin, and two yellow canine incisors, each as long as her forearms, extend from a scaly pink gum. It exhales through its wet, reptilian nose; twin ovals of vapor cloud the window. Saliva hangs from its lower jaw in pendulous bobs. The light veers past; the beast ducks lower. Its pleated throat convulses; it peers at her with one eye, spider-webbed with filigrees of blood vessels, whole tiny river systems trundling blood deeper and deeper into the yellow of its eyeball, unknowable, terrible, wet—it is a demon dredged up from some black corner of memory; even from across the gallery, she can see into the crypt of its eye, huge and unblinking, and she can smell it, too; the creature smells like a swamp, riparian, of mire and ooze, and a thought, a scrap, a line from a book, rises to her from some abscess of memory and she wakes with a sentence on her lips: *They are coming. They are coming and they don't mean well.*

SATURDAY

The southeaster throws a thick sheet of fog over Table Mountain. In Vredehoek everything looks hazy and tenuous. Cars loom up out of the white and disappear again. Alma sleeps till noon. When she wakes she comes tottering out with her wig in proper alignment, her eyes bright. "Good morning," she says.

Pheko is startled. "Good morning, Mrs. Alma."

He serves her oatmeal, raisins, and tea. "Pheko," she says, enunciating his name as if tasting it. "You're Pheko." She says his name several more times.

"Would you like to sit indoors today, Mrs. Alma? It's awfully damp out there."

"Yes, I'll stay inside. Thank you."

They sit in the kitchen. Alma shovels big spoonfuls of oatmeal into her mouth. The television burbles out news about rising tensions, farm attacks, violence outside a health clinic.

"Now my husband," Alma says suddenly, not quite speaking to Pheko but to the kitchen at large, "his passion was always rocks. Rocks and the dead things in them. Always off to do, as he put it, some grave-robbing. Mine was less obvious. I did care about houses. I was an estate agent before many women were estate agents."

Pheko sets a hand on top of his head. Except for a mild unsteadiness in her voice, Alma sounds much as she did a decade ago. The television drones. Fog presses against the balcony windows.

"There were times when I was happy and times when I was not," continues Alma. "Like anyone. To say a person is a happy person or an unhappy person is ridiculous. We are a thousand different kinds of people every hour." She looks at Pheko then, though not quite directly at him. As if a guest floats behind him and to his left. Fog seeps through the garden. The trees disappear. The lounge chairs disappear. "Don't you think?"

Pheko closes his eyes, opens them.

"Are you happy?"

"Me, Mrs. Alma?"

"You should have a family."

"I do have a family. Remember? I have a son. He is five years old now."

"Five years old," says Alma.

"His name is Temba."

"I see." She drives her spoon into what's left of the oatmeal and lets go and watches its handle slowly fall down to touch the rim of the bowl. "Come with me."

Pheko follows her up the stairs into the guest bedroom. For a full minute she stands beside him, both of them facing her wall of papers and cartridges. She crouches, moving here and there along the wall. Her lips move silently. On the wall in front of Pheko is a postcard of a little island ringed by a turquoise sea. Two years ago Alma worked every day on this wall, posting things, concentrating. How many meals did Pheko bring her up in this room?

She reaches for the photo of Harold and fingers its corner a moment. "Sometimes," she says, "I have trouble remembering things."

Behind her, out the window, the fog cycles and cycles. The sky is invisible. The neighbor's rooftops are gone. The garden is gone. Everything is white. "I know, Mrs. Alma," Pheko says.

VAPOR LIGHTS

It's 9:30 p.m. and the wind is shrieking against the ten thousand haphazard houses in Site C. As soon as he walks in the door, Pheko can tell by the way Miss Amanda has her lips pinched under her teeth that Temba has become ill. A foot away, he can feel the heat radiating off the boy's body. "Little lamb," whispers Pheko.

The queue at the twenty-four-hour clinic is already long, longer than Pheko has ever seen it. Mothers and children sit on upturned onion crates or sleep on blankets. Behind them a bus-length mural depicts Jesus stretching supernaturally long arms across a wall. Dried leaves and plastic bags scuttle down the road.

Two separate times over the next few hours Pheko has to get out of line because Temba has soiled his clothes. He cleans his son, wraps him in a towel, and returns to wait outside the clinic. The vapor lights on their towers above Site C rock back and forth like some aggregation of distant moons. Scraps of paper and skeins of dust fly through the air beneath them.

By 2 a.m. Pheko and Temba are still nowhere near the front of the line. Every hour or so a bleary nurse walks up and down the queue and says, in Xhosa, how grateful she is for everybody's patience. The clinic, she says, is waiting for antibiotics.

Pheko can feel Temba's sweat soaking through the towel around him. The boy's cheeks are the color of dishwater. "Temba," Pheko whispers. Once the boy raises his face weakly and Pheko can see the wobbling pinpoints of the light towers reflected in the sheen of his eyes.

THAT SAME HOUR

Roger and Luvo enter Alma Konachek's house in the earliest hours of Sunday morning. Alma doesn't wake. Her breathing sounds steadily from the bedroom. Roger wonders if perhaps the houseboy has given her a sedative.

Luvo tromps upstairs. Roger opens the refrigerator and closes it; he contemplates stepping out into the garden to smoke a cigarette. He feels, very keenly tonight, that he is almost out of time. Down below the balcony, somewhere past the fog, Cape Town sleeps.

Absently, for no reason, Roger opens the drawer beside the dishwasher. He has stood in this kitchen on seventeen different nights but has never before opened this drawer. Inside Roger can see butane lighters, coins, a box of staples. And a single beige polymer cartridge, identical to the hundreds upstairs.

Roger picks up the cartridge and holds it to the window. Number 4510.

"Kid," Roger calls, raising his voice to the ceiling. "Kid." Luvo does not reply. Roger walks upstairs and waits. The boy is hooked into the machine. His torso seems to vibrate lightly.

After another minute the machine sighs, and Luvo's eyes flit open. The boy sits back and grinds his palms into his eyesockets. Roger holds up the new cartridge.

"Look at this." There is a shakiness in Roger's voice that surprises them both.

Luvo reaches and takes it. "Have I seen this before?"

CARTRIDGE 4510

Alma is in a movie theater with Harold. They are perhaps thirty years old. The movie is about scuba divers. Onscreen, white birds with forked tails soar above a beach. Light touches the tops of breaking waves. Alma and Harold sit side by side, Alma in a bright green dress, green shoes, green plastic earrings, Harold in an expensive brown shirt. The side of Harold's knee presses against the side of Alma's. Luvo can feel a dim electricity traveling between them.

Now the camera slips underwater. Rainbows of fish flit across the screen. Reefs scroll past. Alma's heart does its steady work.

The memory jerks forward; Alma and Harold are in a cab, Alma's camera bag on the bench seat between them. They travel through a place that looks to Luvo like Camps Bay. Everything out the windows is vague; it is as if, for Alma, there is nothing to look at all. There is only feeling, only anticipation, only her young husband beside her.

In another breath they are climbing the steps of a regal, cream-colored hotel, backed by moonlit cliffs. Gulls soar everywhere. A little gold-lettered sign reads *Twelve Apostles Hotel*. Inside the lobby a willowy woman in a white shirt and white pants with a gold belt buckle gives them a key on a brass chain; they pad down a series of hallways.

In the hotel room Alma lets out a succession of bright, genuine laughs. She gulps wine. Everything is pristine; two spotless windows, a wide white bed, richly ruffled lampshades. Harold switches on a music player and takes off his shoes and dances clumsily in his socks. Out the windows, range after range of spotlit waves fold over onto a beach.

After what might be a few minutes Harold leaps the balcony railing and takes off his shirt and socks. "Come with me," he calls, and Alma takes her camera bag and follows him down onto the beach. Alma laughs as Harold charges into the wavebreak. He splashes around a bit, grinning hugely. "Freezing!" he shouts. As he walks out of the water, Alma raises her camera, and takes a photograph.

If they say anything more to one another, it is not remembered, not recorded on the cartridge. In the memory Harold makes love to Alma twice. Luvo feels he should leave, should yank out the cartridge, send himself back into Alma's house in Vredehoek, but the room is so clean, the sheets are so cool beneath Alma's back. Everything is soft; everything seems to vibrate with possibility. Alma tastes the sea on Harold's skin. She feels his big-knuckled hands hold onto her ribs, his fingertips touch the knobs of her spine.

Near the end of the memory Alma closes her eyes and seems to slip underwater, as if back into the film at the moviehouse, watching a huge black urchin wave its spines, noticing how the water is not silent but full of soft clicks, and soon the pastels of coral are scrolling past her vision, and little slashes of needlefish are dodging her fingers, and Harold's body seems not to be on top of hers at all, but drifting instead beside her; they are swimming together, floating slowly away from the reef toward a place where the sea floor falls away and the bottom is too far away to see, and there is only light filtering into deep water, bottomless water, and Alma's blood seems to swell out to the very edges of her skin.

SUNDAY, 4 A.M.

Alma sits up in bed. From the ceiling comes the unmistakable sounds of footfalls. On her nightstand there is a glass of water, its bottom daubed with miniature bubbles. Beside it is a hard-cover book. Though its jacket is missing and half the binding is torn away, the title appears sparkling and whole in her mind. *Treasure Island.* Of course.

From the ceiling comes another creak. Someone is in my house, Alma thinks, and then some still-functional junction in her brain coughs up an image of a man. His teeth are orange. His nose looks like a small brown gourd. His trousers are khaki and stained and a tear in the left shoulder of his shirt shows his darker skin beneath. A faded jaguar winds up the underside of his wrist.

Alma jerks herself onto her feet. A demon, she thinks, a bur-glar, a tall man in the yard.

She hurries across the kitchen into the study and opens the heavy, two-handled drawer at the bottom of Harold's fos-sil cabinet. A drawer she has not opened in years. Toward the bottom, beneath a stack of paleontology magazines, is a cigar box upholstered with pale orange linen. Even before she finds it, she is certain it is there. Indeed, her mind feels particularly clear. Oiled. Operable. You are Alma, she thinks. I am Alma.

She retrieves the box, sets it on the desk that once was Harold's and opens it. Inside is a nine-millimeter handgun.

She stares at it a moment before picking it up. Blunt and colorless and new-looking. Harold used to carry it in his glove compartment. She does not know how to tell if it is loaded.

Alma carries the gun in her left hand through the kitchen to the living room and sits in the silver armchair that offers her a view up the stairwell. She does not turn on any lights. Her heart flutters in her chest like a moth.

From upstairs winds a thin strand of cigarette smoke. The pendulum in the grandfather clock swings back and forth. Out the windows there is only a dim whiteness: fog. Everything seems irradiated with a meaning she is only now recognizing. My house, she thinks. I love my house.

If Alma keeps her eyes straight ahead, and does not look to her right or left, it is possible to believe Harold is about to settle into the matching chair beside her, the lamp and table between them. She can just sense the weight of his body shifting over there, can smell something like rock powder in his clothes, can perceive the scarcely perceptible gravitational tug one body exerts upon another. She has so much to say to him.

She sits. She waits. She tries to remember.

LEAVING THE QUEUE

At 4:30 a.m. Pheko and Temba are still twenty or so people from the clinic entrance. Temba is sleeping steadily now, his arms and legs limp, his big eyelids sealing him off from the world. The wind has settled down. Clouds of gnats materialize above the shacks. Pheko squats against the wall with his son in his lap. The boy looks emptied out, his cheeks depressed, the tendons in his throat showing.

Above them the painted Jesus stretches his implausibly long arms. The light towers have been switched off and a dull orange glow reflects off the undersides of the clouds.

My last day of work, Pheko thinks. Today the accountant

will pay me. A second thought succeeds that one: Mrs. Alma has antibiotics. He is surprised he did not think of this sooner. She has piles of them. How many times has Pheko refreshed the little army of orange pill bottles standing in her bathroom cupboard?

Bats cut silent loops above the shanty rooftops. A little girl beside them unleashes a chain of coughs. Pheko can feel the dust on his face, can taste the earth in his molars. After another minute he lifts his sleeping son and abandons their place in the queue and carries the boy down through the noiseless streets to the bus station.

HAROLD

"Maybe it's something the houseboy didn't want her to see?" murmurs Roger. "Something that made her upset?"

Luvo waits for the memory to fade. He studies Alma's wall in the dimness. *Treasure Island. Gorgonops longifrons. Porter Properties.* "That's not it," he says. On the wall in front of them float countless iterations of Alma Konachek: a seven-year-old sitting cross-legged on the floor; a brisk, thirty-year-old estate agent; a bald old lady. An entitled woman, a lover, a wife.

And in the center Harold walks perpetually out of the sea. His name printed below it in shaky handwriting. A photograph taken on the very night when Harold and Alma seemed to reach the peak of everything they could be. Alma had placed that picture in the center on purpose, Luvo is sure of it, before her endless rearranging had defaced the original logic of her project. The one thing she wouldn't move.

The photograph is faded, slightly curled at the edges. It must be forty years old, thinks Luvo. He reaches out and takes it from the wall.

Before he feels it, he knows it will be there. The photograph is slightly heavier than it should be. Two strips of tape cross over its back; something has been fixed underneath.

"What's that?" asks Roger.

Luvo carefully lifts away the tape so as not to tear the photograph. Beneath is a cartridge. It looks like the others, except it has a black X drawn across it.

He and Roger stare at it a moment. Then Luvo slides it into the machine. The house peels away in slow, deciduous waves.

Alma is riding beside Harold in a dusty truck: Harold's Land Cruiser. Harold holds the steering wheel with his left hand, his face sunburned red, his right hand trailing out the open window. The road is untarred and rough. On both sides grassy fields sweep upward into crumbled mountainsides.

Harold is talking, his words washing in and out of Alma's attention. "What's the one permanent thing in the world?" he's saying now. "Change! Incessant and relentless change. All these slopes, all this scree—see that huge slide there?—they're all records of calamities. Our lives are like a fingersnap in all this." Harold shakes his head in genuine wonderment. He swoops his hand back and forth in the air out the window.

Inside Alma's memory a thought rises so clearly it's as if Luvo can see the sentence printed in the air in front of the windshield. She thinks: Our marriage is ending and all you can talk about is rocks.

Occasional farm cottages rush past, white walls with red roofs; derelict windpumps; sun-ravaged sheep pens; everything tiny against the backdrop of the peaks growing ever larger beyond the hood ornament. The sky is a swirl of cloud and light.

Time compresses; Luvo feels jolted forward. One moment a rampart of cliffs ahead glows chalk-white, flickering lightly as if composed of flames. A moment later Alma and Harold are in among the rocks, the Land Cruiser ascending long switchbacks. The road is composed of rust-colored gravel, bordered now and then by uneven walls of rock. Sheer drops open off the left, then right sides. A sign reads, *Swartbergpas.*

Inside Alma, Luvo can feel something large coming to a head. It's rising, frothing inside her. Heat prickles her under her blouse; Harold downshifts as the truck climbs through a nearly impossible series of hairpin turns. The valley floor with its quilting of farm fields looks a thousand miles below.

At some point Harold stops at a pullout surrounded by rockfall. He produces sandwiches from an aluminum cooler. He eats ravenously; Alma's sandwich sits untouched on the dash. "Just going to have a poke around," Harold says, and does not wait for a reply. From the back of the Land Cruiser he takes a jug of water and his ebony walking stick with the elephant on the handle and climbs over the drystone retaining wall and disappears.

Alma sits, bites back anger. Wind plays in the grasses on both sides of the road. Clouds drag across the ridgetops. No cars pass.

She'd tried. Hadn't she? She'd tried to get excited about fossils. She'd just spent three days with Harold in a game lodge outside Beaufort West: a cramped row of rooms encircled by rocks and wind, ticks on her pant legs, a lone ant paddling slow circles atop her tea. Lightning storms scoured the horizon. Scorpions patrolled the kitchenette. Harold would leave at dawn and Alma would sit in a fold-up chair outside their room with a mystery novel in her lap and the desolation of the Karoo shimmering in all directions.

A glitter, a madness. The Big Empty, people in Cape Town called the Karoo, and now she saw why.

She and Harold had not been talking, not sleeping in the same bed. Now they were driving over this pass toward the coast to spend a night in a real hotel, a place with air-conditioning and white wine in silver buckets. She would tell him how she felt. She would tell him she had reached a certain threshold. The prospect of it made her feel simultaneously lethargic and exhilarated.

The sun lapses across the ridgelines. Shadows swing across the road. Time skids and ripples. Luvo begins to feel nauseous, as if he and Alma and the Land Cruiser are teetering on the edge of a cliff, as if the whole road is about to slough off the mountain and plunge into oblivion. Alma whispers to herself about snakes, about lions. She whispers, "Hurry up, goddamn it, Harold."

But he does not come back. Another hour passes. Not a single car comes over the pass in either direction. Alma's sandwich disappears. She urinates beside the Land Cruiser. It's nearly dusk before Harold clambers back over the wall. Something is wrong with his face. His forehead is crimson. His words come fast, quick convoluted strings of them, as if he is hacking them out.

"Alma, Alma, Alma," he's saying. Spittle flies from his lips. He has found, he said, the remains of a *Gorgonops longifrons* on a ledge halfway down the escarpment. It is toothy, bent, big as a lion. Its long, curved claws are still in place; its entire skull is present, its skeleton fully articulated. It is, he believes, the biggest fossilized gorgon ever found. The holotype.

His breathing seems only to pick up pace. "Are you okay?" asks Alma, and Harold says, "No," and a second later, "I just need to sit for a moment."

Then he wraps his arms across his chest, leans against the side of the Land Cruiser, and slides into the dust.

"Harold?" shrieks Alma. A slick of foamy, blood-flecked saliva spills down the side of her husband's throat. Already dust begins to cling to the wet surfaces of his eyeballs.

The light is low, golden, and merciless. On the veld far below, the zinc rooftops of distant farmhouses reflect back the dying sun. Every shadow of every pebble seems impossibly stark. A tiny rockslide starts beneath Alma's ribs. She turns Harold over; she opens the rear door. She screams her husband's name over and over.

When the memory stimulator finally spits out the cartridge, Luvo feels as if he has been gone for days. Patches of rust-colored light float through his vision. He can still feel the monotonous, back-and-forth motion of the Land Cruiser in his body. He can still hear the wind, see the silhouettes of ridgelines in his peripheral vision, feel the gravity of the heights. Roger looks at him; he flicks a cigarette out the open window into the garden. Strands of fog pull through the backyard trees.

"Well?" he says.

Luvo tries to raise his head but it feels as if his skull will shatter.

"That was it," he says. "The one you've been looking for."

Tall Man in the Yard

Alma is thirsty. She would like someone to bring her some orange juice. She runs her tongue across the backs of her teeth. Harold is here. Isn't Harold in the chair beside her? Can't she hear his breathing on the other side of the lamp?

There are footfalls on the stairs. Alma raises her eyes. She is almost giddy with fear. The gun in her left hand smells faintly of oil.

Birds are passing over the house now, a great flock, harrying across the sky like souls. She can hear the beating of their wings.

The pendulum in the grandfather clock swings left, swings right. The traffic light at the top of the street sends its serial glow through the windows.

The fog splits. City lights wink between the garden palms. The ocean beyond is a vast, curved shield. It seems to boom outward toward her like a loudspeaker, a great loudspeaker of reflected starlight.

First there is the man's right shoe: laceless, a narrow maw between the toe and sole. Then the left shoe. Dark socks. Unhemmed trouser legs.

Alma tries to scream but only a faint, animal sound comes out of her mouth. A man who is not Harold is coming down the stairs and his shoes are dirty and his hands are out and he is opening his mouth to speak in one of those languages she never needed to learn.

His hands are huge and terrible. His beard is white. His teeth are the color of autumn leaves.

His hat says Ma Horse, Ma Horse, Ma Horse.

VIRGIN ACTIVE FITNESS

The bus grinds to a halt in Claremont and Temba sits up and looks out bleary-eyed and silent at Virgin Active Fitness, not yet open for the day. His gaze tracks the still-lit, unpopulated swimming pools through his eyeglasses. Submerged lights radiating out through green water.

The bus lurches forward again. Looking up through the window, the boy watches the darkness drain out of the sky. The first rays of sun break the horizon and flow across the east-facing valleys of Table Mountain. Fat tufts of fog slide down from the summit.

A woman in the aisle stands with her back very straight and peers down into a paperback book.

"Paps?" Temba says. "My body feels loose."

His father's arm closes around his shoulders. "Loose?"

The boy's eyes shut. "Loose," he murmurs.

"We're going to get you some medicine," Pheko says. "You just rest. You just hang on, little lamb."

Dawn

Luvo is detaching himself from the remote device when he hears Roger say, from the stairwell, "Now, wait one minute." Then something explodes downstairs. Every molecule in the upstairs bedroom feels as if it has been jolted awake. The windows rattle. The cartridges on the wall quiver. In the shuddering concussion afterward Luvo hears Roger fall down the stairs and exhale a single sob, as if expelling all of his remaining breath at once.

Luvo sits paralyzed on the edge of the bed. The grandfather clock resumes its metronomic advance. Someone downstairs says something so quietly that Luvo cannot hear it. His gaze catches on a small, inexplicable watercolor of an airborne boat among the hundreds of papers on the wall in front of him, a sailboat gliding through clouds. He has seen it a hundred times before but has never actually looked at it. Sails straining, clouds floating happily past.

Gradually the molecules in the air around Luvo seem to return to their former states. He hears no more from down-

ANTHONY DOERR

stairs except the grandfather clock, banging away in the living room. Roger has been shot, he thinks. Someone has shot Roger. And Roger has the cartridge with the *X* on it in his shirt pocket.

A low breeze drifts through the open window. The pages on Alma's wall fan out in front of him like a flower, like a mind turned inside out.

Luvo listens to the clock, counts to a hundred. He can still see Harold in the gravel beside the Land Cruiser, his face a mask, dust stuck to his eyes, saliva gleaming on his chin and throat.

Eventually Luvo crawls across the floor and peers down the stairwell. Roger's tall body is at the bottom, slumped over onto itself, folded almost in half. His hat is still on. His arms are crimped underneath him. A portion of his face is gone. A halo of blood has pooled around his head on the tile.

Luvo lies back on the carpet, sees Alma's immaculate room at the Twelve Apostles Hotel, sees a mountain range rush past the dusty windscreen of a truck. Sees Harold's legs twitching beneath him in the gravel.

What is there in Luvo's life that makes sense? Dusk in the Karoo becomes dawn in Cape Town. What happened four years ago is relived twenty minutes ago. An old woman's life becomes a young man's. Memory-watcher meets memory-keeper.

Luvo stands. He plucks cartridges off the wall and sticks them in his pockets. Forty, fifty of them. Once his pockets are full he moves toward the stairwell, but pauses and looks back. The little room, the spotless carpet, the washed window. On the bedspread a thousand identical roses intertwine. He takes the photograph of Harold walking out of the sea and slips it inside his shirt. He sets Cartridge 4510 in the center of the coverlet where someone might find it.

Then he stands at the top of the stairwell, collecting himself. From the living room—from Roger—rises a smell of blood

56

and gunpowder. An odor more grim and nauseating than Luvo expected.

Luvo is about to walk down the stairs when the rape gate rattles and he hears a key slip into the deadbolt of the front door.

CLOCK

Perhaps the last thing in the world Pheko is prepared to see is a man facedown at the bottom of Alma's stainless steel staircase lying in a puddle of blood.

Temba is asleep again, a hot weight across his father's back. Pheko is out of breath and sweating from carrying the boy up the hill. He sees the dead man first and then the blood but still it takes him several more seconds to absorb it all. Parallelograms of morning light fall through the balcony doors.

Down the hallway, in the kitchen, Alma is sitting at the kitchen table, steadily turning the pages of a magazine. She is barefoot.

The questions come too quickly to sort out. How did this man get in? Was he killed with a gun? Did Mrs. Alma do the killing? Where is the gun? Pheko feels the heat radiating off his son into his back. He wants suddenly for everything to go away. The whole world to go away.

I should run, he thinks. I should not be here. Instead he carries his son over the body, stepping over the blood, past Alma in the kitchen. He continues out the back door of the kitchen and into the garden and sets the boy in a lounge chair and returns inside to retrieve the white chenille blanket off the foot of Alma's bed and wraps the boy in it. Then inside again for Alma's pill bottles. His hands shake as he tries to read the labels. He ends up choosing two types of antibiotic of which

ANTHONY DOERR

there are full bottles and crushing them together into a spoon-ful of honey. Alma does not look up from the pages as she turns them, one, then the next, then the next, her stare lost and unknowable and reptilian.

"Thirsty," she says.

"Just a moment, Mrs. Alma," says Pheko. In the garden he sticks the spoon in Temba's mouth and makes sure the boy swallows it down and then he goes back into the kitchen and pockets the antibiotics and listens to Alma snap the pages for-ward awhile, and puts on the coffeepot, and when he is sure he will be able to speak clearly he pulls his telephone from his pocket and calls the police.

BOY FALLING FROM THE SKY

Temba is looking into the shifting, inarticulate shapes of Alma's backyard leaves when a boy falls from the sky. He crashes into some hedges and clambers out onto the grass and places his head in the center of the morning sun and peers down at Temba with a corona of light spilling out around his head.

"Temba?" the silhouette says. His voice is hoarse and unsteady. His ears glow pink where the sunlight passes through them. He speaks in English. "Are you Temba?"

"My glasses," says Temba. The garden is a sea of black and white. The face in front of him shifts and a sudden avalanche of light pierces Temba's eyes. Something bubbles inside his gut. His tongue tastes of the sweet, sticky medicine his father spooned into his mouth.

Now hands are putting on Temba's glasses for him. Temba squints up, blinking.

"My paps works here."

58

"I know." The boy is whispering. Fear travels through his voice.

Temba tries whispering, too. "I'm not supposed to be here."

"Me either."

Temba's eyesight comes back to him. Big palms and rose-bushes and a cabbage tree loom against the garden wall. He tries to make out the boy standing over him against the back-drop of the sun. He has smooth brown skin and a wool cap over his lightly felted head. He reaches down and tugs the blanket up around Temba's shoulders.

"My body is sick," says Temba.

"Shhh," whispers the boy. He takes off his hat and presses three fingers against his temple as if reining in a headache. Temba glimpses strange outlines on the boy's scalp, but then the boy puts his cap back on and sniffs and glances nervously toward the house.

"I'm Temba. I live at B478A, Site C, Khayelitsha."

"Okay, Temba. You should rest now."

Temba looks toward the house. Its sleek profile looms up above the hedges, cut with silver windowframes and chrome balcony railings.

"I'll rest now," he says.

"Good," whispers the boy with the smooth skin and the glowing ears. Then he takes five quick steps across the back-yard and leaps up between the trunks of two palms and scales the garden wall and is gone.

THE DAYS FOLLOWING

Harold's dying face, Roger's crumpled frame, and the filmy eyes of Temba all rotate through Luvo's thoughts like some appalling picture show. Death succeeding death in relentless concatenation.

He spends the rest of Sunday hiding inside the labyrinthine paths of the Company Gardens, crouched among the leaves. Squirrels run here and there; city workers string Christmas lights through a lane of oaks. Are people looking for him? Are the police?

Monday Luvo crouches in the alley outside a chophouse watching the news on a bar television through an open window. It takes several hours before he sees it: An elderly woman has shot an intruder in Vredehoek. A reporter stands on Alma's street, a few houses away, and talks into a microphone. In the background a stripe of red-and-yellow police tape stretches across the road. The reporter says nothing about Alma's dementia, nothing about Pheko or Temba, nothing about accomplices. The whole report lasts perhaps twenty-five seconds.

He does not return to Roger's apartment. No one comes for him. No Roger shaking him awake in the night, hustling him into a taxi. No Pheko come to demand answers. No ghosts of Harold or Alma. Tuesday morning Luvo rides a bus up to Derry Street and walks up onto the slopes of Table Mountain, through the sleek, hushed houses of Vredehoek. There is a blue van in front of Alma's house and the garage door is open. The garage is absolutely empty. No Mercedes, no realty sign. No lights. The police tape is still there. As he stands beside the gutter a moment a dark-skinned woman passes behind a window pushing a vacuum cleaner.

That afternoon he sells Alma's memory cartridges to a trader named Cabbage. Cabbage calls a red-eyed teenager out from the trees to run them through a ramshackle memory machine. The transaction takes more than two hours. "They real," affirms the teenager finally, and Cabbage looks Luvo up and down before offering him 3,300 rand for the whole batch.

Luvo studies the cartridges in the bottom of his backpack. Sixty-one of them. Pinpoints of a life. He asks the trader if he can buy the remote device, with its dirty-looking, warped headgear, but Cabbage only grins and shakes his head. "Costs more than you'll ever have," he says, and snaps his bag shut.

Afterward Luvo walks back up through the Company Gardens to the South African Museum and stands in the fossil room with his money in his pocket. He gazes into every display case. Brachiopod, paper mussel, marsh clam. Horsetail, liverwort, seed fern.

Outside a light rain starts to fall. A warder ambles through, announces to no one in particular that it's closing time. Two tourists come through the door, glance about, and leave. Soon the room is empty. Luvo stands in front of the gorgon a long time. It's a slender-headed skeleton, stalking something on its long legs, its huge canine incisors showing.

At the street market in Greenmarket Square Luvo buys the following things: a kelly green duffel bag, nine loaves of white bread, a paint scraper, a hammer, a sack of oranges, four two-liter bottles of water, a polyester sleeping bag, and a puffy red parka that says *Kansas City Chiefs* across the back. When he's done, he has 900 rand in his pocket, all the money left him in the world.

B478A

Pheko gazes up into the darkness of his little house and listens to the rain rattle on the roof. Beside him Temba blinks his big eyes, waiting for sleep to fall away. The boy's fever has broken; he is slowly coming back into himself.

Pheko is thinking about his cousin who says he might be able to find him work loading powdered cement into bags for shipping. He's thinking about the fur of dead insects on the window screens, the tracks of ants marching along the floor. And he's thinking about Alma.

For six hours the police asked Pheko questions. He did not know where Temba had been taken; he hardly knew where he was. Then they released him. They let him keep the antibiotics, they even paid his train fare. After leaving her kitchen that morning with the police, Alma still turning the pages of that thick, five-year-old fashion magazine, he has not seen Alma again.

All around the little house are things he has been given by Harold and Alma over the years, castoffs and hand-me-downs: a dented soup pot, a plastic comb, an enameled mug that says *Porter Properties Summer Picnic.* A dish towel, a plastic colander, a thermometer. How many hours had Pheko spent with Alma over the past twenty years? She is engraved into him; she is part of him.

"I saw a boy," Temba says. "He looked like an angel from church."

"In your dream?"

"Maybe," says Temba. "Maybe it was a dream."

SWARTBERG PASS

On the morning bus heading east from Cape Town there's the impossible straightness of the N1 cutting across the desert all the way to the horizon. The road is swallowed by the bus's big

tinted windscreen like an infinite black ribbon. On either side
of the N1, dry grasslands run away from the highway's edges
into sheaves of brown mountains. Everywhere there is light
and stone and unimaginable distance.

Luvo feels simultaneously frightened and awed. As far as
he can remember, he has never been outside of Cape Town,
though he has Alma's memories riding along inside him, the
bright blue coves of Mozambique, rain in Venice, a line of trav-
elers in suits standing in a first-class queue in a Johannesburg
train station.

He pulls the photograph of Harold from his backpack. Harold, half-grinning, half-grimacing, walking out of the sea. He
thinks of Roger, lying dead on the floor of Alma's living room.
He hears Chefe Carpenter say, "You owe money, don't you?"

It's afternoon when Luvo clambers off at the intersection for
Prince Albert Road. A gas station and a few aluminum trailers
huddle under a brass-colored sun. Black eagles trace slow ovals
a half-mile above the road. Three friendly-looking women sit
beneath a vinyl umbrella and sell cheese and marmalade and
sticky rolls. "It's warm," they tease. "Take off your hat." Luvo
shakes his head. He chews a roll and waits with his duffel bag.
It's nearly dusk before a Bantu sales representative in a rented
Honda slows for him.

"Where you going?"

"The Swartberg."

"You mean over the Swartberg?"

"Yes, sir."

The driver reaches across and pushes the door open. Luvo
climbs in. They turn southeast. The sun goes down in a wash
of orange and moonlight spills onto the Karoo.

The pavement ends. The man drives the last hour through
the badlands in silence, with the startled eyes of bat-eared foxes

reflecting now and then in the high beams and a vast spread of stars keeping pace above and curtains of dust floating up behind the rear tires.

The car vibrates beneath them. Soon there is no traffic in either direction. Great walls of stone rear up, darker than the sky. They come around a turn and a rectangular brown sign, its top half pocked from a shotgun blast, reads *Swartbergpas*. Luvo thinks: Harold and Alma saw this same sign. Before Harold died they drove right past this spot.

Fifteen minutes later the Honda is climbing past one of the road's countless switchbacks when Luvo says, "Please stop the car here."

The man slows. "Stop?"

"Yes, sir."

"You sick?"

"No, sir."

The little car shudders as it idles. Luvo unclips his seat belt. The man blinks at him in the darkness. "You're getting out here?"

"Yes, sir. Just below the top."

"You're joking."

"No, sir."

"Ag, it gets cold up here. It *snows* up here. You ever seen snow?"

"No, sir."

"Snow is terrible cold." The man tugs at his collar. He seems about to asphyxiate with the strangeness of Luvo's request.

"Yes, sir."

"I can't let you out here."

Luvo stays silent.

"Any chance I can talk you out of this?"

"No, sir."

Luvo takes his big duffel and four bottles of water from the backseat and steps out into the darkness. The man looks at him a full half-minute before pulling off. It's warm in the moonlight but Luvo stands shivering for a moment, holding his things, and then walks to the edge of the road and peers over the retaining wall into the shadows below. He finds a thin path, cut into the slope, and hikes maybe two hundred meters north of the road, pausing every now and then to watch the twin red taillights of the salesman's Honda as it eases up the switchbacks high above him toward the top of the pass.

Luvo finds a lumpy, level area of dry grass and rocks roughly the size of Alma Konachek's upstairs bedroom. He unrolls his sleeping bag and urinates and looks out over the starlit talus below, running mile after mile down onto the plains of the Karoo far beneath him.

He takes a drink of water and climbs into his sleeping bag and tries to swallow back his fear. The rocks on the ground are still warm from the sun. The stars are bright and impossibly numerous. The longer he looks into a patch of sky, the more stars emerge within it. Range upon range of suns burning out beyond the power of his vision.

No cars show themselves on the road. No airplanes cross the sky. The wind makes the only sound. What's out here? Millipedes. Buzzards. Snakes. Warthogs, ostriches, bushbuck. Farther off, on the northern tablelands: jackals, wild dogs, leopards. A last few rhinos.

First Day

Dawn finds Luvo warm and bareheaded inside his sleeping bag with a breeze washing over the ports in his scalp. A truck grinds up the switchbacks of the road in the distance, *Happy Chips* painted across its side.

He sits up. Around his sleeping bag are rocks, and beyond his little level spot of grasses are more rocks. The slopes below him and above him are littered with rocks in every size, pressed half into the earth like grave markers. Beyond them cliffs have calved off slabs the size of houses. Indeed, there seem to be sandstone and limestone blocks everywhere, an infinity of rocks.

The *Happy Chips* truck disappears around another hairpin. No souls, only a few spindly trees—only boulders and distances. On its pedestal at the museum, the gorgon had seemed huge, big as a dinosaur, but out here the scale of things feels new. What was a dinosaur compared to cliffs like these? Without turning his head Luvo can see ten thousand rocks in which a gorgon might be hidden.

Why did he think he could find a fossil out here? A fifteen-year-old boy who knows only adventure novels and an old woman's memories? Who has never found a fossil in his life?

Luvo eats two pieces of bread and walks slow circles around his sleeping bag, turning over stones with his toes. Splotches of lichen grow on some, pale oranges and grays, and the rocks include grains of color, too, striations of black, flecks of silver. They are lovely but they contain nothing that looks like the fossils in the museum, in Harold's cabinet, in Alma's memories.

All that first day Luvo makes wider and wider circles around his little camp, carrying a bottle of water, watching his shadow slip across the hillsides. Clouds drift above the mountain range at the horizon and their shadows drag across the farms far below. Luvo remembers Harold talking to Alma about time. Younger was "higher in the rocks." Things that were old were deep. But what is higher and lower here? This is a wilderness of rocks. And every single stone Luvo turns over is plain and carries no trace of bone.

Maybe one car comes over the pass every two hours. Three eagles soar over him in the evening, calling to one another, never once flapping their wings as they float over the ridge.

The Great Karoo

In dreams Luvo is Alma: a white-skinned estate agent, pain-free, well-fed. He strides through the Gardens Centre; clerks rush to help him. Everywhere circular racks gleam with clothes. Air-conditioning, perfumes, escalators. Clerks open their bright, clean faces to him.

His headaches seem to be intensifying. He has a sense that his skull is slowly being crushed, and that the metallic taste seeping into his mouth is whatever is being squeezed out.

On his second day up on Swartberg Pass, ants chew a hole through one of his bread bags. The sun roasts his arms and neck. Lying there at night Luvo feels as if the gorgon is at the hub of a wheel out of which innumerable spokes rotate. Here comes Luvo on one spoke, and Roger on another, and Temba on the next, and Pheko and Harold and Alma after that. Every-thing coursing past in the night, revolving hugely, almost unfathomably, like the wheel of the Milky Way above. Only the center remains in darkness, only the gorgon.

From his memory Luvo tries to summon images of the gorgon at the museum, tries to imagine what one might look like out here, in the rocks. But his mind continually returns to Alma Konachek's house.

Roger is dead. Harold is dead. Alma is either in jail or tucked into a home for the rich and white-skinned. If there's anything left of who she was, it's a scrap, a shred, some scribbled note that a cleaner or Pheko has guiltily unpinned from her wall and thrown into the trash. And how much longer can Luvo be any better off, with these ports throbbing in his skull? A few more months?

Here is the surprise: Luvo likes the strange, soothing work of looking into the rocks. He feels a certain peace, clinging to the side of Swartberg Pass: The clouds are like huge silver battleships, the dusks like golden liquids—the Karoo is a place of raw light and monumental skies and relentless silence. But beneath the silence, he's learning, beneath the grinding wind, there is always noise: the sound of grass hissing on the cliffsides and the clattering of witgat trees tucked here and there into clefts. As he lies in his sleeping bag on his third night he can hear an almost imperceptible rustling: night flowers unveiling their petals to the moon. When he is very quiet, and his mind has stilled the chewing and whirling and sucking of his fears, he imagines he can hear the coursing of water deep beneath the mountains, and the movements of the roots of the plants as they dive toward it—it sounds like the voices of men, singing softly to one another. And beyond that—if only he could listen even more closely!—there was so much more to hear: the supersonic screams of bats, and, on the most distant tablelands, the subsonic conversations of elephants in the game reserves, grunts and moans so deep they carry between animals miles apart, forced into a few isolated reserves, like castaways on distant islands, their calls passing through the mountains and then shuttling back.

That night he wakes to the quivering steps of six big antelope, shy and jittery, the keratin of their hooves clacking against the rocks, the vapor of their breath showing in the moonlight as they file past his sleeping bag, not fifty feet away.

On Luvo's fourth morning, wandering below the pass, perhaps a half mile from the road, he turns over a rock the size of his hand and finds pressed into its underside the clear white outline of what looks like a clam shell. The shell is lighter than the stone around it and scalloped at the edges. The name of the fossil rises from some corner of his brain: brachiopod. He sits in the sun and runs the tips of his fingers over the dozens of grooves in the stone. An animal that lived and died eons ago, when this mountainside was a seabed, and galaxies of clams flapped their shells at the sun.

Luvo hears Harold Konachek's big, enthusiastic voice: *Two hundred fifty million years ago this place was lush, filled with ferns and rivers and mud.* Flesh washing away, minerals penetrating bones, the weight of millennia piling up, bodies becoming rock.

And now this one little creature had risen to the surface, as the earth was weathered away by wind and rain, in the way a long-frozen corpse sometimes bobs to the surface of a glacier, after being mulled over in the lightless depths for centuries.

What Endures?

His dreams stray farther and farther from his reality, dreams that feel as if they emerge not from his own forgotten childhood but from lives that have been passed to him through his blood. Dreams of ancestors, dreams of long ago men who dragged their own aching heads through this arid place, centuries of nations pursuing herds across the sands, whole bands passing in the haze with ocher on their faces and spears in their fists and great ragged tents folded and strapped to their backs, the long poles nodding as they marched, dogs trotting at their feet, tongues lolling. Thick-bodied herds, rain-animals and handprints, lines of dots descending from a sky and plugging into a rhinoceros horn. Men with antelope heads. Fish with the faces of men. Women dissolving into mists of red.

The fifth morning on Swartberg Pass finds Luvo exhausted and hollow and in too much pain to rise from his sleeping bag. He pulls the curled photograph of Harold from his duffel and studies it, running his fingers over the man's features. Pinpoints of sky show through the little holes in each corner.

Luvo tries to cut through his headache, tries to coax his memory back toward the moments before Harold's death. Harold was talking about geology, about death. "What's the permanent thing in the world? Change!" Windpumps, sheep pens, a sign that reads *Swartbergpas*.

Luvo remembers Alma's sandwich on the dashboard, the wind in the grass beside the road, Harold finally returning over the apron of the road, staggering as he muttered Alma's name. Pink foam coming out of his mouth. Alma punching telephone buttons in vain. Gravel pushed into Harold's cheek and dust on his eyeballs.

Luvo stares at the photograph of Harold. He has begun to feel as if Alma's wall of papers and cartridges has been reiterated out here a hundredfold on the mountainside, these legions of stones like identical beige cartridges, each pressed out of the same material. And here he is doomed to repeat the same project over and over, hunting among a thousand things for a pattern, searching a convoluted landscape for the remains of one thing that has come before.

Dr. Amnesty's cartridges, the South African Museum, Harold's fossils, Chefe Carpenter's collection, Alma's memory wall—weren't they all ways of trying to defy erasure? What is memory anyway? How can it be such a frail, perishable thing?

The shadows turn, shorten; the sun swings up over a ridge. Luvo remembers for the first time something Dr. Amnesty told Alma on one of the cartridges. "Memory builds itself without any clean or objective logic: a dot here, another dot here, and plenty of dark spaces in between. What we know is always evolving, always subdividing. Remember a memory often enough and you can create a new memory, the memory of remembering."

Remember a memory often enough, Luvo thinks. Maybe it takes over. Maybe the memory becomes new again.

In Luvo's own memory a gun explodes. Roger slumps down the stairs and lets out a last breath. A five-year-old boy sits in a lounge chair wrapped in a blanket blinking up at the sky. Alma tears out a page of *Treasure Island* and nails it to a wall. Everything happens over and over and over.

A body, Harold told Alma once, vanishes quickly enough to take your breath away. As a boy, he said, his father would put a dead ewe on the side of the road and in three days the jackals would have reduced it to bones and wool. After a week, even the bones would be gone.

"Nothing lasts," Harold would say. "For a fossil to happen is a miracle. One in fifty million. The rest of us? We disappear into the grass, into beetles, into worms. Into ribbons of light."

It's the rarest thing, Luvo thinks, that gets preserved, that does not get erased, broken down, transformed.

Luvo turns the photograph in his hands and a new thought rises: When Harold was leaning against the Land Cruiser, clutching his chest, his breath coming faster and faster, his heart stopping in his chest, he was not holding his walking stick. The tacky ebony walking stick with the elephant on top. The stick that used to drive Alma mad. When Harold left the Land Cruiser, he took his walking stick from the back of the truck. And when he returned, a couple of hours later, he no longer had it.

Maybe he'd dropped it on the way back to the Land Cruiser. Or maybe he'd left it in the rocks to mark the gorgon's location. Four years had passed and the walking stick could have been picked up, or washed over a cliff in a storm, or Luvo could be remembering things wrong, but he realizes it had been here once, on the north side of Swartberg Pass, somewhere below the road. Near where Luvo is camped. And it might be here still.

Luvo wants to find the gorgon, needs to find it, for himself, for Alma, for Pheko, for Roger, for Harold. If the walking stick is still here, he thinks, it will not be too hard to find. There are no trees up here so big, no branches nearly as long as that walking stick. No wood as dark as ebony.

It's a small thing, perhaps, but it's enough to get Luvo on his feet, and start him searching again.

THE GORGON

For that whole day and the next, Luvo walks the sea of stones. He has only one two-liter bottle of water left and he rations it carefully. He works in circles, in rectangles, in triangles. Belts and swaths and carpets of stones. He looks now for something dark, bleached by sun perhaps, a few red beads strung around its handle, the wooden elephant carved on top. Such staffs he has seen sold by children along the airport road and at tourist shops and in Greenmarket Square.

The sixth evening it starts to rain and Luvo drapes his sleeping bag over a bush and crawls beneath it and sleeps a dreamless sleep and around him spiders draw their webs between the branches. When he wakes, the sky is pale.

He stands, shakes the water drops off his sleeping bag. His head feels surprisingly light, almost painless. It's morning, Luvo thinks. I slept through an entire rainstorm. He climbs perhaps fifty feet onto a flat, smooth rock and sits chewing a slice of bread and then sees it.

Harold's walking stick is sticking up from between two boulders two hundred meters away. Even from where he sits Luvo can see the hole almost near the top, a tiny space carved between the elephant's legs and its torso.

Every second, walking those two hundred meters, is like leaping into very cold water, in that first instant when the body goes into shock, and everything you are, everything you call your life, disintegrates for an instant, and all you have around you is the water and the cold, your heart trying to send splinters through a block of ice.

The walking stick is sun-bleached and the beads are no longer on the handle but it's still standing upright. As if Harold has left it there for Luvo to find. He stares at it awhile, afraid to touch it. The morning light is sweet and clear. The hillside trickles quietly around him with last night's rain.

There is a carefully stacked pile of stones right beside it and even after Luvo has clawed most of them away, it takes him a few minutes to realize he is looking down at a fossil. The gorgon is white against the grayer limestone and the outline of the animal inside seems interrupted in places. But eventually he can make out its form from one foreleg to the tip of its tail: It is the size of a crocodile, tilted onto its side, and sunk as if into an enormous bathtub of cement. Its big, curved claws are still in place. And its skull sits separate from the rest of the stone entirely, as if it has been set there by the recession of a flood. It is big. Bigger, he thinks, than the one at the museum.

Luvo lifts away more rocks, sweeps away gravel and dust

with his hands. The skeleton is fully articulated, looped into the stone. It is perhaps ten feet long. His heart skids.

With the hammer it takes Luvo only about two hours to break the skull free. Little chips of darker rock fly off as he strikes it and he hopes he is not damaging the thing he has come to find. As big as an old box-television, made entirely of stone, even once it's free of the matrix surrounding it, the skull seems impossible for him to lift. Even the eyeholes and nostrils are filled with rock, a lighter color than the surrounding skull. Luvo thinks: I won't be able to move it by myself.

But he does. He unzips the sleeping bag and folds it over the skull, padding it over on all sides, and using the walking stick as a lever, begins to roll the skull, inches at a time, toward the road. It's dark and Luvo is out of water before he gets the skull to the bottom of the retaining wall. Then he goes back to the rest of the skeleton, covers it again with rocks and gravel, marks it with the walking stick, and brings his camp up to the road.

His legs ache; his fingers are cut. Rings of starlight expand out over the ridgeline. The insects in the grass around him exult in their nighttime chorus. Luvo sits down on his duffel bag with the last of his oranges in his lap and the skull waiting six feet below, wrapped in a sleeping bag. He puts on his bright red parka. He waits.

The moon swings gently up over the mountains, huge, green, aswarm with craters.

RETURN

Three English-speaking Finnish women stop for Luvo after midnight. Two are named Paula. They seem mildly drunk.

They ask shockingly few questions about how ragged Luvo looks or how long he has been sitting on the side of one of the most remote roads in Africa. He keeps his hat on, tells them he has been fossil hunting, asks them to help him with the skull. "Okay," they say, and work together, pausing now and then to pass around a bottle of Cabernet, and in fifteen minutes have heaved the skull over the wall and made room for it in the back of their van.

They are traveling across South Africa. One of them has recently turned forty and the others are here to celebrate with her. The floor of their camper van is knee-deep with food wrappers and maps and plastic bottles. They pass around a thick, half-hacked-apart shank of cheese; one of the Paulas cuts wedges of it and stacks them on crackers. Luvo eats slowly, looking at his torn fingernails and wondering how he must smell. And yet, there is reggae music washing out of the dashboard, there is the largeness of these women's laughter. "What an adventure!" they say, and he thinks of his paperbacks sitting in the bottom of his duffel. When they stop at the top of the pass and pile out and ask Luvo to take their photograph beside the beaten brown sign that reads *Die Top*, Luvo feels as if perhaps they have been sent to him as angels.

Dawn finds them eating scrambled eggs and chopped tomatoes in the rickety and deserted dining room of the Queens Hotel in a highway town called Matjiesfontein. Luvo drinks an ice-cold Fanta and watches the women eat. Their trip is ending and they show each other photos on the camera's screen. Ostriches, wineries, nightclubs.

When he's done with the first Fanta Luvo drinks another one, the slow fans turning above, and the kind, sweaty smiles of the three women turn on him now and then, as if in their worlds black and white are one and the same, as if the differences between people didn't matter so much anymore, and then they get up and pile into the van for the drive back to Cape Town.

One of the Paulas drives; the other two women sleep. Out the windows communication wires sling past in shallow parabolas from pole to pole. The road is relentlessly straight. Paula-the-driver looks back now and then at Luvo in the backseat.

"Headache?"

Luvo nods.

"What kind of fossil is it?"

"Maybe something called a gorgon."

"Gorgon? Like the Medusa? Snakes for hair, all that?"

"I'm not sure."

"Well, those are the gorgons all right. Medusa and her sisters. Turn you to stone if you look them in the eyes."

"Really?"

"Really," says forty-year-old Finnish Paula.

"This gorgon is very old," says Luvo. "From when this whole desert was a swamp, and big rivers ran all through it."

"I see," says Paula. She drives awhile, tapping her thumb on the wheel in time with the music. "You like that, Luvo? Going out and digging up old things?"

Luvo looks out the window. Out there, beyond the fence-lines, beneath the starlit, flat-topped hills, beneath the veld, beneath the dwarf scrub, beneath the endless running wind of the Karoo, what else remains locked away?

"Yes," he says. "I like it."

THE TWELVE APOSTLES HOTEL

Paula parks the van outside Chefe Carpenter's stucco wall and the four of them get out and Luvo waves at the security camera but nothing seems to happen so they sit on the curb waiting. Not ten minutes later Chefe in his robe comes up the street walking his two collies. He regards Luvo and then the women with their matted hair and wrinkled shirts and when they open the back of the van and lift away the shredded remains of Luvo's sleeping bag, he looks at the fossil for a full minute without saying anything. His eyes seem both incredulous and dreamy, as if he is not entirely sure that what is happening is real. With his trembling lip and soft eyes he looks to Luvo as if he is about to cry.

Twenty minutes later they stand in Chefe's spotless garage drinking coffee with the skull sitting naked on the painted floor. This one huge head retrieved from the past and stripped from its context. Chefe makes a call and an Indian man comes over and looks at the skull with his hand on his chin and then makes several more telephone calls. His excitement is obvious. Within an hour three more men come in to look at the skull and the three yawning Finnish women and the strange boy in the wool cap.

Eventually Chefe disappears into the house and reemerges dressed in a trim blue suit. He says he can offer 1.4 million rand. The jaws of the Finnish women drop simultaneously. They thump Luvo on the back. They shriek and jump around the garage. Luvo asks what he can give him now and Chefe says, "Now? As in today?"

"That's what he said," says one of the Paulas. After another half hour of waiting Chefe gives Luvo 30,000 rand in cash. There is enough money that he has to give it to Luvo in a paper shopping bag. Luvo asks that the remainder be sent in a complete sum to Pheko Garrett, B478A, Site C, Khayelitsha.

"All of it?" Chefe asks and Luvo says, "All of it."

"How do we know you'll do that?" asks Paula, and Chefe

Carpenter looks up at all three of them, taking his eyes off the skull for the first time in several minutes, as if he is not sure who has spoken. He blinks his eyes once. "You can go now," he says.

Three blocks away Luvo says goodbye to the Finnish women, who hug him each in turn and give him their email addresses on little white cards, and one of the Paulas is crying softly to herself as they watch Luvo climb out of their rented camper van.

Near the entrance to the Company Gardens is a little English bookshop. Luvo walks inside with his paper shopping bag full of money. He finds a paperback of *Treasure Island* and pays for it with a 1,000-rand note.

Then he flags down a waterfront cab and tells the driver to take him to the Twelve Apostles Hotel. The driver gives him a look, and the woman at the desk at the hotel gives him the same look, but Luvo has cash and once he has paid she leads him down a hundred-meter-long cream-colored runner of carpet to a black door with the number 7 on it.

The room is as clean and white as it was in Alma's memory. Off the balcony jade-colored waves break onto a golden beach. In the bathroom tiny white tiles line the floor in diamond shapes. Crisp white towels hang on nickel-plated rods. There's a big, spotless, white toilet. White fluffy bathmats sit on the floor. A single white orchid blooms in a rectangular vase on the toilet tank.

Luvo takes a forty-five-minute shower. He is somewhere around fifteen years old and he has perhaps six months left to live. After his shower he lies on the perfect white sheets of the bed and watches the huge afternoon sky flow like liquid out the window. Rafts of gulls sail above the beach. He thinks of Alma's memories, both those carried inside his head and the ones somewhere out in the city—Cabbage will have traded them away by now. He thinks of Alma's memory of this place, of the movie about the fish, gliding out into the great blue. He sleeps.

When he wakes, hours later, he stares awhile into cobalt squares of night out the windows and then he turns on his lamp and opens *Treasure Island*.

I remember him as if it were yesterday, he reads, *as he came plodding to the inn door, his sea chest following behind him in a hand-barrow; a tall, strong, heavy, nut-brown man . . .*

The Gorgon

It takes six weeks for a crew of six men to excavate the skeleton. They work in daylight only and park their cars two bends away from the easiest route and when they have to bring in the crane they do it at night. They bring it back to Cape Town in an unmarked truck. The dealer who buys it from Chefe Carpenter brings it to a blackmarket auction house in London. In London it is cleaned and prepared and varnished and mounted on a titanium brace. It sells at an anonymous cloak-and-dagger auction for 4.5 million dollars, the fourth-highest sum anyone has ever paid for a fossil. The skeleton travels from London on a container ship through the Mediterranean and the Suez Canal and across the Indian Ocean to Shanghai. A week later it is installed by trained preparators on a pedestal in the lobby of a fifty-eight-story hotel.

No fake vegetation, no color, just a polyvinyl acetate sprayed along the joints and a Plexiglas cube lowered down over it. Someone sets two big potted palms on either side but two days later the hotel's owner asks for them to be taken away.

Pheko

In late February Pheko goes to the post office behind the spaza shop and in his mailbox is a single envelope with his name on it. Inside is a check for almost 1.4 million rand. Pheko looks up. He can hear, all of a sudden, the blood trundling through his head. The ground swivels out from underneath him. Madame Gecelo, behind the counter, looks over at him and looks back at whatever form she is filling out. A bus with no windows passes. Dust rides up over the little post office.

No one is looking. The floor steadies. Pheko peeks again into the envelope and reads the amount. He looks up. He looks back down.

On the subject line the check says, *Fossil Sale.* Pheko locks his post office box and hangs his key around his neck and stands with his eyes closed awhile. When he gets home he shows Temba his two fists. Temba looks at him through his little eyeglasses, then looks back at the fists. He waits, thinking hard, then taps the right fist. Pheko smiles.

"Try the other one."

"The other one?"

Pheko nods.

"You never say to try the other one."

"This time I say try the other one."

"This isn't a trick?"

"Not a trick." Temba taps the left hand. Pheko opens it. "Your bus card?" says Temba. Pheko nods.

"Your bus card?" repeats Temba.

They stop in the market on the way to the station and buy swimming shorts, red for Pheko and light blue for Temba. Then they ride the Golden Arrow toward the city. Pheko carries the plastic shopping bag containing the swimming trunks in his right hand but will not let Temba see inside. It is a warm March day and the edges of Table Mountain are impossibly vivid against the sky.

Pheko and Temba disembark at the Claremont stop and walk two blocks holding hands and enter a branch of the Standard Bank of South Africa two storefronts down from Virgin Active Fitness. Pheko opens an account and shows his identification and the clerk spends ten minutes typing various things into his computer and then he asks for an initial deposit. Pheko slides the check across.

A manager shows up thirty seconds later and looks at the check and takes it back behind a glass-walled office. He speaks into a phone for maybe ten minutes.

"What are we doing?" whispers Temba.

"We're hoping," whispers Pheko.

After what seems like an hour the manager comes back and smiles at Pheko and the bank deposits the check.

Ten minutes later Temba and Pheko stand in the glaring, cloudless sunlight in front of the glass walls of Virgin Active Fitness. Above them they can see people on treadmills, toiling away, and straight ahead, down through the walls, through their own reflections, they can see the three indoor pools, swimmers toiling through lanes, lifeguards in chairs, and children shooting through the channels of the twisting green waterslide.

At the entry Pheko gives the attendant a 1,000-rand note and she grumbles for a minute about change but passes some over and Pheko fills out a form on a clipboard and then they walk into a big locker room, lined with mahogany-fronted lockers, a few men here and there shaving or lacing tennis shoes or knotting ties and here comes Pheko with Temba trotting behind, adjusting his little eyeglasses with a happy incredulousness, and Temba chooses locker number 55 and they pull on their brand-new swim trunks, red for Pheko and light blue for Temba. Then they pass through a tile hallway lined with dripping showers and descend twelve steps and step through a glass door and into the roiling, chlorinated air of the indoor pools.

Temba whispers something to himself that Pheko cannot hear. Lifeguards in red polo shirts sit in chairs. The slide gushes; the shouts of children echo off the ceiling.

Pheko leads Temba up the long waterslide staircase, holding his little hand, the pools below growing smaller, the pink backs of the children in front of them wet with drops of water. Toward the top there is a short wait, each person in front of them climbing into place, then releasing, shooting down the slide, sweeping through the turns, and within a minute Pheko and Temba have climbed the last few steps and they stand together at the top of the waterslide.

Pheko sits in the slide and lifts his son and sets him between his legs. Warm water rushes through their trunks and races down the slide and disappears beyond the first turn. Pheko takes off his son's glasses and holds them in his fist.

Temba looks back at him, his eyes naked. "It looks very fast, Paps."

"It sure does."

Pheko looks down the steep channel into the first turn and then over the wall to where the pool looks very, very far below, the swimmers like little drowsy bees, the pure sunlight pouring through the windows, the traffic gliding noiselessly past.

He says, "Ready?"

"Ready," says Temba.

ALMA

Alma sits in the community dining room in a yellow armchair. Her hair is short and silver and stiff. The clothes she is wearing are not hers; clothing seems to get mixed up in this place. Out the window to her left she can see a concrete wall, the top half of a flagpole, and a polygon of sky.

The air smells of cooked cabbage. Fluorescent lights buzz softly in the ceiling. Nearby two women are trying to play rummy but they keep dropping the cards. Somewhere else in the building, perhaps the basement, someone might be howling. It's hard to say. Maybe it's only the air, whistling out of heating ducts.

A ghost of a memory flits past Alma: there, then gone. A television at the front of the room shows a man with a microphone, shows a spinning wheel, shows an audience clapping.

Through the door walks a big woman in a white tank top and white jeans. In the light of the entryway her dark skin is almost invisible to Alma, so that it looks as if a white outfit has become animated and is walking toward her, white pants and a white top and white eyeballs floating. She walks straight toward Alma and begins emptying boxes onto the long table beside her.

A nurse in a flowered smock behind Alma claps her hands together. "Time for fine arts class, everyone," she says. "Anyone who would like to work with Miss Stigers can come over."

Several people start toward the table, one pushing a walker on wheels. The woman in white clothes is setting out buckets, plates, paints. She opens a big Tupperware bin. She looks over at Alma.

"Hi, sweetheart," she says.

Alma turns her head away. She keeps quiet. A few minutes later some others are laughing, holding up plaster-coated hands. The woman in white clothing sings quietly to herself as she tends to the residents' various projects. Her voice rides beneath the din.

Alma sits in her chair very stiffly. She is wearing a red sweater with a reindeer on it. She does not recognize it. Her hands, motionless on her lap, are cold and look to her like claws. As if they, too, might have once belonged to someone else.

The woman sings in Xhosa. The song is sweet and slow. In a back room across town, inside a memory clinic in Green Point, a thousand cartridges containing Alma's memories sit gathering dust. In her bedside drawer, among earplugs and vitamins and crumpled tissues, is the cartridge Pheko gave her when he came to see her, Cartridge 4510. Alma no longer remembers what it is or what it contains or even that it belongs to her.

When the song is done a man at the table in a blue sweater breaks into applause with his plaster-coated hands. The piece of sky out Alma's window is warm and purple. A jetliner tracks across it, winking a golden light.

When Alma looks back, the woman in white is standing closer to her. "C'mon, sweetheart," she says with that voice. A voice like warm oil. "Give this a try. You'll like it."

The woman places a foil pie plate in front of Alma. There is newspaper over the tablecloth, Alma sees, and paint and silk flowers and little wooden hearts and snowmen scattered here and there in plastic bowls. The singing woman pours smooth, white plaster of Paris out of her Tupperware and into Alma's pie plate, wiping it clean with a Popsicle stick.

The plaster of Paris possesses a beautiful, creamy texture. One of the residents has spread it all over the tablecloth. Another has some in her hair. The woman in white has started a second song. Or perhaps she is singing the first song again,

Alma cannot be sure. *Kuzo inzingo zalomhlaba,* she sings. *Amanda noxolo, uxolo kuwe.*

Alma raises her left hand. The plaster is wet and waiting. "Okay," she whispers. "Okay."

She thinks: I had somebody. But he left me here all by myself.

Kuzo inzingo zalomhlaba. Amanda noxolo, uxolo kuwe, sings the woman.

Alma sinks her hand into the plaster.

Procreate, Generate

Imogene is tiny, all-white. Spun-sugar hair, pale forehead, chalky arms. Imogene the Ice Queen. Imogene the Milk Princess. A black spiderweb is tattooed on her left biceps. She is a resource allocation manager for Cyclops Engineering in Laramie, Wyoming.

Herb is medium-sized, bald, and of no special courage. His smile is a clumsy mosaic of teeth. Veins trail like root formations down his forearms. He teaches molecular phylogeny to undergraduates. He and Imogene live in a single-story brick-and-cedar on five acres fifteen miles from town. Sage, most of it is, and cheatgrass, but they have a few cottonwoods in a dry creekbed, and a graveyard of abandoned tires Herb is trying to clear, and whole bevies of quail that sometimes sprint across the driveway in the early morning. Imogene has twenty-two birdfeeders, some pole-mounted, some suspended from eaves, platform feeders and globe feeders, coffee can feeders and feeders that look like little Swiss chalets, and every evening, when she comes home from work, she drags a stepladder from one to the next, toting a bucket of mixed seeds, keeping them full.

In September of 2002, Imogene swallows her last birth control tablet and she and Herb go out to the driveway so she can crush the empty pill container with the flat edge of the wood maul. This excites Herb: the shards of plastic in the gravel, the taut cords in Imogene's throat. He has been thinking about children all the time lately; he imagines himself coming home from class to find offspring on all the furniture.

Over the next thirty mornings Herb and Imogene have sex twenty times. Each time, afterward, Imogene tilts her hips toward the ceiling and shuts her eyes and tries to imagine it as Herb described: vast schools of his sperm streaming through her cervix, crossing her uterus, scaling her fallopian tubes. In her imagination their chromosomes stitch themselves together with the smallest imaginable sound: two teeth in a zipper locking.

Then: sun at the windows. Herb makes toast. A zygote like a tiny question mark drifts into her womb.

Nothing happens. One month, one period. Two months, two periods. After four months, on New Year's Eve, wind hurling sleet across the driveway, Herb cries a bit.

"I'm just getting the pill out of my system," Imogene says. "This stuff doesn't happen overnight."

Then it's 2003. Imogene begins to notice pregnant women everywhere. They clamber out of minivans at the Loaf 'N Jug; they hunker in Walmart aisles holding infant-sized pajamas to the light. A pregnant repairwoman services the office copier; a pregnant client spills orange juice in the conference room. What defects does Imogene have that these women do not?

She reads on the internet that it takes couples, on average, one year to get pregnant. So. No problem. Plenty of time. She is only thirty-three years old, after all. Thirty-four in March.

At Herb's prompting, Imogene begins sticking a thermometer in her mouth every morning when she wakes up. He plots her temperatures on a sheet of graph paper. We want, he tells her, to time the ovulation spike. Each time they have sex, he draws a little X on their chart.

Three more months, three more periods. Four more months, four more periods. Herb assaults Imogene's peaking temperature with platoons of X's. She lies in the bed with her toes pointed to the ceiling and Herb rummages around on top of her and grunts and the spermatozoa paddle forth.

And nothing happens. Imogene cramps, finds blood, whispers into the phone, "I'm a fucking Swiss timepiece."

The university lets out. The brewer's blackbirds return. The lark sparrows return. Imogene plods through the backyard filling her feeders. Not so long ago, she thinks, I'd be stoned in public for this. Herb would divorce me. Our crops would be razed. Shamans would stick garlic gloves into my reproductive tracts.

In August, the biology department administrator, Sondra Juetten, gives birth to a girl. Herb and Imogene bring carnations to the hospital. The infant is shriveled and squinty and miraculous-looking. She wears a cotton hat. Her skull is crimped and oblong.

Herb says, "We're *so* excited for you, Sondra."

And he is excited, Imogene can see it; he bounces on his toes; he grins; he asks Sondra a series of questions about the umbilical cord.

Imogene stands in the doorway and asks herself if she is generous enough to be excited for Sondra, too. Nurses barge past. Drops of dried blood are spattered on the linoleum beside the hospital bed; they look like tiny brown sawblades. A nurse unwraps the infant and its diaphragm rises and falls beneath the thin basket of its ribs and its tiny body seems to Imogene like the distillation of a dozen generations, Sondra's mother's mother's mother, an entire pedigree stripped into a single flame and stowed still burning inside the blue tributaries of veins pulsing beneath its skin.

She thinks: Why not me?

Wyoming tilts away from the sun. Goodbye, wood ducks. Goodbye, house wrens. Goodbye to the little yellow warbler who landed on the window feeder yesterday and winked at Imogene before continuing on. The abandoned tires freeze into the earth. The birds make their brutal migrations.

"What about you two?" Herb's brother asks. This is Thanksgiving, in Minnesota. Herb's mother cocks her head, suddenly interested. Herb's nephews clack their silverware against the table like drummers. "You guys thinking about kids?"

Herb looks at Imogene. "Sure. You never know."

Imogene's bite of pumpkin pie turns to cement in her mouth. Herb's sister-in-law says, "Well, don't wait too long. You don't want to be rolling to flute recitals in a wheelchair."

There are other moments. Herb's two-year-old nephew climbs uninvited into Imogene's lap and hands her a book called *Big Fish, Little Fish.* "Biiig!" he says, turning the pages. "Biiiig fish!" He squirms against her chest; his scalp smells like a deep, cold lake in summer.

A day later Herb tugs Imogene's sleeve in the airport and points: There are twins by some newspaper machines with tow heads and overalls. Maybe three years old. They are jumping on the tips of their toes and singing about a tiny spider getting washed out of a waterspout and when they are done they clap and grin and sprint in circles around their mother.

When Imogene was twenty-one, her parents were killed simultaneously when their Buick LeSabre skidded off Route 506 a mile from home and flipped into a ditch. There was no ice on the road surface and no coming traffic and her father's Buick was in good repair. The police called it an accident. For two weeks Imogene and Herb stood in a variety of overheated, overdecorated living rooms holding Triscuits on little plates and then Imogene graduated from college and promptly moved to Morocco.

She lived three years in a one-room apartment in Rabat with no refrigerator and one window. She could not wear shorts or skirts and could not go outside with her hair wet. Some days she spent the whole day in her kitchen, reading detective novels. Her letters from that time were several pages long and Herb would read them again and again, leaning over the dashboard of his truck.

There are two kinds of pigeons here. There are the thick-looking ones, rock pigeons, the ones we see back home. They moan on the roof at night. But there are also these other pigeons with white patches on their necks. They're big birds and gather in huge wheels and float above the rooftops, dark and gleaming, turning up there like big mobiles made of metal. Some mornings crows divebomb them and the pigeons will start shrieking and from my bed it sounds like little airborne children shouting for help.

She never mentioned her parents. Once she wrote: *No one here wears seat belts.* Another time: *I hope you're keeping bags of salt in the back of the truck.* That was as close as she came. Eventually she attached herself to a Peace Corps initiative and began working with blind women.

More than once in those years Herb stopped outside Destinations Travel in downtown Laramie and watched the four-foot plastic Earth turn in the window but could not bring himself to buy an airplane ticket. They had been dating only four months before her parents died. And she had not invited him.

He wrote his mundane replies: a hike to a lake, a new cereal he liked. *Love, Herb,* he'd conclude, feeling resolute and silly at the same time. He worried he wrote too much. He worried he did not write enough.

In 2004, after sixteen months of failing to get pregnant, Imogene tells her gynecologist. He says workups can be scheduled. Endocrinologists can be contacted. Urologists can be contacted. They have plenty of options.

"It's not time," he says, "to despair."

"Not time to despair," Imogene tells Herb.

"I'm not despairing," he says.

They have AIDS tests. They have hepatitis tests. Two days

later Herb masturbates into an eight-ounce specimen cup and drives sixty-six miles east on I-80 to a urologist in Cheyenne with the cup in a little Christmas bag meant for office gifts because he and Imogene have run out of brown paper bags. The bag rides shotgun on the bench seat beside him, little Santas grinning all over it. His sample barely covers the bottom. He wonders: Do some men fill up that whole cup?

The same afternoon Imogene leaves work early to have carbon dioxide pumped into her insides. She has radio-opaque dye injected through her cervix into her uterus and all the way up her fallopian tubes. Then she is wheeled into an X-ray room where a nurse with peanut butter breath and Snoopy earrings drapes a lead apron over Imogene's chest and asks her to remain completely motionless. The nurse steps away; Imogene hears the machine come to life, hears the high whine of electrons piling up. She closes her eyes, tries not to move. The light pours into her.

The phone rings six days later. The doctors have discussed the situation. Dual-factor infertility. Imogene gets three words: polycystic ovary syndrome. Herb gets two words: severe deficits. In motility, in density, in something else. Only three percent of his sperm are rated viable.

Herb's face appears to crumple. He sets his half-eaten wedge of cantaloupe on the counter and goes into the bathroom and shuts the door. Imogene finds herself staring into the space between the countertop and the refrigerator. There is dust down there, and a single Cheerio. A groan comes from the bathroom. Then a flush. With one hand Imogene gently probes her abdomen with her fingers.

*   *   *

All morning she sits at her computer and drowns in memory. A bus climbs through layers of cold air, mountains the color of cardboard, a phosphorous sky. Gazelles in a courtyard pick through rubbish. Sheepdogs doze on village rooftops.

"No parents, no husband, no children," a blind woman once told her. Her gaze was a vacuum. Imogene did not know where to look. "I am a tribe of one."

Her computer screen swims. She rests her forehead on the desk.

"Are you mad? Are you mad at me, Imogene?" Herb cannot help himself: The refrain becomes almost visible, a whirl of haze, like fan blades turning in front of his face.

"I'm not mad," she says. Their failures, she decides, were inevitable from the start. Prewritten. Genetic. Their inadequacies, their timidities, their differences from everybody else. She had always been confused, always living far from town, always reading, always saying no to junior high dance invitations. Imogene the Ice Queen. Imogene the Pipedream. Too petite, too pale, too pretty. Too easily scorched.

"Everything is fine," she tells Herb during dinner, during *Jeopardy!* Ten years of trying not to get pregnant and now it turns out they never could.

Herb develops his own theory: It's the tires out in the yard. A whole graveyard of them, seventeen metals, sixteen types of hydrocarbons, and they've gotten into the well water, the shower, the pasta, and now the poisons are *inside their bodies.*

More tests. Imogene has a laparoscopy during which a doctor punctures her ovaries a dozen times with an electrosurgical needle. Herb masturbates into another cup, makes another hour-and-a-half drive to Cheyenne, drops his pants in front of another urologist.

Wait another six days. Get another phone call. Confirmed diagnosis. Imogene studies herself in the bathroom mirror. She had been thinking she could quit her job. She had been thinking she could start cooking Moroccan food, Tunisian food: an infant strapped to her chest, pots steaming atop the range. Maybe raise some hens. Instead she starts a regimen of glucophage and gets diarrhea for a week.

This is not real suffering, she tells herself. This is only a matter of reprogramming her picture of the future. Of understanding that the line of descendancy is not continuous but arbitrary. That in every genealogy someone will always be last: last leaf on the family tree, last stone in the family plot. Hasn't she learned this before?

After school Herb walks out into the big pasture behind the house and works on the tires. They lie so deep in places, so much dust and snow blown into them, that as he hacks out one, or the pieces of it, he inevitably finds another beneath. Sometimes he wonders if there are tires all the way down to the center of the world. He chops them into pieces with an axe, shovels the pieces into his truck. It's cold and there is only the wind in the grass, and the ice clinking softly in the cottonwoods. After a couple of hours, he straightens, looks at the house, small from there, a matchbox beneath the sky. The tiny figure of Imogene trudges through the sage, filling her feeders, dragging a five-gallon bucket with one arm, stepladder with the other, her legs lost in the haze.

*   *   *

They agree to visit a fertility clinic. It is eighty minutes away in good weather. Parked nearest the entrance is a Mercedes with the license plate BBYMKR.

The doctor sits behind a glass-topped desk and draws upside-down. He draws a uterus, fallopian tubes, two ovaries. He draws instruments going in and harvesting eggs. On the wall is a framed poster of a giant vagina and its inner workings. Beside it, a framed photo of three chubby daughters leaning against a Honda.

"Okay," Herb is saying. "All right."

Does Imogene have any questions? Imogene has no questions. She has a thousand questions.

"You draw upside-down really well," she says, and tries a laugh.

The doctor gives a quarter-smile.

"Practice," he says.

The finance lady is nice, smells like cigarettes. They can get loans. Interest rates are swell. Her daughter did three "cycles." She points to photos.

The procedure, including medications, embryo lab, and anesthesiologist, will cost thirteen thousand dollars. On the drive home acronyms twist through their brains: IUI, ICSI, HCG. IVF. A herd of antelope stands in the scraps of snow just off the interstate, their shadows crisp and stark on the slope behind them, their eyes flat and black. They flash past: there, then gone. Herb reaches for Imogene's hand. The sky is blue and depthless.

They sign up. A box of drugs arrives. Herb unpacks it into the cabinet in their bathroom. Imogene can't look. Herb can hardly look. There are four different ziplocks of syringes. Vials and pill bottles. Videocassettes. Containers for used needles. Four hundred alcohol wipes. Fourteen hundred dollars of synthetic hormones.

Imogene's protocol starts with, of all things, oral contraceptives. To regulate her cycle, the booklet says. She pours a glass of milk and studies the little pink tablet.

Dusk falls across the range. Herb grades quizzes at the kitchen table. The clouds deepen, darken. Imogene walks out into the yard with her stepladder and seed bucket and the pill dissolving in her gut and the silence extends and the sky dims and the birdfeeders seem miles apart and it is a feeling like dying.

Each time she hears a syringe tear away from its wrapper, Imogene feels slightly sick. Seventeen days of an ovarian stimulator called Lupron. Then two weeks of progesterone to prepare her uterus for pregnancy. Then vaginal suppositories. If she does get pregnant, eight more weeks of daily injections. Sometimes a little dot of blood follows the needle out and Herb covers it with an alcohol wipe and holds it there and closes his eyes.

After the shots, he lays out her pills, five of them. She eats toast spread with applesauce before work and swallows the capsules on her way out the door.

"Tell me you love me, Imogene," Herb calls from the kitchen, and in the garage, the car window up, Imogene may or may not hear. The Corolla starts. The garage door rolls up, rolls down. Her tires hiss in the cinders. The prairie shifts under its carpet of ice.

*   *   *

Springtime. Imogene's ovaries inflate on schedule. They become water balloons, dandelion heads, swollen peonies. The doctor measures her follicles on an ultrasound monitor: Her interior is a blizzard of pixels. Nine millimeters. Thirteen millimeters. The doctor wants them to grow to 16, to 20. They root for numbers: 30 eggs, 20 embryos. 3 blastocysts. 1 fetus.

Halfway through April, Ed Collins, the regional manager at Cyclops Engineering, calls Imogene into his office and chides her for taking off too many afternoons.

"How many doctors' appointments can a person have?" He fingers buttons on his polo shirt.

"I know. I'm sorry."

"Are you sick?"

She looks at her shoes. "No. I'm not sick."

The more estrogen floods Imogene's body, the prettier she gets. Her lips are almost crimson, her hair is a big opalescent crown. Down both arms Herb can see the purple spiderwork of her veins.

Hormones whirl through her cells. She sweats; she freezes. She limps around in sweatpants with her ovaries stuffed full of follicles and her follicles stuffed with ova. "It's like having two full bladders," she says. Before potholes she has to slow the Corolla to a crawl.

Herb rides beside her with his scrotum throbbing between his thighs, traitorous, too warm. On his desk he has eighty-three protein structure papers to grade. He is fairly sure he will have to charge this month's house payment on his credit card. He tells himself: Other people have it worse. Other people, like Harper Ousby, the women's basketball coach, get their ribs sawed open and the valves of their hearts replaced with parts from the hearts of *animals.*

Clouds pile up at the horizon, plum-colored and full of shoulders.

On May Day Herb masturbates into another cup and drives Imogene and his sample to the fertility clinic and the doctor goes into Imogene's ovaries, aspirating her follicular fluid with what looks like a stainless steel hydra: a dozen or so segmented steel snakes at one end and a vacuum at the other. Herb sits in the waiting room and listens for its hiss but hears only the whirr and click of the heat register, and the receptionist's radio: Rod Stewart.

After an hour they call him back. Imogene is shivering on a chair in the RN's office. Her lips are gray and slow and she asks him several times if she threw up. He says he's not sure but doesn't think so.

"I remember throwing up," she says. She sips Gatorade from a paper cup. He puts a pad in her panties and unties her gown and pulls her sweatpants up over her legs.

For three days they want the eggs to grow, one cell cleaving into two, two into four. The delicacy of mitosis: a snow crystal settling on a branch, the single beat of a moth's wings.

"I was in Africa," Imogene says. "There were all these vultures in the sky."

Two days later a nurse calls to tell them only six eggs have successfully fertilized, but two have become viable eight-cell embryos. Again they drive to Cheyenne. The doctor installs both embryos inside Imogene with a syringe and a long tube like a half-cooked spaghetti noodle. The whole process takes thirty seconds.

She rides back to Laramie lying across the bench seat, the sky racing past the windshield. At the doctor's instructions, she lies in bed for three days, eating yogurt, turning her hip to Herb every twelve hours for her injections, wondering if something tiny is happening inside her, some microscopic spark flaring and fading and flaring again. Then she goes back to work, bruised, still full, an invisible puncture wound in each ovary. She finds herself walking very carefully. She finds herself thinking: Twins? A week later Herb drives her back to the clinic for a blood test.

The results are negative. Implantation did not occur. No pregnancy. No twins. No baby. Nothing.

Things between Herb and Imogene go quiet. Invoices arrive in the mail, one after another. For extra income Herb teaches a summer section of general biology. But he is continually losing his train of thought in the middle of lectures. One afternoon, halfway through a chalk drawing of basic protein synthesis, maybe twenty-five seconds go by during which all he can imagine are doctors scrabbling between Imogene's legs, dragging golf ball–size eggs from her ovaries.

There are snickers. He drops the chalk. A tall sophomore in the front, a scholarship swimmer named Misty Friday, is wearing camouflage shorts and a shirt with about a hundred laces in front of her breasts, like something a knight might wear under his armor. Her calves are impossibly long.

"Professor Ross?"

She chews the ends of the laces on her shirt. Herb's vision skews. The floor seems to be making slow revolutions beneath him. The ceiling tiles inch lower. He dismisses class.

Imogene and Herb buy their groceries, eat their dinners, watch their shows. One evening she crouches at the edge of the driveway and watches a mantis dribble eggs onto a stalk of weed, pushing out a seemingly endless stream of them, tapioca pearls in an amber goo. Three minutes later a squadron of ants has carried off the whole load in their tiny jaws. What, she wonders, happened to those two embryos? Did they slip out of her and get lost in the bedsheets? Did they fall out at work, go tumbling down her pant leg, and get crushed into that awful beige carpet?

Herb tries her in June, and again on the fourth of July: "Do you think we could try another cycle, Imogene?"

Needles. Telephone calls. Failure. "Not yet," she mutters. "Not right now."

They lie awake beside each other, speechless, and look for patterns in the ceiling plaster. Ten years of marriage and hadn't they imagined children by now? A fetus curled in an ocean of amniotic fluid, a daughter standing at the back door with mud on her sneakers and a baby bird in her palm? Seventy-five trillion cells in their bodies and they can't get two of them together.

Here is another problem: the clichés. There are too many clichés in this, armies of them. Imogene's least favorites are the most obvious and usually come from the mothers at work: You're not getting any younger. Or: I envy your freedom—you can do whatever you want!

Equally bad is the moment at the biology department

summer picnic when Goss, the new hire in plant sciences, announces that his wife is pregnant. "My boys can *swim*," he declares, and pushes his glasses higher on his nose and claps Herb on the shoulder.

There is the cliché when Imogene tells Herb (Saturday night, Sunday night) that she's fine, that she doesn't need to talk about it; when Herb overhears a student in the hall call him a "pretty ballsy professor"; when Imogene passes by two receptionists at lunch and hears one say, "I can't even *walk* past Jeff without getting pregnant."

Stretchmarks, baby formula, stroller brands; if you're listening for something, it's all you'll hear.

"Tell me anything, Imogene," Herb says. "But please don't tell me you're fine."

She keeps her attention on the ceiling. Her name hangs in the space between them. She does not answer.

The chapter about human reproduction in the textbook on Herb's desk is called *The Miracle of Life*. Imogene looks up *miracle: An event that appears to be contrary to the laws of nature.*

She looks up *fine: Made up of tiny particles. Or: Very thin, sharp, or delicate.*

Herb calls his brother in Minnesota. His brother tries to understand but has problems of his own, layoffs, a sick kid. His brother's last Christmas card had a photo of a golf hole on the front. Inside it said: *The distance to success is measured by your own drive. Happy Holidays.*

"At least you must be having lots of fun trying," his brother says. "Right?"

Herb makes a joke, hangs up. A room away, Imogene rests

her head against the refrigerator. Outside the wind is flying down from the mountains, and there haven't been headlights on the road all night, and all Imogene can hear is the whirring of the dishwasher, and her husband's low sobbing, and the hot wind tearing through the sage.

Laramie: a film of dust on the windshield, a ballet of cars turning in acres of parking lot, The Home Depot, Office Depot, the Dollar Store, sun filtering through distant smoke, battered men scratching lottery tickets on a bus stop bench. Two brisk ladies in long dresses hold salads in plastic boxes. An airplane whines past. Everything deadeningly normal. How much longer can she live here?

They fight. He says she is detached. He says she is not good at dealing with grief. In her eyes leaves blow back and forth. Detached, Imogene thinks, and remembers a time-lapse video she saw once of a starfish detaching from a dock post and roaming the sea floor on its thousand tiny feet.

She retreats to the garage and runs her hands through her buckets of seeds.

He chops tires out of the yard until little stars burst behind his eyes. In a parallel world, he thinks, I'm a father of nine. In a parallel world I'm waiting beneath an umbrella for my children to come out of the rain.

The summer session winds down. The swimmer in the front row, Misty Friday, wants to conference about her take-home exam. Her tank top is sheeny and her shoulders are freckled

and her hair is baled up in golden elastics. The classroom empties. Herb takes a seat in the desk beside Misty's and she leans
across the gap and they put their heads over a paragraph she has
written about eukaryotes, and soon the building is completely
empty. A lawnmower drones somewhere outside. Houseflies
buzz against the windows. Misty smells like skin lotion and
pool chlorine. Herb is looking at the perfect, fat loops of her
cursive, feeling as if he is about to fall forward into the page,
when he calls her—completely by accident—sweetheart.

She blinks twice. Licks her lips, maybe. Hard to tell.

He stumbles: "All cells have what, Misty? Cell membrane,
cytoplasm, and genetic material, right? In yeast, mice, people,
it doesn't matter . . ."

Misty smiles, taps the tip of her pen against the desk, gazes
down the aisle.

The mountains turn brown. Range fires ring the sun with
smoke. Imogene finds herself unable to summon the energy
to drive home from work. She cannot summon even the will
to get up from her desk. Screensaver fish swim across the computer monitor and the daylight fades to dimness and then to
black and still Imogene sits in her plastic chair and feels the
weight of the building settling all around her.

A person can get up and leave her life. The world is that big.
You can take a $4,000 inheritance and walk into an airport and
before your heartache catches up with you, you can be in the
middle of a desert city listening to dogs bark and no one for
three thousand miles will know your name.

Nothingness is the permanent thing. Nothingness is the
rule. Life is the exception.

It is almost midnight when she drives the dark road home and in the garage she leans against the steering wheel before going in and feels shame draw up her torso and leach through her armpits.

It should be straightforward, she thinks. Either I can have babies or I can't have babies. And then I move on. But nothing is straightforward.

In August Herb gets an email from Misty45@hotmail.com. Subject: *Neurons*.

so if like you were saying the other day in class neurons are what make us feel everything we feel and each receptor works the same pumping those ions back and forth why do some things hurt and some things sort of prickle and some things feel cold?? what makes some things feel good professor ross and why if nerve fibers are what make us feel can I feel so MUCH without the receptor being stimulated at all professor ross without any part of me ever being touched at all??

Herb reads it again. Then again. It's Wednesday morning and his piece of toast, slathered with strawberry jam, remains halfway to his mouth. He imagines replies: *It's complicated, Misty,* or *See, there are photoreceptors, mechanoreceptors, and chemoreceptors,* or *Let's talk further,* or, *Friday, 4 p.m., my car, don't worry because I CAN'T GET YOU PREGNANT,* but then he imagines he *could* get her pregnant, that all he'd have to do is want to, a few words here, a smile there, her twenty-year-old ovaries practically foaming with eggs anyway, so healthy, so ripe, ova almost half the age of Imogene's, basically outfitted with tractor beams, even his dying sperm, that feeble three percent, could make it in there. He thinks of Misty's ankles, Misty's collarbone; a twenty-year-old with glitter on her eyelids and a name like a weather forecast.

From the kitchen comes the sound of Imogene's chair being pushed back. Herb deletes the message, sits red-faced in front of the screen.

Six months after Imogene returned from Morocco, they got married. He drove her to Montana for a honeymoon and led her up a trail beneath a string of ski-lift towers, a drizzle coming down on her bare arms and the dry grass swishing around her knees, and the procession of lift towers beneath them standing silently under the rain. He'd brought a bottle of wine; he'd brought chicken salad.

"You know," he told her, "I think we'll be married forever."

Now it's 2004 and they've been married almost eleven years. He submits the summer session's final grades to the registrar and takes a corner stool at Cole's and drinks a pitcher of sweet, dark beer.

Then he drives to the Corbett Pool. A few folks in short sleeves sit in the bleachers beneath a forty-foot mural of a cowboy. Misty Friday is easy to spot: taller than the rest of the women, sleek in a navy one-piece trimmed with white. Her bathing cap is gold. Herb sweats in his khakis. The swimmer in Misty's lane makes the turn, starts back. Misty climbs onto a starting platform, lowers her goggles. Everywhere voices echo: off the ceiling, off the churning water. *C'mon Tammy, Go Becky.* It feels to Herb as though he is pumping through the interior of a living cell, mitochondria careering around, charged ions bouncing off membranes, everything arranging and rearranging.

And yet, from another perspective, everything is motionless. Misty's knees are bent; her arms poised above her head. The moment before her teammate touches the wall, before Misty leaps, stretches out into a minute, an hour. The chlorine in the air touches the very back of Herb's throat.

Misty enters the water; Herb hurries back to his truck. He tells himself it's just biology, the chemical fist of desire, his spine quaking in it like a sapling. The truth. The questions. No transgression if there is no action. Isn't that what they taught in Sunday school? Misty was right to wonder how people can make other people feel without touching one another.

He starts the truck toward home. The sun sinks behind Medicine Bow to the west and sends up streamers of gold and silver.

"You never know," Herb's mother once told him, the skin beneath her eyes streaked with mascara, "all the things that go into making a marriage last. You never know what goes on behind closed doors."

When Herb walks inside, Imogene is sitting at the kitchen table with tears on her cheeks. In the fading light her hair is as white as ever, almost translucent.

"Okay," she says. "I'll do it. I want to try one more time."

It's early October before the clinic can schedule them in again. This time they know the nurses' names, the schedule, the dosages; this time the language is not so impenetrable. The box of drugs is smaller; they already have specimen cups, alcohol wipes, syringes. Imogene pulls down the waistband of her pajamas; Herb drives in the first needle.

At Cyclops Engineering, receptionists string fake spiderwebs across the ceilings. Goss, the plant sciences professor, comes by Herb's office with sandwiches: turkey, tomatoes, vinegar. He talks about his wife's pregnancy, how she vomits in the kitchen sink, how his unborn daughter is the size of an avocado by now.

"Isn't it crazy," he says, "that every student in this school, every person in town, every single human who has ever lived, existed because of two people fucking?"

Herb smiles. They eat. "Be fruitful and multiply!" shouts Goss, and scatters shreds of lettuce across Herb's desk.

At night Imogene dreams: She and Herb sit in a blind woman's parlor on a floral print couch and drink cold tea and the blind woman asks them questions about their sexual history. Imogene's mother walks in, dragging two old tires. The blind woman gives Imogene an ultrasound. Doves flutter against the ceiling.

Subcutaneous. Intramuscular. Herb unscrews the used needles, drops them in the sharps container. He lines up Imogene's rosary of pills. Out in the yard a ground fog clings to the sage, sealing off the earth. A few finches swoop between feeders like ghosts.

At work Imogene tells Ed Collins, the regional manager, why she will need to miss more afternoons. She lifts the hem of her shirt and shows him the spectrum of injection bruises above her panty line like slow purple fireworks.

"I've seen worse," he says, but both know this isn't true. Ed has two daughters and a waterslide in his backyard and gets hopelessly drunk playing putt-putt golf every Friday night.

Fifteen miles away, at the kitchen table, Herb signs away his 401K.

Again Imogene's ovaries swell. Again the season begins to turn; leaves blowing across the field of old tires, the sky seamed with a vast, corrugated backbone of cloud.

"So our two frogs make Baby Tadpole," Herb tells his Thursday lab, "and Baby Tadpole will turn out like his parents but not *exactly* like them: Reproduction is not replication."

After class he erases Baby Tadpole, then the arrows of descendancy, parent frog A, parent frog B. The body has one obligation, he thinks: *procreate.* How many male *Homo sapiens* are right now climbing atop their brides and groaning beneath the weight of the species?

Tomorrow, the doctor will go into Imogene and retrieve her eggs. Herb drives home, cooks chicken breasts. The roof moans in the wind.

"Do you think they'll let me wear socks this time?"

"We'll bring some."

"Do you think all my hair will fall out?"

"Why would it do that?"

Imogene cries then. He leans across the table and holds her hand.

It starts to snow. It snows so much it seems the clouds will never empty of it and in the morning they make the sixty-six-mile drive in a whiteout and do not talk for any of it, not a single word. Trucks are overturned every few miles. The snow blows in hypnotic sheets through the headlights and the interstate looks as if it has ignited into ten-foot-tall white flames. Herb leans forward, squinting hard. Imogene cradles his sperm sample between her thighs. The heads of her ovaries sway heavily inside her. Something in the way the snow swirls and checks up and swirls again reminds her of the way she'd pray for snowy days as a girl, how she'd go through an Our Father and enunciate every word and she wonders how she can be a thirty-five-year-old orphan when just yesterday she was a nine-year-old in Moon Boots.

When Herb finally pulls into the clinic, they've been in the truck three hours. He has to pry his fingers off the wheel.

The anesthesiologist wears all black and is extremely short. They are late so everything goes very quickly.

"I'm just going to give you some candy now," he tells Imogene through his mask, and drives the Pentothal in.

Herb tries to grade lab reports in the waiting room. Slush melts in dark pools on the carpet. No matter what, he tells himself, no matter how bad things seem to be going, someone always has it worse. There are cancer patients out there incandescing with pain, and toddlers starving to death and someone somewhere is deciding to load a pistol and use it. You ran a marathon? Good for you. Ever hear of an ultra-marathon? It might be cold where you live but it's colder in Big Piney.

After a while he gets called back in. He kneels beside Imogene in the RN's office, refilling her cup of Gatorade, watching the lights in her eyes come back on. Fifty feet away, for the second time this year, an embryologist rinses Imogene's eggs and weakens the zona pellucida and injects one good sperm into each one.

A nurse comes into the office, says, "You two are so cute together."

"We don't have it so bad," Imogene hears Herb say, as he half walks, half carries her through the slush to the car. "We don't have it bad at all."

The sky has broken and the sun fuses the entire parking lot with light. In the truck she dozes, and dreams, and wakes up thirsty.

In Minnesota, across the country, Herb's parents send prayers into the naked trees outside their bedrooms. Herb's nephews toast Herb and Imogene with their milk. At Cyclops Engineering Ed Collins sets an African violet in a plastic pot on Imogene's desk.

The telephone rings. Twenty fertilized eggs. Fourteen embryos. An entire brood. Imogene smiles in the doorway, says, "I'm the old woman in the shoe."

Two days later, three embryos have divided into eight cells and look strong enough to transfer. The snow melts on the roof; the whole house comes alive with dripping water.

If there's a sadness in this, Herb thinks, it's about the embryos that don't even make it three days, the ones that get discarded, lumpy and fragmented, rated unviable. Nucleated cells, wrapped in coronas like little suns. Little sons. Little daughters. Herb and Imogene, father and mother, the DNA already unzipped, paired, and zipped back up, proficiencies at piano playing and field hockey and public speaking predetermined. Pale eyes, veiny limbs, noses shaped like Herb's. But not good enough. Not viable.

Herb and Imogene and the birds at the feeders and Goss the plant sciences professor and Misty Friday the swimmer—all of them were once invisible, too small to see. Motes in a sunbeam.

A cross-section of a single hair. Smaller. Thousands of times smaller.

"The stars," a junior high science teacher once told Herb, "are up there during the day, too." And understanding that changed Herb's life.

"Even if we get pregnant this time," Imogene says, "you think we'll stop worrying? You think we'll have more peace? Then we'll want to find out if the baby's got Down syndrome. We'll want to know why it's crying, why it won't eat, why it won't sleep."

"I'd never worry," Herb says. "I'd never forget." They drive the sixty-six miles back to Cheyenne. The doctor gives them photos of their three good embryos: gray blobs on glossy paper.

"All three?" he asks, and Imogene looks at Herb.

Herb says, "It's your uterus."

"All three," Imogene says.

The doctor pulls on gloves, gets out the half-cooked spaghetti noodle. He implants the embryos. Herb carries Imogene to the truck. The interstate skims past, cinders chattering in the wheelwells. He carries her up to the bedroom. Her feet bump the lampshade. Her hair spreads across the pillow like silk. She is not supposed to get up for three days. She is supposed to imagine little seeds attaching, rootlets creeping through her walls.

In the morning, at the university, Herb hands out midterm exams. His students hunch in their rows of desks, snow on their boots, anxieties fluttering in their chests.

"All you have to do," he tells them, navigating the rows, "is show me you understand the concepts."

They look at him with open eyes, with faces like oceans.

Fifteen miles away, Imogene rolls over in bed. Inside her uterus three infinitesimal embryos drift and catch, drift and catch. In ten days, a blood test will tell if any of them have attached.

Ten more days. For now there is only the quiet of the house. The birds. The tires in the field. She studies her palms, their rivers and valleys. A memory: Imogene, maybe six years old, had broken her front teeth on the banister. Her father was looking for pieces of tooth in the hall rug. Her mother's bracelets were cold against Imogene's cheek.

The telephone starts to ring. Out the bedroom window a pair of slate-colored juncos flap and flutter at a feeder.

"Tell me it's going to be okay," Herb whispers, the receiver of his office phone clamped to his ear. "Tell me you love me."

Imogene starts to tremble. She shuts her eyes and says she does.

The Demilitarized Zone

Paper my son has carried with him, touched a pen to. I press it to my nose but it smells like notebook paper, nothing more:

Dad—the birds. Sea eagles. Ducks like mallards only more beautiful. Egrets, but not like our egrets—taller, wilder. I watch them with the spotting scope and they look dirty and ragged, like deposed kings. They stab the mud with their long beaks.

I want to know their names—I ask everybody but no one knows or cares. I even shout questions at the North Koreans, but what do they know. Grandpop, I think, would know.

I've learned that the huge, short-tailed bird with the black neck is called a red-crowned crane. Ahn told me; he calls the crane turumi, bird of peace. But Northerners, he says, call it something else, something like "messenger of death." He says the KPA have built huge birdfeeders that they stock with poisoned snails. Ahn hates the Northerners though, and it's hard to know out here what is true and what is made up.

And then there is this diarrhea. Painful, awful. I haven't been to the Doc. Don't tell Mom. Tell her I'm fine.

"Pop," I say, "wake up," and I read him the letter. Between sentences I glance at his face, but there's no way to tell if any of it is getting through. He blinks. He brings a hand to his mouth and adjusts his teeth.

Pop was in Korea, too. He spent twelve months there in 1950, doing things he never talked to any of us about, not once. Now, with the Alzheimer's, I doubt he can recall much of it. Where do memories go once we've lost our ability to summon them?

It's October here in Idaho, cardboard spiders taped up in store windows. I make Pop dinner, give him his bath, put him in bed. Before I fall asleep, I take a letter at random from the shoebox beside the bed and read:

> Both sides have loudspeakers everywhere, in trees, on towers, and they blare propaganda at each other all night, so loud I doubt anyone can make any sense of it. Mom would hate it. Remember when we went to Seattle for Christmas and she had to sleep with cotton stuffed in her ears?

The next night I hear her keys in the lock, her boots in the hall. "I need to get into the crawlspace," she hollers, and disappears into the basement. When she comes back up she is holding a blonde wig I have never seen before.

"For my costume," she says. She goes to the freezer and pours herself a drink. I still don't understand how any of this works: Can she just walk in here? Do I change the locks? A week ago I took all the photographs down, then put them back up, then took down just the ones with her in them.

We stand on opposite sides of the kitchen island. Pop colors with oil pastels at the table. She asks, "What are you going as?"

"You actually think I'd go to that party?" I imagine the boyfriend, waiting for her at his condo: He'll dress up as a vampire, maybe, or an axe-murderer, something involving fake blood.

"Let me see a letter," she says.

"Maybe you should get going," I say.

"Just show me one letter. Christ. He's my son, too."

I bring her one from August. I know what it says: *I think of Grandpop out there in the mud, carrying a full load, the hills lit with artillery. I want to ask him: Grandpop, were you scared? Did you take a single minute for granted?*

She looks up. "You're not going to let me see a new one?"

"That is a new one."

"Don't lie to me, Davis."

"Yeah. Well."

She shakes her head and swears. Pop makes small blue circles, slowly filling the body of a cartoon jack-o'-lantern.

"You know," she says, "this little bleeding-martyr thing you're doing is wearing me out."

They're real estate agents, my wife and he. I found them in the worst, most hackneyed way: in his Chevy Tahoe, in the parking lot of the Sun Valley Lodge. I was driving past and saw her truck (next to his) and thought I'd stop to ask what she wanted for dinner.

She moved out the next week. That was in July. Our son still doesn't know.

Mom & Dad: Today I was in the fore bunker when a flock of gulls—a thousand of them at least—came wheeling out of the mist, so low I could see individual feathers in their wings. It took a couple of minutes for them to pass over me. Maybe it was the diarrhea pills, or the silence of the morning, but I felt invisible out there, like a ghost, those birds sailing over me like they've probably sailed over this spot for millions of years, their eyes registering me as no more important than a stump, a patch of dirt. I thought: They are more involved in the world than I will ever be.

It's snowing now, back at the garrison, and everything is gray and dismal. Behind me, toward Seoul, I can see a line of tail-lights fading all the way down the highway.

I buy him books on birds and Asian mammals and wrap them in Christmas paper and ship them out. At night I dream: tiger tracks in the snow—a thousand birds spilling over trees. Asiatic bears, Amur leopards. Above and to both sides is thick netting. I wake thinking: We are all animals, pacing a hallway, sea-to-sea.

On Thanksgiving I go out after Pop is tucked in and walk the cold, brilliant road over the saddle toward the Big Wood Condos where she and the boyfriend live. His place is on the first floor, backed against the sage, and I leave the road and climb well above it until I can descend through the darkness and peer through his patio door.

They're around a big table with some others: his family maybe. He's wearing a cashmere vest. She waves a wineglass as she talks. Her pants are shiny and gold; I've never seen them before. On the counter behind them sits a ravaged turkey.

He says something, she throws back her face and laughs, laughing hard and genuine, and I watch them a bit longer before I retreat, back through the moonlight, the way I came.

Mom, Dad: There are rumors again that the North has made a bomb. Everyone is a little more tense, dropping things, yelling at each other. From Gamma Post I used to watch the sky-line of Kaesong through a range finder—I could see the roof of a temple, three smokestacks, one cement building. Roads wind-

ing in and out. But nothing: no one. No smoke lifting from the stacks, no cars winding up the roads.

Ahn comes to see me in the field clinic and asks why I am here and I say because I have parasites in my intestines, and he says, no, why in Korea. I think a bit and then say to serve my country. He groans and shakes his head. He says he's here because he has to give three years of service or they'll kill him.

The first Saturday in December I strap Pop into snowshoes and we go up into the hills with a treesaw and a plastic toboggan. The snow is already deep in places and Pop founders a bit but he does well: His heart is as strong as ever. Halfway up the valley below Proctor Mountain, high above the golf course mansions, we find a tree that is about right and I clear the snow from its base and cut it down.

Later, as I drag it home through the snow, the toboggan tips on a slope and the tree rolls off. I turn, but before I can even take a step, Pop has gone to his knees and wrestled it back onto the sled and lashed it down with a piece of cord he must have had in his coat pocket. As if he understood—as if he, too, didn't want to see this one particular tradition fail.

I'm in the crawlspace going through boxes when I realize she has taken all the ornaments.

On the tenth of December I get this:

Dad: Yesterday morning I was out of my cot, looking out the window, when two cranes came soaring out of the DMZ, as silent as gods. They were maybe forty feet away when one hit a communication wire and went down, cartwheeling. I couldn't believe how fast it fell. The wires shook and trembled. The sound was like a bundle of sticks getting crushed. The bird lay there on the pavement squirming a bit.

I watched it for maybe three minutes and it didn't stop squirming and no one came by. Finally I pulled on my boots and went out.

The crane was maybe five feet tall. Its beak was working back and forth, like it was chewing, but the top portion no longer matched up with the bottom portion. I think part of it was paralyzed because its legs didn't move.

Its partner flapped down from a tree and watched me from a Dumpster like some ancient white monk. I crouched over the wounded one for maybe five minutes. It was working its huge beak and its eyes were panicking and only one Jeep passed in all that time and the other bird just watched me from the Dumpster.

You'll think I'm crazy but I picked the crane up. It weighed more than you'd think a bird would, maybe twenty pounds. I was worried it would fight but it just lay limp in my arms, watching me. It smelled like the rice paddies do here, like slugs and snails. I carried it across the road, past the first post and to Ahn, who was just finishing his watch in Delta Tower. "Ahn," I said, "what can I do with this?" But he just looked at the bird and looked at me and would not touch it. While we were standing there the crane died—its eye stopped moving, and I could feel something go out of it. Ahn looked at me a minute, and opened the gate and without quite knowing what I was doing, I carried the bird out past the wire into the DMZ.

I stopped maybe three hundred yards out, beneath a scrubby patch of oak. There are mines all over the place that far out and I couldn't bring my feet to go any farther. Across the way the forest was still and dark.

The ground was frozen, but if you want to dig a hole, I guess, you can always dig one. I set the crane in and kicked dirt over it and covered it up.

Unauthorized Absence, AWOL, I know. I was so scared of mines that after I got it buried I didn't move much. It was cold. I watched the blank face of the forest to the North.

The ROK came after me about twenty minutes later. They had dogs. I am lucky, I guess, that they didn't shoot. There was a lot of shouting and rifle-cocking and writing things down on clipboards. I don't know what will happen: They say court martial but the Doc tells me not to sweat it. As I write now the loudspeakers start up, metallic and loud. I miss Idaho; I miss mom.

I dial the only number I have for Camp Red Cloud, in Uijongbu, South Korea, and a night sergeant tells me to wait and comes back and says I should try next week sometime. I stare at our wispy, illegal tree in the corner; it is already losing needles. I take one of Pop's coloring books, a Christmas one, and cut out the pictures he has finished. A blue reindeer, an orange Joseph, a green infant Jesus: all meticulously colored. With tape I fix them to the branches: shepherds there, Mary here. I give Jesus the top.

The next afternoon I get this:

Dad: Do you remember Grandpop's job at the tree farm? Near Boardman? All those poplars. I remember driving the service roads with him on a four-wheeler. What was I, seven? Grandpop drove fast, acre after acre of poplars going past on both sides, and I remember that as I looked down the rows, for a half-second I could see all the way to the back of the farm, maybe a mile deep, to a pocket of light—like a distant grove, almost imaginary—and it would flash each time at the end of every row, long lines of white trunks whisking by between, and that light repeating at the back, like one of those flip-books where you flip the pages and make a horse look like it's running.

They have IVs in my arms. The diarrhea is awful; I can feel everything flowing out. Giardia lamblia, Doc tells me. When it gets very bad it's a feeling like watching those poplars of Grandpop's rush past, and that light at the end repeating like that.

There won't be a court martial, anything like that. Word is they'll send me home. Ahn will be okay, too—his sergeant likes birds.

It is a day before the solstice, and just after dark, when the phone rings and my son is on the other end. Already I can feel the tears starting, somewhere in the backs of my eyes. "Day after tomorrow," he says, and all I can think of is Christmas morning, and his mother, how she used to sit on the stairs, looking down at the tree, waiting for us to wake up so we could start in on the gifts.

"About Mom," I say, but he has already hung up. Upstairs I get the shoebox of letters and tie it shut with ribbon. I put Pop in his coat and gloves, and together we leave the house and climb toward the saddle.

The snow falls softly, just enough to carry a little light in it. Pop climbs steadily, stepping in my footprints.

At the Big Wood Condos we walk to the end of the first floor. I listen a moment—it is quiet—and leave the shoebox at the door.

Then we turn, climb back to the saddle, and make the top of the hill, our breath standing out in front of us. From there we can see the lights of Ketchum below: the dark spread of the golf course, the Christmas lights along the fence into town, the headlights of snowcats roving the flanks of the ski mountain, packing the snow in—and the town itself, twinkling in the valley, the little roof of our house small among the snowy rooftops, and all the mountains of Idaho beyond it. Somewhere, above it all, our boy is crossing over the ocean, coming home.

Village 113

THE DAM

The Village Director stands under an umbrella with the façade of the Government House dripping behind him. The sky is a threadbare curtain of silver. "It's true," he says. "We've been slated for submergence. Property will be compensated. Moving expenses will be provided. We have eleven months." Below him, on the bottom stair, his daughters hug their knees. Men shuffle in their slickers and murmur. A dozen gulls float past, calling to one another.

On project maps, amidst tangles of contour lines, the village is circled with a red submergence halo scarcely bigger than a speck of dust. Its only label is a number.

One-one-three, one-thirteen, one plus one plus three is five. The fortune-teller crouches in her stall and shakes pollen across a field of numbers. "I see selfishness," she says. "I see recompense. The chalice of ecstasy. The end of the world."

Far-off cousins from other river towns, already relocated, send letters testifying to the good life. Real schools, worthwhile

ANTHONY DOERR

clinics, furnaces, refrigerators, karaoke machines. Resettlement districts have everything the villages do not. Electricity is available twenty-four hours a day. Red meat is everywhere. You will leapfrog half a century, they write.

The Village Director donates kegs; there's a festival. Generators rumble on the wharf and lights burn in the trees and occasionally a bulb bursts and villagers cheer as smoke ascends from the branches.

The dam commission tacks photos of resettlement districts to the walls of the Government House—two girls ride swings, pigtails flying; models in khaki lean on leather furniture and laugh. *The river bottled,* a caption says, *the nation fed. Why wait?* Farmers on their way back from market pause, rest their empty baskets across their shoulders, and stare.

QUESTIONS

Teacher Ke shakes his cane at passersby; his coat is a rag, his house a shed. He has lived through two wars and a cultural purge and the Winter of Eating Weeds. Even to the oldest villagers Teacher Ke is old: no family, no teeth. He reads three languages; he has been in the gorges, they say, longer than the rocks.

"They spread a truckload of soil in the desert and call it farmland? They take our river and give us bus tickets?"

The seed keeper keeps her head down. She thinks of her garden, the broad heads of cabbages, the spreading squash. She thinks of the seeds in her shop: pepper seeds, cream and white; kurrat seeds, black as obsidian. Seeds in jars, seeds in funnels, seeds smaller than snowflakes.

"Aren't you betrayed?" the schoolteacher calls after her. "Aren't you angry?"

October

Blades of light slip between clouds; the air smells of flying leaves, rain, and gravel. Farmers drag out their wagons for harvest. Orchardists stare gray-eyed down their rows of trees.

The dam has been whispered about for years: an end to flooding in the lower reaches, clean power for the city. Broken lines, solid lines, a spring at the center of every village—wasn't all this foretold in the oldest stories? The rivers will rise to cover the earth, the seas will bloom, mountains become islands; the word is the water and the earth is the well. Everything rotates back to itself. In the temple such phrases are carved above the windows.

The seed keeper ascends the staircases, past women yoked with firewood, past the porters in their newspaper hats, past the benches and ginkgo trees in the Park of Heroes, onto the trails above the village. Soon forest closes around her: the smell of pine needles, the roar of air. Above are cliffs, tombs, caves walled in with mud.

Here, a thousand years ago, monks lashed themselves to boulders. Here a hunter stood motionless sixteen winters until his toes became roots and his fingers twigs.

Her legs are heavy with blood. Below, through branches, she can see a hundred huddled rooftops. Beyond them is the river: its big, sleek bend, its green and restless face.

Li Qing

After midnight the seed keeper's only son appears in her doorway. He wears huge eyeglasses; a gold-papered cigarette is pinched between his lips.

He lives two hundred miles downriver in the city and she has not seen him in four years. His forehead is shinier than she remembers and his eyes are damp and rimmed with pink. In one hand he extends a single white peony.

"Li Qing."

"Mother."

He's forty-four. Stray hairs float behind his ears. Above his collar his throat looks as if it is made of soft, pale dough.

She puts the peony in a jar and serves him noodles with ginger and leeks. He eats carefully and delicately. When he finishes he sips tea with his back completely straight.

"First-rate," he says.

Outside a dog barks and falls quiet and the air in the room is warm and still. The bottles and sachets and packets of seeds are crowded around the table and their odor—a smell like oiled wood—is suddenly very strong.

"You've come back," she says.

"For a week."

A pyramid of sugar cubes rises slowly in front of him. The lines in his forehead, the sheen on his ears—in his nervous, pale fingers she sees his boyhood fingers; where his big, round chin tucks in against his throat, she sees his chin as a newborn—blood whispering down through the years.

She says, "Those are new glasses."

He nods and pushes them higher on his nose. "Some of the other guards, they make fun. They say: 'Don't make spectacles of yourself, Li Qing,' and laugh and laugh."

She smiles. Out on the river a barge sounds its horn. "You can sleep here," she says, but her son is already shaking his head.

SURVEY

All the next day Li Qing walks the staircases talking to villagers and writing numbers in a pad. Surveying, he says. Assessing. Children trail him and collect the butts of his cigarettes and examine the gold paper.

Again he does not appear in her doorway until close to midnight; again he eats like an aging prince. She finds imperfections she didn't notice the day before: a fraying button thread, a missed patch of whiskers. His glasses are cloudy with smudges. A grain of rice clings to his lower lip and she has to restrain herself from brushing it free.

"I'm walking around," he says, "and I'm wondering: How many plants—how much of the structure of this village— came from your seeds? The rice stubble, the fields of potatoes. The beans and lettuce the farmers bring to market, their very muscles. All from your seeds."

"Some people still keep their own seeds. In the old days there was not even a need for a seed keeper. Every family stored and traded their own."

"I mean it as a compliment."

"Okay," she says.

He jogs a pencil up and down in his shirt pocket. The lantern is twinned in his glasses. When he was a boy he would fall asleep with a math book beneath his cheek. Even then his hair was the color of shadows and his pencils were cratered with teethmarks. She marvels at how having her son at her table can be a deep pleasure and at the same time a thorn in her heart.

The lantern sputters. He lights a cigarette.

"You are here to see how we feel about the dam," she says. "No one cares. They only want to know who will get the biggest resettlement check."

His index finger makes small circles on the table. "And you? Do you care?"

Out the window a rectangle of paper, a letter, or a page of a book, spins past, blowing up the street and hurtling out over the roof toward the river. She thinks of her mother, cleaving melons with her knife—the wet, shining rind, the sound of yielding as the hemispheres came apart. She thinks of water closing over the backs of the two stone lions in the Park of Heroes. She does not answer.

ALL THAT WEEK

Dam commission engineers pile ropes and tripods and blueprint tubes onto the docks. At night they throw noisy, well-lit banquets; during the day they spray-paint red characters—water level markers—on houses.

The seed keeper disembowels pumpkins and spreads the pulp across ragged sheets of plastic. The seeds are shining and white. The insides of the pumpkins smell like the river.

When she looks up Teacher Ke is standing in front of her, thin, impossibly old. "Your son," he says. "He is one of them."

It is drizzling and the garden is damp and quiet. "He's a grown man. He makes his own decisions."

"We're numbers to him. We're less than that."

"It's okay, Teacher," she says. "Here." She drags a wet hand across her forehead. "I'm almost done. You must be cold. I'll make some tea."

The schoolteacher backs away, palms up. The wind moves in his coat and she has the sudden impression his whole body is made of cloth and could blow away at any moment.

"He's here to arrest me," he hisses. "He's here to kill me."

NUMBERS

Memory is a house with ten thousand rooms; it is a village slated to be inundated. The seed keeper sees six-year-old Li Qing wading in mud at the edges of the docks. She sees him peering past the temple eaves at stars.

He was born with hair so thick and black it seemed to swallow light. His father drowned three months later and she brought up the boy alone. Math was the only schoolwork he cared for: algebra, geometry, graphs, and diagrams; incorruptible rules and explicit conclusions. A world not of mud, trees, and barges, but of volumes, circumferences, and surface areas.

"Equations are complete," he told her once. "If they have a solution, the solution is the same for everybody. Not like"—he gestured at her seedlings, the house, the gorge beyond—"*this place.*" At fourteen he started school in the city. By seventeen he had enrolled in civil engineering school and had no time for anything else. *I am so busy,* he would write. *The environment here is very competitive.*

He joined Public Security; he patrolled the aisles of train cars wearing a handgun, a short-brimmed cap, and trousers with stripes down the legs. Each time he returned, he looked slightly different, not merely older, but changed: a new accent, the cigarettes, three sharp knocks on the door. It was as if the city was entering his body and remaking it; he'd look at the low dark houses and wandering hens and farmers with their rope belts as if at film from another century.

There was no dramatic falling-out, no climactic fight. He'd send teapots for her birthdays. On New Year's he'd send a little glass dolphin, or an electric toothbrush, or seven clouds made from sequins. Whatever space existed between them somehow extended itself, growing invisibly, the aerial roots of ivy burrowing into mortar. A year would revolve. Then another.

Now it is dusk again and Li Qing sits at her table in his jacket and tie and recites numbers. The dam will be made from eleven million tons of concrete: Its parapet will be a mile long; its impoundment will swallow a dozen cities, a hundred towns, a thousand villages. The river will become a lake and the lake will be visible from the moon.

"The size of the thing," he says, and smoke rises past his glasses.

THE LEAVING

Heads of families are summoned to the Government House in groups of six. The choice is a government job or a year's wages in cash. Apartments in resettlement towns will be discounted. Everyone takes the money.

The ore factory closes. The owner of the noodle restaurant leaves. The barber leaves. Every day wedding armoires and baskets of cloth and boxes and crates trundle past the seed keeper's window on the backs of porters.

Hardly anyone buys seeds for winter wheat. The seed keeper stares at her containers and thinks: It would be easier if I had traveled. I could have gone to see Li Qing in the city. I could have climbed onto a ferry and seen something of the world.

By the end of the week the engineers are gone. The uppermost row of red markers bisects the rock face above town. The river will rise sixty-four meters. The tops of the oldest trees won't reach the surface; the gable of the Government House's roof won't come close. She tries to imagine what her garden will look like through all that water—China pear and persimmon, the muddy elbows of pumpkin vines, the underside of a barge passing fifty feet above her roof.

Outside her chicken wire the neighbor boys whisper stories that revolve around Li Qing. He has killed men, they say; his job is to remove anyone who does not support the dam. A list is folded into his back pocket, and on the list are names; when he puts a body to a name, he takes you to the wharf and the two of you go upriver but only he comes back.

Stories, only stories. Not every story is seeded in truth. Still, she lies in bed and falls through the surfaces of nightmares: The river climbs the bedposts; water pours through the shutters. She wakes choking.

THE NIGHT BEFORE LI QING LEAVES

They descend the old staircases to the docks and cross the Bridge of Beautiful Glances, and the buoys of fish traps welter and drag in the rapids and a half dozen skiffs skim against their tethers.

The wind carries the smell of rain. Occasionally Li Qing loses his footing in front of her and little stones go tumbling off into the water.

The river swallows all other sounds. There are only the faintly visible swoops of bats coming down from the high walls and the moonlight landing on rows of distant corn and the silver lines of riffles where the river wrinkles along its banks.

"Here we are," he says.

The cinder of his cigarette flares and his hand slips into his back pocket and a sudden coil of panic seizes around her throat and she thinks: He knows. My name is on his list. But he only produces a little square of cloth and wipes the lenses of his glasses.

With his eyes exposed Li Qing looks into the darkness as if he is standing on the edge of a cold and deep abyss but then he replaces the glasses and he is merely Li Qing once more, forty-four, unmarried, deputy security liaison for Dam Commission Engineers' Division Three.

"I noticed you didn't collect your resettlement payment," he says.

He speaks carefully; he is, she realizes, testing his words for balance. "You're getting older, Mother. All these staircases, all those hours you spend bent over your garden. Life is hard here. The cold, the wind. No one has electric heat. No one even has a telephone."

A drizzle starts to blow onto the river and she listens to it come. Within a few seconds it is on them and speckling his glasses. "A cash settlement or a government job. Plus your son living nearby. They aren't terrible options. Every day people leave the countryside for less."

Up and down the gorge the sound of the rain echoes and reechoes and the wind slips into caves and comes spiraling out again. The small orange point of his cigarette sails out over the river in an arc and disappears. She says, "What about a third choice?"

Li Qing sighs. "There is no third choice."

THE SCHOOLTEACHER

In the darkness, a half mile away, Teacher Ke stands in front of the Government House. Rain blows past the lanterns. He holds a candle inside a jar; its flame buffets back and forth. The wind flies and a plastic poncho draped over his shoulders flares behind him, rising in the rain like the wings of a wraith.

November

There is little work. She eats alone. Midnights feel emptier without Li Qing in them; she hangs his peony upside-down over the doorway and the petals fall off one by one.

The dwarf oak behind her house drops its last acorns and she listens to high rustlings in the branches, the whistle and thud of the big seeds striking the roof. *Here,* the trees seem to say, and *here.*

A letter:

> *Mother—I wish we'd been able to talk. I wish a lot of things. We should start searching for your apartment. Something not too far away from me, something with an elevator. There are things here that will make your life easier. What I wanted to say is that you don't have to remain loyal to one place all your life.*
>
> *It would be a great help if you would please send in your relocation claim. 31 July isn't far away. The waiting lists get longer every day.*

Land transactions stop. Marriage proposals stop. Every afternoon another barge clanks into the docks and another family piles on their possessions—bedframes and naked dolls and slavering little dogs and aquatints of long-gone sons in uniform.

The Village Director's wife comes into the seed room and gazes into the mouths of a dozen envelopes. All summer her garden behind the Government House spilled over with asters: purple, magenta, white. Now she goes away with fifty seeds. "They say we'll have a balcony," she says, but her eyes are full of questions.

There is almost nothing, it seems, people cannot take with them: roofs, drawers, felt carpets, window moldings. A neighbor spends all day on a ladder extracting shingle nails; another hacks flagstones out of the streets. A fisherman's wife exhumes the bones of three generations of housecats and rolls them in an apron.

They leave things, too: cracked makeup cases and spent strings of firecrackers and graded arithmetic homework and dustless circles on a mantel where statuettes once stood. All she can find inside the restaurant are the broken pieces of an aquarium; all she finds in the cobbler's shop are three blue stockings and the top half of a female mannequin.

That whole month the seed keeper does not see Teacher Ke once. She is starting, she realizes, to look for him. Her feet take her past the schoolteacher's tiny, slumping shed, but the door is closed and she cannot tell if anyone is inside.

Maybe he has already left. Li Qing's letter sits on her table, small and white. *July isn't far away. You don't have to remain loyal to one place all your life.*

Some evenings, sitting alone among the thousand dim shapes of the seed containers, she feels slightly nauseous, off-balance, as though her son is pulling at her from one end of a huge and invisible cable, as though thousands and thousands of individual wires have been set into her body.

THE CHILDREN

Here is the Park of Heroes; here are the ginkgo trees, a procession in the dark. Here are the ancient lions, their backs polished from five centuries of child-riders. Every full moon, her mother used to say, the lions come to life and pad around the village, peering in windows, sniffing at trees.

Fog drags through the streets and moonlight pours into it like milk. Always, before first light, the lions would creep back to their pedestals and cross their paws and become stone once more. Don't disbelieve what you can't see. She turns down the old alley with its collapsing walls. The schoolteacher's shed is barely a shape. The door is open.

"Hello?"

A cat hurries past. She ascends one stair, then the other. The doorway is all darkness. The wood groans. "Teacher Ke?"

Inside are stacks of papers and a half-barrel stove, coal-stained and cold. Two pots hang from a nail; the cot is empty, the blanket folded.

The fog rolls. Down by the river a ferry blows its horn, a sound like the lowing of a bull, huge and prehistoric. She hurries away, shivering.

In the morning it is colder and outside her chicken wire the neighbor boys stack skim ice in piles and whisper.

You hear? You didn't hear? He took him upriver. The old teacher. He took him a hundred miles into the mountains. In a boat? In a boat. Then he dropped him off. No food? Gave him a gold cigarette. Made him swim for it. Miles from anyplace. That old man? He took him into nowhere and left him to die.

She leans back against the wire. She sits there a long time until the garden is bearded with shadow and dusk fills the sky with trenches and wounds.

Downriver

White cliffs flicker past in the mist. Within fifteen minutes the seed keeper is passing through country she has seen maybe five times in her life. The gorge opens and peels back: Terraces of croplands slide past, winter potatoes and mustard tubers and the yellow stubble of harvested rice.

All day the boat travels through gorges and all day the river gains strength, gathering tributaries—it is fifty meters across, then pinched between cliffs and surging. She can feel its power in her feet. The image of the schoolteacher's empty bed winks across the face of a passing village; it holds steady in the reflection of the overcast sun, flaking and shoaling and accusatory on the water.

She does not leave the deck. A family shares its rice. Daylight hurries into gloom and one by one the passengers retreat into the cabin to sleep. A dozen villages pass in the night, card parlors, tumbledown hotels, the skiffs of fishermen, lamps swinging above wharfs like wayward stars. She thinks: The two of you go upriver but only he comes back. She thinks: In six months, all of this will be underwater.

The City

A soaring black façade, sheathed in glass, an exoskeleton of balconies. His apartment is on the forty-eighth floor. The kitchen gradually fills with light. Li Qing heats dumplings in a microwave; he pours tea into mugs with engineering logos stamped onto them.

"Eat," he says. "Take my robe." Out the window, beyond a balcony, the sunrise is lost behind a convulsion of rooftops and antennas.

His mattress is small and firm. She breathes and listens to the muted roar of traffic, to her son moving lightly about the room, putting on a suit, knotting his tie. Everything seems to take on the motion of the river, the bed rocking back and forth, a current drawing her forward.

"You rest," Li Qing says, and his face looms over her like a moon. "It's good you came."

When she wakes it's evening. A beetle traverses the ceiling, wallowing in the whorls of plaster. Water travels the walls, the flushing of neighbors' toilets, the unstoppering of sinks.

She sits at the table and waits for her son. Sleep is slow to leave her. The drawn curtains are thick and heavy.

He is home before eight. He throws his jacket across the couch. "Did you sleep? I'll order some food." One of his socks has a hole in it and his heel shows through.

"Li Qing." She clears her throat. "Sit down."

He puts on the kettle and sits. His eyes are very steady. She tries to hold his gaze.

"Did you ever interview Teacher Ke? While you were in the village?"

"The retired teacher?"

"Yes. What did you say to him?"

The kettle groans as it heats. "I presented the case of the dam. He had some questions, I think. I tried to answer them."

"That's all?"

"That's all."

"You only talked to him?"

"I only talked to him. And gave him his resettlement check."

The balcony rails vibrate in the wind and the seed keeper swallows. Her son pulls a cigarette from his pocket, sticks it in his mouth, and strikes a match.

Days to Come

He lets her wear his sweaters; he buys her a towel. She watches the clothes in his dryer spin and spin. After meals he smokes on his balcony and the wind comes pouring over him and lifts his tie and flaps its loose end against the glass. The cigarette butts sail down in spirals until they disappear.

Maybe Teacher Ke left like everybody else. Maybe, she thinks, I've got this all wrong. Maybe at some point a person should stop accumulating judgments and start letting them go.

She rides with him to work in his black sedan. In the lobby of his office building a model of the dam sits on a massive table. Tourists crowd the Plexiglas and the flashes of cameras blink on and off.

The cool, uniform sweep of the model dam's buttress is the size of Li Qing's car. It is studded here and there with elaborate cranes, swiveling back and forth and raising and lowering their booms. The riverbanks are crawling with toy bulldozers and a convoy of tiny trucks slides along a mechanical track. Miniature shrubs and pines dot the hills; everywhere there are glowing lights and electric towers. Water flows through sluicegates, rattles down a spillway, sits placidly in the reservoir, all of it dyed a fabulous blue.

Welcome, a voice from the ceiling says, over and over. *Welcome.*

District 104

He drives her through a resettlement district. Vast new apartment structures, a block long, straddle central plazas. One after another they whisk past: white concrete, blue glass, neon, bird markets and meat stalls and growling, whirling street scrubbers and the cheery names of intersections: Radiance Way, Avenue of Paradise. Construction sheeting flaps in the wind; buckets swing from scaffolding. Everything is streaked with coal dust.

"This district here," Li Qing says, "is one of the nicest. Most of these people are from the First Twenty."

They stop at a traffic light. Motorbikes rattle on either side. Beyond them she can hear the boom of dull bass and the clinking of chisels and the drumming of a jackhammer. Li Qing is saying more, about how exciting it is for city engineers to construct neighborhoods from scratch, to plan proper sewers, wide roads, but she finds she can no longer pay attention. Women slip past on bicycles and a car alarm squeals to life and dies and the idling tailpipes of the motorbikes exhale steadily. The traffic light turns green; televisions flare blue simultaneously in a thousand windows.

After dinner he wants to know what she thinks: Did she notice the high windows? Would she like to go back and look through a model apartment? Three-year-old Li Qing appears on the undersides of her eyelids; he rolls a pinecone across the floor and practices telling lies: The wind spilled the seeds; a ghost stained his blanket.

Then he was twelve and tying centipedes to balloon strings and watching them rise up between the cliffs. How can he be forty-four years old?

"Some people do think the dam is a bad idea," he says. "They call the radio stations; they organize. In one village they've threatened to chain themselves into their houses and drown against the rafters."

Words rise to her mouth but she finds she cannot assemble them into sentences. The whole city stretches beyond Li Qing's balcony, a riddle of rooftops and fire escapes, a haze of antennas. The wind wraps itself around the building; everything rocks back and forth.

"But really this is just a tiny percentage," Li Qing says. "Most everybody is in favor of the dam. The flooding downstream is awful, you know. It killed two thousand people last summer. And we can't keep burning all this coal. Talk is good. It is healthy. I encourage it."

Selfishness, recompense, and the chalice of ecstasy. Her son wants to know about his father; what does she think his father would have thought about the dam? But everything reels; she is floating through rapids, trapped between the walls of a gorge. Limestone walls flash past, white and crumbling.

RETURN

In the village, two hundred miles away, another neighbor leaves: mother, father, son, daughter, a parade of furniture, a guinea pig, rabbit, and ferret, their cages suspended from the bamboo poles of porters, their black eyes peering into a snowfall, their breath showing in little spirals.

She has been in the city nine days when she rises and dresses and walks out into the other room, where her son sleeps crammed onto his polyester couch. His glasses are folded on the floor beside him. His nostrils flare slightly with each breath; his eyelids are big and blue and traced with tiny capillaries.

She says his name. His eyes flutter.

"How does the water come, when it comes?"

"What do you mean?"

"Does it come fast? Does it surge?"

"It comes slowly." He blinks. "First the currents will go out of the river, and then the water will become very calm. The rapids will disappear. Then, after a day, the wharfs. To reach high water will take eight and a half days, we think."

She closes her eyes. The wind hisses through the rails on the balcony, a sound like electricity.

"You're going back," he says. "You're leaving."

THE VILLAGE

Nothing new has been built in months. Windows break and are left broken. Rocks as big as dogs fall into streets and no one bothers to remove them. She ascends the long staircase and creeps down the crumbling alley to the schoolteacher's house. His door is open; a kerosene lantern hangs from a beam. Teacher Ke sits over a sheet of paper in a shaft of light. A blanket hangs over his lap; he dips a brush in a bottle of ink. His beard wags over the paper.

He has not been arrested; he has not been killed. Maybe he was never gone at all—maybe he was in a nearby town drinking *mao tai*.

"Good evening, Teacher," she calls, and continues up the street.

Her house sits unmolested. Her seeds are where she left them. She drags the coal bucket across the floor and opens the mouth of the stove.

There are maybe a hundred villagers left, some old fishermen and a few wives and a handful of rice farmers waiting until their seedlings are big enough to transplant. The children are gone; the Village Director is gone. Excrement sits in the empty shells of houses. But in the morning the seed keeper feels strangely unburdened, even euphoric: It feels right to be here, in the silver air, to stand in her garden amid the scraps of slush and listen to the wind stream through the gorge.

Light pours between clouds, glazing rooftops, splashing into streets. She lugs a pot of stew up the staircases and through the crumbling alley and leaves it steaming on the steps of the house of the schoolteacher.

SPRING

February brings rainstorms and the first scent of rapeseed. Threads of water spill from the canyon walls. Inside the temple six or seven women sing between blasts of thunder. The roof is leaking and rainwater leaches through great brown splotches and drips into pans scattered around the aisles.

There is no Spring Festival, no rowing races down the river, no fireworks on the summits. She would be seeding rice now, a seed in each container of her plastic trays, then earth, then water. Instead she seeds her garden, and the neighbor's garden, and throws handfuls of seeds into the yards of abandoned houses, too: kale, radish, turnip, chives. She is suddenly wealthy: She has the seeds for fifty gardens. In the evenings she cooks—spicy noodles, bean curd soup—and brings the pots to the steps of the schoolteacher and leaves them under lids and collects the pots she has left before, empty, clumsily washed.

Meanwhile the village disappears. The boards of the docks vanish. The wrappings are taken off trees. Clock hands disappear and the doors off the Government House and the guide wires from radio antennas and the antennas, too. Whole groves of bamboo are taken. Magnolia trees are dug up and carted in wheelbarrows onto barges. Hinges and knobs and screws and nuts evaporate. Every ounce of teak in every house is dismantled and packed away in blankets and lugged down the staircases.

In March the few farmers who are left thresh their wheat. When the wind is low she can hear them, the chop-chop of scythes. Every March of her life she has heard that sound.

She cannot remember a spring more colorful. Flowers seem to be exploding out of the mud. By April there is scarlet and lavender and jade everywhere. Behind the Government House zinnias are coming up with a deep, almost unnatural vigor—as if they were pouring up out of the earth. She kneels over them for a half hour, studying the smooth, stout stems of the seedlings.

Soon so many plants in her garden are coming up she has to start pulling them. It is as if someone is underneath the earth, pushing her vegetables up with his fingers. Has spring always been like this? Startling, overpowering? Maybe she is more sensitive to it this year. Bees drift through the alleys with their heavy baskets, seemingly drunk; to stand beneath the sycamores is to stand in a blizzard of seeds.

At night she walks the town and has the sense that the darkness is a great cool lake. Everything seems about to float away. Darkness, she thinks, is the permanent thing.

And silence. With the people gone, and the ore factory quiet, it is as if the village has become a trove of silence, as if the sounds of her shoes on the stairs, and the air passing in and out of her lungs, are the only sounds for miles.

Mail service stops. She does not hear from Li Qing. Any moment, perhaps, he will appear at her door and demand she leave with him immediately. But he never shows. At night there are only three or four lights against the huge background of the gorge and the dark sky and the darker river with its faint avenue of reflected stars.

Fireflies

Every night now thousands of fireflies float up the staircases and hang in the trees, flashing their sequenced trains of light, until the whole gorge looks as if it has been threaded with green bulbs. She bends to exchange a pot of soup for the empty one sitting on the schoolteacher's stair when the door swings open.

"You're watching the beetles," he says. He clambers out the doorway and sits with the point of his cane balanced on the bottom step. She nods.

"I thought you had left. In the winter."

She shrugs. "Everyone is leaving."

"But you're still here."

"So are you."

He clears his throat. Out in his fruit trees the fireflies rise and flash, rise and flash. "My son—" she says.

"Let's not talk about him."

"Okay."

"They're courting females," he says. "The beetles. In some of the big trees along the river, I've seen thousands of them all flashing in synchrony. On, off. On, off."

She stands to go.

"Stay," he says. "Talk a while."

Memory

Every stone, every stair, is a key to a memory. Here the sons of her neighbors flew kites. Here the toothless knife-sharpener used to set up his coughing, smoking wheel. Here, forty years ago, a legless girl roasted nuts in a copper wok and here the seed keeper's mother once let her drink a glass of beer on Old

Festivals Day. Here the river took a clean shirt right out of her hands; here was once a field, furred with green shoots; here a fisherman put his hot, dry mouth on hers. The body odor of porters, the white faces of tombs, the sweet, bulging calves of Li Qing's father—the village drowns in memory.

Again and again her feet take her up the long staircases past the park to the crumbling alley, the tides of fireflies, and the sour perfume of the schoolteacher's yard. She brings a pot of hot water and a bag of sugar cubes, and the schoolteacher joins her on the steps and they drink and watch the beetles pulse and rise as if the whole gorge is smoldering and these are sparks that have shaken free.

Before the construction of the Government House, before mail service, before the ore factory, this was a place of monks, and warriors, and fishermen. Always fishermen. The seed keeper and the teacher talk of presidents and emperors, and the songs of trackers, and the temple, and the birds. Mostly she listens to the old man's voice in the darkness, his sentences parceling out one after another until his frail body beside her seems to disappear in the darkness and he is only a voice, a schoolteacher's fading elocution.

"Maybe," he says, "a place looks different when you know you're seeing it for the last time. Or maybe it's knowing no one will ever see it again. Maybe knowing no one will see it again changes it."

"Changes the place or how you see it?"

"Both."

She sips her sweet water. He says: "Earth is four and a half billion years old. You know how much a billion is?"

One-thirteen, sixty-six, forty-four. A hundred billion suns per galaxy, a hundred billion galaxies in the universe. Teacher Ke writes three letters a day, a hundred words each. He shows them to her; the white paper, his wobbly calligraphy. He addresses them to newspapers, officials, engineers. He shows her a whole roster—hundreds of pages thick—of dam commission employees. She thinks: My son's name is in there.

"What do you say in the letters?"

"That the dam is a mistake. That they're drowning centuries of history, risking lives, working with faulty numbers."

"And do they make a difference?"

He looks at her; the moisture in his eyes reflects the fireflies, the soaring, glossy ruins of the cliffs. "What do you think?"

JULY

Everything accumulates a terrible beauty. Dawns are long and pink; dusks last an hour. Swallows swerve and dive and the stripe of sky between the walls of the gorge is purple and as soft as flesh. The fireflies float higher up on the cliffs, a foam of green, as if they know, as if they can sense the water coming.

Is Li Qing trying to reach her? Is he right now racing up the river in a hydrofoil to take her away?

Teacher Ke asks her to carry his letters to the wharfs and see if passing boats will take them to another village to mail them. The fishermen almost always say no; they squint at the rickety script on the envelopes and sense they are dangerous. She has more luck with the hollow-eyed scavengers who come up on ramshackle motor launches to salvage scrap metal or paving stones; she bribes them with an old dress, or kerosene, or a paper bag heavy with eggplant. Maybe they mail them; maybe they round the bend and pitch them into the rapids.

By now all the unbroken flagstones have been taken and sunflowers begin to rise from the center of the streets. Her improvised gardens in her neighbors' yards are unruly with bees and nettles. "There are hours," the schoolteacher says, "when I think of the shoeshine boys making fun of me, and the piles of trash steaming in the rain, and the burns on my fingers from that old stove, and I cannot wait to see it all go underwater."

The long staircase, one landing after another, the front of each step edged with light. No chisels, no dogs, no engines. Just the sky, and light falling down between the shells of buildings, like a fine rain, and her footfalls echoing through the alleys.

She stands in her house and stares into the mouths of containers, watching little diamonds of light reflect off the smooth polish of seeds, their perfect geometries, their hibernal dreams.

She peers past the schoolteacher into his tiny shed, the scattered piles of papers and the books and his blackened lantern and the husks of beetles in the corners.

She says, "You're going to drown with the village."

"You're the one," he says, "we should be worried about."

FINALLY

There are two nights left in July when the schoolteacher appears in her doorway. He is wearing a suit, his shoes are shined, and his beard is combed. His eyes gleam. Over his shoulder is a knapsack, in one fist is his cane, and in the other the neck of a large plastic bag.

"Look." Inside are hundreds, maybe thousands, of fireflies. "Honey and water. They can't get enough of it."

She smiles. He unloads his knapsack: a bottle of *mao tai* and a stack of thirty or so letters.

"Two glasses," he says, and drags his stiff legs over to her chair and sits and wrestles the cork out of the bottle. They toast.

"To one last mailing."

"To one last mailing."

He explains what he needs and she empties every jar she has, pouring the seeds into buckets and trays. The schoolteacher strips corks with a penknife and rolls letters into the bottles and together they use a paper funnel to shake the fireflies in. The insects fly everywhere and clog the bottlenecks but they manage to get thirty or so into each bottle.

They stack the corked bottles in a basket. Fireflies crawl the glass. The light from the lantern wavers and shadows lap the walls. She can feel the liquor burning in her stomach and down the lines of her arms.

"Good," Teacher Ke is saying, "good, good, good." His voice is a whisper, the hissing revolutions of needle across an old record.

When she extinguishes the lantern the bottles glow softly. She heaves the basket onto her shoulders and carries it down the staircases, and the schoolteacher limps beside her, leaning on his cane.

The air is warm and damp; the sky is a stripe of dark blue ink between the black walls of the cliffs. The basket on her shoulder buzzes softly. They reach what's left of the docks, fifteen or so piles driven into the riverbed, and she sets down the basket and studies it.

"They'll run out of air," she says, but she can feel the liquor working now, and Teacher Ke is breathing hard, already half drunk himself. Everything is silent except for the river.

"Okay," he says. "Let's put them in."

She wades out into the cold water. Pebbles stir beneath her shoes. The current parts lightly around her knees. The schoolteacher is a trembling weight at her elbow. She floats the basket out alongside them. The bottles flash and flash. Eventually the two of them—seed keeper and schoolteacher—are submerged to their waists.

Maybe the river is already beginning to slack, to back up and rise. Maybe ghosts pour out of the Earth, out of the mouths of tombs up and down the gorges, out of the tips of twigs at the ends of branches. The fireflies tap against the glass. More than anything, she thinks, I'll be sad to see the speed go out of the water.

She hands him the first bottle and he sets it in and they watch the river take it, a green-blue light winking out into the current, turning slightly as it picks up pace.

Twenty thousand days and nights in one place, each layered and trapped and folded on top of the last, the creases in her hands, the aches between her vertebrae. Embryo, seed coat, endosperm: What is a seed if not the purest kind of memory, a link to every generation that has gone before it?

The bottle disappears. She hands him the next one. When he turns she can see he is crying.

Everything has trained her to expect this to work out badly. Li Qing with his cigarettes; the schoolteacher with his questions. Our side, their side. But perhaps, she thinks, there is no good and bad to it at all. Every memory everyone has ever had will eventually be underwater. Progress is a storm and the wings of everything are swept up in it.

She leans forward and wipes the schoolteacher's eye with her thumb. The second bottle is gone.

Teacher Ke drags his forearm across his nose. "All this trouble," he says, "and still—doesn't it feel good? Doesn't it make you feel young?"

The river murmurs against their bodies and the bottles go out of the basket one after another. The old man takes his time. The bottles glow and flash in the current and round the bend and are gone. She listens to the current, and the old man sends his letters downstream, and they stand in the water until they cannot tell where their legs end and where the river begins.

JULY 31

On the last day, five or six steady, level-faced servicemen with chainsaws come for the trees. They bring them down in four-foot sections, and load the logs onto handwagons, and bounce the handwagons down what's left of the staircases, past the broken pavement and the sunflowers and the seed keeper's gardens in the neighbors' yards. They take the oaks, the ginkgos, the three old sycamores from the garden behind the Government House. They leave the lions.

All day she does not see the schoolteacher and she hopes he is already gone, making his way upriver on some old trail, or squatting in the canoe of a passing fisherman, watching the gorges drift past. Maybe she is the last person in the village; maybe she is the last person on the river.

In the afternoon three policemen come to sweep the village, shining flashlights into rooms, lifting discarded plywood with the toes of their boots, but it is easy to hide from them and in an hour their hydrofoil is gone, roaring toward the next town.

She spreads a blanket across her table and upends containers of seeds onto it. Mustard tuber, pak choy, cabbage, eggplant, cauliflower. Millet, chestnut, radish. Her mother's voice: *Seeds are the dreams plants dream while they sleep.* Seeds big as coins; seeds light as breath. They all go onto the blanket. When all the containers are empty she folds the corners of the blanket over each other and ties the whole thing into a bundle.

In her arms it is maybe as heavy as a child. The sun rolls down behind the gorge. By now the diversion has been sealed off, and water is piling up behind the dam.

A wool cap. A jacket. She leaves her dishes stacked in the cupboards.

She walks down the staircases for the last time and out to the Bridge of Beautiful Glances and sits on the parapet. The day's heat rises from the stone into the backs of her thighs. Everything is radiant.

Birds are landing on the roof of the Government House. Coming up the river is the low growl of a motor launch, and when it rounds the corner she turns. Behind its windshield is a pilot and beside the pilot is Li Qing, waving at her and wearing his ridiculous eyeglasses.

YEARS LATER

She lives in a blocklong building called New Immigrant 606. Her apartment has three rooms, each with a door and a single-paned window. The walls are white and blank. She never receives a bill.

Sundays Li Qing comes by and sits with her for a few hours, drinking beer. Lately he brings Penny Ou, a divorcée with a gentle voice and a trio of moles mushrooming off the side of her nose. Sometimes they bring her son, a round-faced nine-year-old named Jie. They eat stew, or noodles with bean sprouts, and talk of nothing.

Jie swings his feet back and forth beneath the table. A radio burbles on the sideboard. Afterward Penny takes the dishes to the sink and washes and dries them and stacks them in the cupboard.

The days seem made of twilight, immaterial as shadows. Memories, when they come, are often viscous and weak, trapped beneath distant surfaces, or caught in neurofibrillary tangles. She stands over the full bathtub but cannot remember filling it. She goes to fill the kettle but finds it steaming.

Her seeds sit moldering or cracking or expired altogether in a prefabricated plywood dresser that came with the apartment. Occasionally she stares at it, its unvarnished face, its eight shiny knobs, and a sensation nags at the back of her consciousness, a feeling like she has misplaced something but can no longer remember what it is.

Her mother used to say seeds were links in a chain, not beginnings or endings, but she was wrong: Seeds are both beginnings and ends—they are a plant's eggshell and its coffin. Orchards crouch invisibly inside each one. For a school project Jie brings over six Styrofoam cups filled with peat. The seed keeper offers him six magnolia seeds, each bright as a drop of blood.

The boy pokes a hole into each cupful of dirt with a finger; he drops the seeds in like tiny bombs. They put the cups on her windowsill. Water. Soil. Light. "Now we wait," she says.

We go round the world only to come back again. A seed coat splits, a tiny rootlet emerges. On the news a government official denies reports of cracks in the dam's ship locks. Li Qing calls: He's going to be traveling this week. Things are very busy. Penny Ou will try to stop by.

The seed keeper goes to the window. In the plaza, tides of people drift in a hundred directions; bicyclists, commuters, beggars, trash collectors, shoppers, policemen. Teacher Ke would have aged even more; it would hardly be possible for him to still be alive. And yet: What if he is one of those figures down there, inside one of those cars, one of the shapes on the sidewalk, a head and shoulders, the infinitesimal tops of his shoes?

Out past the square, tens of thousands of lights tremble in the wind, airplanes and shopfronts and billboards, guide lights and lamps behind windows and warning lights on antennas. Above them a handful of stars show themselves for a moment, murky, scarcely visible between clouds, flashing blue and red and white. Then they're gone.

The River Nemunas

My name is Allison. I'm fifteen years old. My parents are dead. I have a poodle named Mishap in a pet carrier between my ankles and a biography of Emily Dickinson in my lap. The flight attendant keeps refilling my apple juice. I'm thirty-six thousand feet over the Atlantic Ocean and out my smudgy little window the whole world has turned to water.

I'm moving to Lithuania. Lithuania is in the upper-right corner of Europe. Over by Russia. On the world map at school, Lithuania is pink.

Grandpa Z is waiting for me outside baggage claim. His belly looks big enough to fit a baby inside. He hugs me for a long time. Then he lifts Mishap out of his carrier and hugs Mishap, too.

Lithuania doesn't look pink. More like gray. Grandpa Z's little Peugeot is green and smells like rock dust. The sky sits low over the highway. We drive past hundreds of half-finished concrete apartment buildings that look as if they've been hit by tornadoes once or twice. There are big Nokia signs and bigger Aquafresh signs.

Grandpa Z says, Aquafresh is good toothpaste. You have Aquafresh in Kansas?

I tell him we use Colgate.

He says, I find you Colgate.

We merge onto a four-lane divided highway. The land on both sides is broken into pastures that look awfully muddy for early July. It starts to rain. The Peugeot has no windshield wipers. Mishap dozes in my lap. Lithuania turns a steamy green. Grandpa Z drives with his head out the window.

Eventually we stop at a house with a peaked wooden roof and a central chimney. It looks exactly like the twenty other houses crowded around it.

Home, says Grandpa Z, and Mishap jumps out.

The house is long and narrow, like a train car. Grandpa Z has three rooms: a kitchen in front, a bedroom in the middle, and a bathroom in the back. Outside there's a shed. He unfolds a card table. He brings me a little stack of Pringles on a plate. Then a steak. No green beans, no dinner rolls, nothing like that. We sit on the edge of his bed to eat. Grandpa Z doesn't say grace so I whisper it to myself. Bless us O Lord and these thy gifts. Mishap sniffs around skeptically between my feet.

Halfway through his steak Grandpa Z looks up at me and there are tears on his cheeks.

It's okay, I say. I've been saying it's okay a lot lately. I've said it to church ladies and flight attendants and counselors. I say, I'm fine, it's okay. I don't know if I'm fine or if it's okay, or if saying it makes anyone feel better. Mostly it's just something to say.

It was cancer. In case you were wondering. First they found it in Mom and she got her breasts cut off and her ovaries cut out but it was still in her, and then Dad got tested and it was in his lungs. I imagined cancer as a tree: a big, black, leafless tree inside Mom and another inside Dad. Mom's tree killed her in March. Dad's killed him three months later.

I'm an only child and have no other relatives so the lawyers sent me to live with Grandpa Z. The Z is for Zydrunas.

Grandpa Z's bed is in the kitchen because he's giving me the bedroom. The walls are bare plaster and the bed groans and the sheets smell like dust on a hot bulb. There's no shade on the window. On the dresser is a brand-new pink panda, which is sort of for babies, but also sort of cute. A price tag is still pinned to its ear: 39.99 Lt. The Lt is for litas. I don't know if 39.99 is a lot or a little.

After I turn off the lamp, all I see is black. Something goes tap tap tap against the ceiling. I can hear Mishap panting at the foot of the bed. My three duffel bags, stacked against the wall, contain everything I own in the world.

Do I sound faraway? Do I sound lost? Probably I am. I whisper: Dear God, please watch over Mom in Heaven and please watch over Dad in Heaven and please watch over me in Lithuania. And please watch over Mishap, too. And Grandpa Z.

And then I feel the Big Sadness coming on, like there's a shiny and sharp axe blade buried inside my chest. The only way I can stay alive is to remain absolutely motionless so instead of whispering Dear God how could you do this to me, I only whisper Amen which Pastor Jenks back home told me means I believe, and I lie with my eyelids closed clutching Mishap and inhaling his smell, which always smells to me like corn chips, and practice breathing in light and breathing out a color— light, green, light, yellow—like the counselor told me to do when the panic comes.

*   *   *

At 4 a.m. the sun is already up. I sit in a lawn chair beside Grandpa's shed and watch Mishap sniff around in Lithuania. The sky is silver and big scarves of mist drag through the fields. A hundred little black birds land on the roof of Grandpa's shed, then take off again.

Each house in Grandpa Z's little cluster of identical houses has lace curtains. The windows are all the same but the lace is different in each one. One has a floral pattern, one a linear pattern, and another has circles butted up against each other. As I look, an old woman pushes aside a zigzag-patterned curtain in one of the windows. She puts on a pair of huge glasses and waves me over and I can see there are tubes hooked through her nose.

Her house is twenty feet away from Grandpa Z's and it's full of Virgin Mary statues and herbs and smells like carrot peels. A man in a track suit in the back room is asleep on a bed with no blankets. The old lady unhooks herself from a machine that looks like two scuba tanks hung on a wheeled rack, and she pats the couch and says a bunch of words to me in Russian. Her mouth is full of gold. She has a marble-sized mole under her right eye. Her calves are like bowling pins and she is barefoot and her toes look beaten and crushed.

She nods at something I don't say and turns on a massive flat-screen television propped up on two cinderblocks, and together we watch a pastor give mass on TV. The colors are skewed and the audio is garbled. In his church there are maybe twenty-five people in folding chairs. When I was a baby Mom talked to me in Lithuanian so I can understand some of the pastor's sermon. There's something about his daddy falling off his roof. He says this means that just because you can't see something doesn't mean you shouldn't believe in it. I can't tell if he means Jesus or gravity.

Afterward the old lady brings me a big hot stuffed potato covered with bacon bits. She watches me eat through her huge, steamy eyeglasses.

Thanks, I say in Lithuanian, which sounds like achoo. She stares off into oblivion.

When I get back to Grandpa Z's house he has a magazine open in his lap with space diagrams in it.

You are at Mrs. Sabo's?

I was. Past tense, Grandpa.

Grandpa Z circles a finger beside his ear. Mrs. Sabo no more remember things, he says. You understand?

I nod.

I read here, Grandpa Z says, clearing his throat, that Earth has three moons. He bites his lower lip, thinking through the English. No, it used to has three moons. Earth used to has three moons. Long time ago. What do you think of this?

You want to know? What it's like? To prop up the dam? To keep your fingers plugged in its cracks? To feel like every single breath that passes is another betrayal, another step farther away from what you were and where you were and who you were, another step deeper into the darkness? Grandpa Z came to Kansas twice this spring. He sat in the rooms and smelled the smells. Now he leans forward till I can see the little red lightning bolts of veins in his eyes. You want to speak?

No thanks.

I mean talk, he says. Talk, Allie?

No. Thanks.

No? But to talk is good, no?

Grandpa Z makes gravestones. Gravestones in Lithuania aren't quite like the ones in America. They're glossy and smooth and made of granite, but most of them are etched with likenesses of the people buried underneath them. They're like black-and-white photos carved right into the stones. They're expensive and everyone spends money on them. Poor people, Grandpa Z says, spend the most. Sometimes he etches faces while other times he does the deceased's whole body, like a tall man standing in a leather jacket, life-size, very realistic, buttons on the cuffs and freckles on the cheeks. Grandpa Z shows me a Polaroid of a tombstone he made of a famous mobster. The stone is seven feet tall and has a life-size portrait of a man with his hands in his pockets sitting on the hood of a Mercedes. He says the family paid extra to have a halo added around the man's head.

Monday morning Grandpa Z goes to his workshop and school doesn't start for two months so I'm left alone in the house. By noon I've looked through all of Grandpa Z's drawers and his one closet. In the shed I find two fishing rods and an old aluminum boat under a tarp and eight jars of Lithuanian pennies and thousands of mouse-chewed British magazines: *Popular Science* and *Science Now* and *British Association for the Advancement of Physics*. There are magazines on polar bears and Mayan calendars and cell biology and lots of things I don't understand. Inside are faded cosmonauts and gorillas hooked up to machines and cartoon cars driving around on Mars.

Then Mrs. Sabo shows up. She shouts something in her derelict Russian and goes over to a chest of drawers and pulls open a cigarette box and inside are photographs.

Motina, she says, and points at me.

I say, I thought you couldn't remember things.

But she is sticking the photos under my nose like she has just remembered something and wants to get it out before she forgets it. Motina means Mom. All the photos contain Mom when she was a girl. Here she is in a polar bear costume and here she is frowning over what might be a lawnmower engine and here she is tramping barefoot through mud.

Mrs. Sabo and I lay out the pictures in a grid on Grandpa Z's card table. There are sixty-eight of them. Five-year-old Mom scowls in front of a rusted-out Soviet tank. Six-year-old Mom peels an orange. Nine-year-old Mom stands in the weeds. Looking at the photos starts a feeling in my gut like maybe I want to dig a shallow hole in the yard and lie down in it.

I separate out twelve of the pictures. In each of them, my mom—my Subaru-driving, cashew-eating, Barry Manilow–listening, Lithuanian-immigrant, dead-because-of-cancer Mom—is either standing in murky water or leaning over the side of a junky-looking boat, helping to hold up some part of a creepy and gigantic shark.

Erketas, Mrs. Sabo says, and nods gravely. Then she coughs for about two minutes straight.

Erketas?

But by now the coughing has shaken all the comprehension out of her. The man in the track suit, her son, comes over and says something and Mrs. Sabo stares at the lower part of his face for a while and eventually he coaxes her back to her house. Grandpa Z comes home from his job at 2:31.

Grandpa, I say, your toilet paper might as well be made out of gravel.

He nods thoughtfully.

And is this my mom, I ask, with all these great whites?

Grandpa looks at the pictures and blinks and puts a knuckle between his teeth. For maybe thirty seconds he doesn't answer.

He looks like he's standing outside an elevator waiting for the doors to open.

Finally he says, Erketas. He goes to a book in a box on the floor and opens it and pages through it and looks up and looks back down and says, Sturgeon.

Sturgeon. Erketas means sturgeon?

River fish. From the river.

We eat sausage for dinner. No bread, no salad. All through the meal the photos of Mom stare up at us.

I rinse the dishes. Grandpa Z says, You walk with me, Allie?

He leads me and Mishap across the field behind the colony of houses. There are neat little vegetable gardens and goats staked here and there. Grasshoppers skitter out in front of us. We clamber over a fence and pick our way around cow dung and nettles. The little trail heads toward some willows and on the other side is a river: quiet and brown, surprisingly far across. At first the river looks motionless, like a lake, but the more I look, the more I see it's moving very slowly.

Mishap sneezes. I don't think he's ever seen a river before. A line of cows saunters along on the far bank.

Grandpa Z says, Fishing. Is where your mother goes. Used to go. Past tense. He laughs an unsmiling laugh. Sometimes with her grandpa. Sometimes with Mrs. Sabo.

What's it called?

River Nemunas. It is called River Nemunas.

Every hour the thought floats to the surface: If we're all going to end up happy together in Heaven then why does anyone wait? Every hour the Big Sadness hangs behind my ribs, sharp and gleaming, and it's all I can do to keep breathing.

Mrs. Sabo, Grandpa Z says, is either 90 years old or 94 years old. Not even her son knows for sure. She has lived through the first Lithuanian independence and the second one, too. She fought with the Russians the first time, against them the second time. Back when all these houses were a collective farm under the Soviets, she used to take a rowboat every day for thirty-five years and row six miles up the river to work in a chemical plant. She went fishing when no women went fishing, he says.

Nowadays Mrs. Sabo has to be hooked up to her oxygen machine every night. She doesn't seem to mind if I come over to watch TV. We turn the volume up really high to hear over the wheezing and banging of her pump. Sometimes we watch the Lithuanian pastor, sometimes we watch cartoons. Sometimes it's so late we only watch a channel that shows a satellite map of the world, rotating forever across the screen.

I've been in Lithuania two weeks when Counselor Mike calls on Grandpa Z's cell phone. Counselor Mike, a lawyer who chews bubblegum and wears basketball shorts. It's two in the morning in Kansas. He asks how I'm adjusting. Hearing his wide-open American voice calls up for me in a sudden rush summertime Kansas. It's like it's right there on the other end of the phone, the air silky, the last porch lights switched off, a fog of gnats hovering above Brown's Pond, the moon coming to earth through sheets and layers and curtains of moisture, streetlights sending soft columns of light onto grocery store parking lots. And somewhere in that sleepy darkness Counselor Mike sits at his clunky kitchen table in his socks and asks an orphan in Lithuania how she's adjusting.

It takes me a full ten seconds to say, I'm fine, it's okay.

He says he needs to talk to Grandpa. We got an offer on the house, he says. Grown-up stuff.

Is the offer good?

Any offer is good.

I don't know what to say to that. I can hear music coming from his end, faraway and full of static. What does Counselor Mike listen to, deep in the Kansas night?

We're praying for you, Allie, he says.

Who's we?

Us at the office. And at church. Everyone. Everyone is praying for you.

Grandpa's at work, I say.

Later I walk Mishap across the field and over the fence and through the rocks to the river. The cows are still on the far side, eating whatever cows eat and whipping their tails back and forth.

Five thousand miles away Counselor Mike is planning to sell the orange plastic tiles Dad glued to the basement floor and the dent I put in the dining room wall and the raspberry bushes Mom planted in the backyard. He's going to sell our warped baking sheets and half-used shampoos and the six Jedi drinking glasses we got from Pizza Hut that Dad said we could keep only after asking our pastor if *Star Wars* would have been "endorsed by Jesus." Everything, all of it, our junk, our dregs, our memories. And I've got the family poodle and three duffel bags of too small clothes and four photo albums, but no one left who can flesh out any of the photos. I'm five thousand miles and four weeks away and every minute that ratchets past is another minute that the world has kept on turning without Mom and Dad in it. And I'm supposed to live with Grandpa Z in Lithuania, what, for the rest of my life?

Thinking about the house sitting there empty back in Kansas starts the Big Sadness swinging in my chest like a pendulum and soon a blue flood is streaming around the edges of my vision. It comes on fast this time and the axe blade is slicing up organs willy-nilly and all of a sudden it feels like I'm looking into a very blue bag and someone's yanking the drawstring closed. I fall over into the willows.

I lie there for who knows how long. Up in the sky I see Dad emptying his pockets after work, dumping coins and breath mints and business cards onto the kitchen counter. I see Mom cutting a fried chicken breast into tiny white triangles and dunking each piece in ketchup. I see the Virgin Mary walk out onto a little balcony between the clouds and look around and take ahold of French doors, one on either side of her, and slam them shut.

I can hear Mishap sniffing around nearby. I can hear the river sliding past and grasshoppers chewing the leaves and the sad, dreamy clanking of faraway cowbells. The sun is tiny and flame-blue. When I finally sit up, Mrs. Sabo is standing beside me. I didn't know she could walk so far. Little white butterflies are looping through the willows. The river glides past. She says something in machine-gun Russian and sets her frozen hand on my forehead. We watch the river, Mrs. Sabo and Mishap and me, in the grass in the sun. And as we watch and breathe and I come back into myself—I swear—a fish as big as a nuclear missile leaps out of the river. Its belly is spotless white and its back is gray and it curls up in midair and flaps its tail and stretches like it's thinking, This time gravity will let me go.

When it comes back down, water explodes far enough across the river that some drops land on my feet.

Mishap raises his ears, cocks his head. The river heals itself over. Mrs. Sabo looks at me from behind her huge eyeglasses and blinks her milky eyes a dozen times.

Did you see that? Please tell me you saw that.

Mrs. Sabo only blinks.

Grandpa Z gets home at 3:29.

I buy you a surprise, he says. He opens the hatchback of the Peugeot and inside is a crate of American toilet paper.

Grandpa, I say. I want to go fishing.

Dad used to say God made the world and everything in it and Grandpa Z would say if God made the world and everything in it, then why isn't everything perfect? Why do we get hernias and why do beautiful healthy daughters get cancer? Then Dad would say, Well, God was a mystery and Grandpa Z would say God was a, what's the word, a security blanket for babies, and Dad would stomp off and Mom would throw down her napkin and blast some Lithuanian words at Grandpa and go jogging after Dad and I'd look at the plates on the table.

Grandpa Z crossed the ocean twice this spring to watch his daughter and son-in-law die. Did God have explanations for that? Now I stand in Grandpa Z's kitchen and listen to him say that there aren't any sturgeon anymore in the River Nemunas. There might be some left in the Baltic Sea, he says, but there aren't any in the river. He says his dad used to take Mom sturgeon fishing every Sunday for years and Mrs. Sabo probably caught a few in the old days but then there was overfishing and pesticides and the Kaunas dam and black-market caviar and his dad died and the last sturgeon died and the Soviet Union broke up and Mom grew up and went to university in the United States and married a creationist and no one has caught a sturgeon in the River Nemunas for twenty-five years.

Grandpa, I say, Mrs. Sabo and I saw a sturgeon. Today. Right over there. And I point out the window across the field to the line of willows.

It is photos, he says. You see the photos of your mother.

I saw a sturgeon, I say. Not in a picture. In the river.

Grandpa Z closes his eyelids and opens them. Then he holds me by the shoulders and looks me in the eyes and says, We see things. Sometimes they there. Sometimes they not there. We see them the same either way. You understand?

I saw a sturgeon. So did Mrs. Sabo. I go to bed mad and wake up mad. I throw the stuffed panda against the wall and stomp around on the porch and kick gravel in the driveway. Mishap barks at me.

In the morning I watch Grandpa Z drive off to work, big and potbellied and confused, and I can hear Mrs. Sabo's machine whirring and thunking in her house next door and I think: I should have asked Grandpa Z to trust me. I should have told him about the pastor's old daddy and the stepladder and Jesus and gravity and how just because you don't see something doesn't mean you shouldn't believe in it.

Instead I wade into Grandpa Z's shed and start pulling out boxes and granite samples and chisels and rock saws and it takes me a half hour to clear a path and another half hour to drag the old aluminum boat into the driveway. It's flat-bottomed and has three bench seats and there are maybe a thousand spiders living beneath each one. I blast them out with a hose. I find a bottle of some toxic Lithuanian cleaner and pour it all over the hull.

After a while Mrs. Sabo comes tottering out in her big eye-glasses with her little arms folded against her chest and looks at me like a praying mantis. She lets off a chain of coughs. Her son comes out in his track suit with a cigarette between his lips and they watch me work for ten minutes or so and then he leads his mother back inside.

Grandpa Z gets home at 3:27. There are boxes and hoses and rakes and tools all over the driveway. The bottle of solvent has left bright, silver streaks across the hull of the boat. I say, Mrs. Sabo and I saw a sturgeon in the river yesterday, Grandpa.

Grandpa Z blinks at me. He looks like maybe he's looking into the past at something he thought had ended a long time ago.

He says, No more sturgeon in the Nemunas.

I say, I want to try to catch one.

They not here, Grandpa Z says. They endangered species. It means—

I know what it means.

He looks from me to the boat to Mishap to me. He takes off his hat and drags his hand through his hair and puts his hat back on. Then he nudges the boat with the toe of his sneaker and shakes his head and Mishap wags his tail and a cloud blows out of the way. Sunlight explodes off of everything.

I use an ancient, flat-tired dolly to drag the boat through the field and over the fence to the river. It takes me three hours. Then I lug the oars and the fishing poles down. Then I walk back and tell Mrs. Sabo's son I'm taking her out on the river and guide Mrs. Sabo by the arm and lead her across the field and sit her in the bow of the boat. In the sunlight her skin looks like old candle wax.

We fish with blunt, seven-foot rods and ancient hooks that

are as big as my hand. We use worms. Mrs. Sabo's face stays completely expressionless. The current is very slow and it's easy to paddle once in a while and keep the boat in the center of the river.

Mishap sits on the bench beside Mrs. Sabo and shivers with excitement. The river slips along. We see a whole herd of feral cats sleeping on a boulder in the sun. We see a deer twitching its ears in the shallows. Black and gray and green walls of trees slide past.

In the late afternoon I pull onto what turns out to be an island and Mrs. Sabo steps out of the boat and lifts up her skirt and has a long pee in the willows. I open a can of Pringles and we share it.

Do you remember my mother? I ask, but Mrs. Sabo only glances over and gives me a dreamy look. As if she knows everything but I wouldn't understand. Her eyes are a thousand miles away. I like to think she's remembering other trips down the river, other afternoons in the sun. I read to her from one of Grandpa Z's nature magazines. I tell her a bald eagle's feathers weigh twice as much as its bones. I tell her aardvarks drink their water by eating cucumbers. I tell her that male emperor moths can smell female emperor moths flapping along six miles away.

It takes me a couple of hours of rowing to get back home. We watch big pivot sprinklers spray rainbows over a field of potatoes and we watch a thousand boxcars go rattling along behind a train. It's beautiful out here, I say.

Mrs. Sabo looks up. Remember? she asks in Lithuanian. But she doesn't say anything else.

We don't catch any fish. Mishap falls asleep. Mrs. Sabo's knees get sunburned.

* * *

That one day is all it takes. Every morning Grandpa Z leaves to go etch dead people's faces into granite, and as soon as he's gone I take Mrs. Sabo out in the boat. An old-timer six houses down tells me I should be using rotten hamburger meat, not worms, and that I should stuff it inside the toes of pantyhose and tie the pantyhose to the hooks with elastic thread. So I get some hamburger and put it in a bucket in the sun until it smells like hell, but the pantyhose won't stay on the hook, and a lady at the convenience store in Mažeikiai says she hasn't seen a sturgeon in fifty years but when there were sturgeon they didn't want rotten food, they wanted fresh sand shrimp on big hooks.

I try deep holes behind rapids and eddies beside fields of bright yellow flowers and big, blue, shadowy troughs. I try clams and nightcrawlers and—once—frozen chicken thighs. I keep thinking Mrs. Sabo will pipe up, will remember, will tell me how it's done. But mostly she sits there with that long-gone look on her face. My brain gradually becomes like a map of the river bottom: gravel bars, two sunken cars with their rust-chewed rooftops just below the surface, long stretches of still water seething with trash. You'd think the surface of a river would be steady but it isn't. There are all these churnings and swirls and eddies, bubblings and blossomings, submerged stumps and plastic bags and spinning crowns of light down there, and when the sun is right sometimes you can see thirty feet down.

We don't catch a sturgeon. We don't even see any. I begin to think maybe Grandpa Z is right, maybe sometimes the things we think we see aren't really what we see. But here's the surprising thing: It doesn't bother me. I like being out there with Mrs. Sabo. She seems okay with it, her son seems okay with it, and maybe I'm okay with it, too. Maybe it feels as if the wretchedness in my gut might be getting a little smaller.

When I was five I got an infection and Dr. Nasser put some drops in my eyes. Pretty soon all I could see were blurs and colors. Dad was a fog and Mom was a smudge and the world looked like it does when your eyes are full of tears. A couple of hours later, right around when Dr. Nasser said it would, my eyesight came back. I was riding in the backseat of Mom's Subaru and the world started coming back into focus. I was myself again and the trees were trees again, only the trees looked more alive than I'd ever seen them: The branches above our street were interlaced beneath an ocean of leaves, thousands and thousands of leaves scrolling past, dark on the tops and pale on the undersides, every individual leaf moving independently but still in concert with the others.

Going out on the Nemunas is sort of like that. You come down the path and step through the willows and it's like seeing the lights in the world come back on.

Even when there's not much of a person left, you can still learn things about her. I learn that Mrs. Sabo likes the smell of cinnamon. I learn she perks up any time we round this one particular bend in the river. Even with her little gold-capped teeth she chews food slowly and delicately, and I think maybe her mom must have been strict about that, like, Sit up straight, Chew carefully, Watch your manners. Emily Dickinson's mom was like that. Of course, Emily Dickinson wound up terrified of death and wore only white clothes and would only talk to visitors through the closed door of her room.

Mid-August arrives and the nights get hot and damp. Grandpa Z keeps the front door open. I can hear Mrs. Sabo's oxygen machine wheezing and murmuring all night. In half-dreams it's a sound like the churning of the world through the universe.

Yellow, green, red runs the flag flapping in front of the post office. Sun up top, Grandpa Z says, land in the middle, blood down below. Lithuania: doormat of a thousand wars.

I miss Kansas. I miss the redbud trees, the rainstorms, how the college kids all wear purple on football Saturdays. I miss Mom walking into the grocery store and pushing her sunglasses up on her forehead, or Dad pedaling up a hill on his bicycle, me a little person in a bike trailer behind him, his maroon backpack bobbing up and down.

One day in late August Mrs. Sabo and I are drifting downstream, our lines trailing in the river, when Mrs. Sabo starts talking in Lithuanian. I've known her forty days and not heard her say so much in all of them combined. She tells me that the afterworld is a garden. She says it's on a big mountain on the other side of an ocean. This garden is always warm and there are no winters there and that's where the birds go in the fall. She waits a few minutes and then says that death is a woman named Giltine. Giltine is tall, skinny, blind, and always really, really hungry. Mrs. Sabo says when Giltine walks past, mirrors splinter, beekeepers find coffin-shaped honeycombs in the hives, and people dream of teeth being pulled. Anytime you have a dream about the dentist, she says, that means death walked past you in the night.

One of Grandpa Z's magazines says that when a young albatross first takes wing, it can stay in the air without touching the ground for fifteen years. I think when I die I'd like to be tied to ten thousand balloons, so I could go floating into the clouds, and get blown off somewhere above the cities, and then the mountains, and then the ocean, just miles and miles of blue ocean, my corpse sailing above it all.

Maybe I could last fifteen years up there. Maybe an albatross could land on me and use me for a little resting perch. Maybe that's silly. But it makes as much sense, I think, as watching your Mom and Dad get buried in boxes in the mud.

At night Mrs. Sabo and I start watching a show called *Boy Meets Grill* on her big TV. I try cooking zucchini crisps and Pepsi-basted eggplant. I try cooking asparagus Francis and broccoli Diane. Grandpa Z screws up his eyebrows sometimes when he comes in the door but he sits through my Bless us O Lord and eats everything I cook and washes it all down with Juozo beer. Some weekends he drives me up the road to little towns with names like Panemunė and Pagėgiai and we buy ice cream sandwiches from Lukoil stations, and Mishap sleeps in the hatchback and at dusk the sky goes from blue to purple and purple to black.

Almost every day in August Mrs. Sabo and I fish for sturgeon. I row upriver and drift us home, dropping our cinderblock anchor now and then to fish the deep holes. I sit in the bow and Mrs. Sabo sits in the stern and Mishap sleeps under the middle bench, and I wonder about how memories can be here one minute and then gone the next. I wonder about how the sky can be a huge, blue nothingness and at the same time it can also feel like a shelter.

It's the last dawn in August. We are fishing a mile upstream from the house when Mrs. Sabo sits up and says something in Russian. The boat starts rocking back and forth. Then her reel starts screaming.

Mishap starts barking. Mrs. Sabo jams her heels against the hull and jabs the butt of her rod into her belly and holds on. The reel yowls.

Whatever is on the other end takes a lot of line. Mrs. Sabo clings to it and doesn't let go and a strange, fierce determination flows into her face. Her glasses slide down her nose. A splotch of sweat shaped like Australia blooms on the back of her blouse. She mutters to herself. Her little baggy arms quiver. Her rod bends into an upside-down U.

What do I do? There's nobody there to answer so I say, Pray, and I pray. Mrs. Sabo's line disappears at a diagonal into the river and I can see it bending away through the water, dissolving into a coffee-colored darkness. The boat seems like it might actually be moving upriver and Mrs. Sabo's reel squeaks now and then and it feels like what the Sunday school teacher used to tell us during choir practice when she'd say we were tapping into something larger than ourselves.

Slowly the line makes a full circuit of the boat. Mrs. Sabo pulls up on her rod, and cranks her reel, gaining ground inch by inch, little by little. Then she gets a bit of slack so she starts reeling like mad, taking in yards of line, and whatever is on the other end tries to make a slow run.

Bubbles rise to the surface. The swivel and weight on Mrs. Sabo's line become visible. It holds there a minute, just below the surface of the water, as if we are about to see whatever is just below the leader, whatever is struggling there, when, with a sound like a firecracker, Mrs. Sabo's line pops and the swivel and broken leader fly over our heads.

Mrs. Sabo pitches backward and nearly falls out of the boat. She drops the rod. Her glasses fall off. She says something like Holy, holy, holy, holy.

Little ripples spread across the face of the river and are pulled downstream. Then there's nothing. The current laps quietly against the hull. We resume our quiet slide downriver. Mishap licks Mrs. Sabo's hands. And Mrs. Sabo gives me a little gold-toothed smile as if whatever was on the other end of her fishing line has just pulled her back into the present for a minute and in the silence I feel my mom is here, together with me, under the Lithuanian sunrise, both of us with decades left to live.

Grandpa Z doesn't believe me. He sits on the edge of his bed, elbows on the card table, a moderately renowned Lithuanian tombstone maker, with droopy eyes and broken blood vessels in his cheeks, a plate of half-eaten cauliflower parmesan in front of him, and wipes his eyes and tells me I need to start thinking about school clothes. He says maybe we caught a carp or an old tire or a sunken cow carcass but that for us to catch a sturgeon would be pretty much like catching a dinosaur, about as likely as dredging a big seventy-million-year-old Triceratops out of the river muck.

Mrs. Sabo hooked one, I say.

Okay, Grandpa Z says. But he doesn't even look at me.

Mažeikiai Senamiesčio Secondary School is made of sand-colored bricks. The windows are all black. A boy in the parking lot throws a tennis ball onto the roof and waits for the ball to roll down and catches it and does this over and over.

It looks like every other school, I say.

It looks nice, Grandpa Z says.

It starts to rain. He says, You are nervous, and I say, How

come you don't believe me about the fish? He looks at me and looks back at the parking lot and rolls down the window and swipes raindrops from the windshield with his palm.

There are sturgeon in the river. Or there's one. There's at least one.

They all gone, Allie, he says. You only break your heart more with this fishing. You only make yourself more lonely.

So what, Grandpa, you don't believe in anything you can't see? You believe we don't have souls? You put a cross on every headstone you make, but you think the only thing that happens to us when we die is that we turn into mud?

For a while we watch the kid throw and catch his tennis ball. He never misses. Grandpa Z says, I come to Kansas. I ride airplane. I see tops of clouds. No people up there. No gates, no Jesus. Your mother and father are in the sky sitting on clouds? You think this?

I look back at Mishap, who's curled up in the hatchback against the rain. Maybe, I say. Maybe I think something like that.

I make friends with a girl named Laima and another girl named Asta. They watch *Boy Meets Grill*, too. Their parents are not dead. Their mothers yell at them for shaving their legs and tell them things like, I really wish you wouldn't chew your hangnails like that, Laima, or, Your skirt is way too short, Asta.

At night I lie in bed with Grandpa Z's unpainted plaster slowly cracking all around me and no shade on the window and Mrs. Sabo's machine wheezing next door and stars creeping imperceptibly across the windowpane and reread the part in my Emily Dickinson biography when she says, "To live is so startling it leaves little time for anything else." People still remember Emily Dickinson said that, but when I try to remember a sentence Mom or Dad said I can't remember a single one. They probably said a million sentences to me before they died but tonight it seems all I have are prayers and clichés. When I shut my eyes I see Mom and Dad at church, Mom holding a little maroon songbook, Dad's little yachting belt and penny loafers. He leans over to whisper something to me—a little girl standing in the pew beside him. But when his mouth opens, no sound comes out.

The willows along the river turn yellow. Our history teacher takes us on a field trip to the KGB museum in Vilnius. The KGB used to cram five or six prisoners into a room the size of a phone booth. They also had cells where prisoners had to stand for days in three inches of water with no place to sit or lie down. Did you know the arms of straitjackets used to be twelve or fourteen feet long? They'd knot them behind your back.

Late one night Mrs. Sabo and I watch a program about a tribe in South America. It shows a naked old guy roasting a yam on a stick. Then it shows a young guy in corduroys riding a moped. The young guy, the narrator lady tells us, is the old guy's grandson. No one wants to do the traditional tribe stuff anymore, the narrator lady says. The old people sit around on their haunches looking gloomy and the youngsters ride buses and move to the cities and listen to cassette tapes. None of the young people want to speak the original language, the narrator says, and no one bothers to teach it to their babies. The village used to have 150 people. All but six have moved away and are speaking Spanish now.

At the end the narrator says the tribe's old language has a word for standing in the rain looking at the back of a person you love. She says it has another word for shooting an arrow into an animal poorly, so that it hurts the animal more than is necessary. To call a person this word, in the old language, the lady says, is the worst sort of curse you could imagine.

Fog swirls outside the windows. Mrs. Sabo stands and disconnects herself from her machine and takes a bottle of Juozo beer from the refrigerator. Then she goes out the front door and walks into the yard and stands at the far edge of the porch light and pours some beer into her cupped hand. She holds it out for a long time, and I'm wondering if Mrs. Sabo has finally drifted off the edge until out of the mist comes a white horse and it drinks the beer right out of her cupped hand and then Mrs. Sabo presses her forehead against the horse's big face and the two of them stay like that for a long time.

That night I dream my molars come loose. My mouth fills with teeth. I know before I open my eyes that Mrs. Sabo is dead. People come over all day long. Her son leaves the windows and doors open for three days so that her soul can escape. At night I walk over to her house and sit with him and he smokes cigarettes and I watch cooking shows.

You are okay? he says in Lithuanian, two nights after she's gone. I shrug. I'm worried that if I open my mouth something wretched will come out. He doesn't say anything else.

The following day Grandpa drives me home from school and looks at me a long time and tells me he wants to go fishing.

Really? I say.

Really, he says. He walks across the field with me; he lets me bait his hook. For three straight afternoons we fish together. He tells me the chemical plant where Mrs. Sabo worked used to make cement and fertilizer and sulfuric acid, and under the Soviets some days the river would turn mustard yellow. He tells me that the farms here were collectives, where many families worked a large area, and that's why the houses are in clusters and not spread out, each to its own plot, like farmhouses in Kansas.

On the fourth day, I'm fishing with a chicken carcass when my line goes tight. I count to three and try to yank my rod up. It doesn't budge. It's a feeling like I've hooked into the river bottom itself, like I'm trying to pull up the bedrock of Lithuania.

Grandpa Z looks over at my line and then at me.

Snagged? he says. My arms feel like they're going to tear off. The current pulls the boat slowly downstream and soon the line is so tight drops are sizzling off it. Every once in a while a little line cranks off the reel. That's all that happens. If I were to let go of my rod, it would shoot upriver.

Something pulls at me and the boat pulls at it and we stay like that for a long time, locked in a tug-of-war, my little fishing line holding the entire boat and me and Mishap and Grandpa Z steady against the current, as if I've hooked into a big, impossible plug of sadness resting on the bottom of the river.

You pull, I whisper to myself. Then you crank. Like Mrs. Sabo did. Pull, crank, pull, crank.

I try. My arms feel like they're disappearing. The boat rocks. Mishap pants. A bright silver wind comes down the river. It smells like wet pine trees. I close my eyes. I think about the new family that's moving into our house, some new Mom hanging her clothes in Mom's closet, some new Dad calling to her from Dad's office, some teenage son tacking posters to my walls. I think about how Grandpa Z says the sky is blue because it's dusty and octopuses can unscrew the tops off jars and starfish have eyes at the tips of their arms. I think: No matter what happens, no matter how wretched and gloomy everything can get, at least Mrs. Sabo got to feel this.

Grandpa Z says, It's not a snag. He says it twice. I open my eyes. Bubbles are rising from whatever is on the other end of my line. It's as if I'm going to separate at the waist. But gradually, eventually, I seem to be gaining some ground. The boat rocks as I pull it a yard upstream. I heave the rod up, crank in a couple turns of line.

Pull, then crank. Pull, then crank. We skid another yard upstream. Grandpa Z's eyes seem about to bulge out of their sockets.

It's not a fish. I know it's not a fish. It's just a big lump of memory at the bottom of the River Nemunas. I say a prayer Dad taught me about God being in the light and the water and the rocks, about God's mercy enduring forever. I say it quickly to myself, hissing it out through my lips, and pull then crank, pull then crank, God is in the light, God is in the water, God is in the rocks, and I can feel Mishap scrabbling around the boat with his little claws and I can even feel his heart beating in his chest, a little bright fist opening and closing, and I can feel the river pulling past the boat, its tributaries like fingernails dragging through the entire country, all of Lithuania draining into this one artery, five hundred sliding miles of water, all the way to the Baltic, which Grandpa Z says is the coldest sea in Europe, and something occurs to me that will probably seem obvious to you but that I never thought about before: A river never stops. Wherever you are, whatever you're doing, forgetting, sleeping, mourning, dying—the rivers are still running.

Grandpa Z shouts. Something is surfacing twenty feet away from the boat. It comes up without hurrying, like a submarine, as if from a dream: breathtakingly huge, the size of a desk. It's a fish.

I can see four barbells under his snout, like snakes. I see his fog-colored belly. I see the big hook stuck through his jaw. He moves slowly, and eases his head back and forth, like a horse shaking off a wasp.

He is huge. He is tremendous. He is ten feet long.

Erketas, says Grandpa Z.

I can't hold it anymore, I say.

Grandpa Z says, You can.

Pull, crank. Breathe in light, breathe out color. The sturgeon comes to us upside down. His mouth sucks and opens, sucks and opens. His back is covered with armor. He looks fifty thousand years old.

For a full minute the fish floats beside the boat like a soft white railroad tie, the boat rocking gently, no Mrs. Sabo, no Mom and Dad, no tape measures or hanging scales, no photographs, my arms ablaze with pain and Mishap barking and Grandpa Z looking down as if he's looking over the rim of a cloud and is witnessing a resurrection. The sturgeon's gills open and close. The flesh inside is a brilliant, impossible crimson.

I hold him there for maybe ten more seconds. Who else sees him? The cows? The trees? Then Grandpa Z leans over, unfolds his pocketknife, and cuts the line. The fish floats beside the boat for a few seconds, stunned and sleepy. He doesn't flick his tail, doesn't flex his huge body. He simply sinks out of sight.

Mishap goes quiet. The boat wobbles and starts downriver. The river pours on and on. I think of those photos of Mom, as tall and thin as a blade of grass, a bike rider, a swimmer, a stranger, a suntanned sixth-grader who might still come pedaling up the driveway of her father's house some afternoon with a jump rope over her shoulder. I think of Mrs. Sabo, how her memories slipped away one by one into the twilight and left her here in a house in a field in the middle of Lithuania waiting for skinny, ravenous Giltine to carry her to a garden on the other side of the sky.

I feel the tiniest lightening. Like one pound out of a thousand has been lifted off my shoulders. Grandpa Z dips his hands in the water and rubs them together. I can see each drop of water falling off his fingertips. I can see them falling in perfect spheres and reflecting back tiny pieces of light before returning to the river.

We hardly ever talk about the fish. It's there between us, something we share. Maybe we believe talking about it will ruin it. Grandpa Z spends his evenings etching Mrs. Sabo's face into her tombstone. Her son has offered several times to pay but Grandpa does it for free. He puts her on the granite without her glasses and her eyes look small and naked and girlish. He draws a lace-collared dress up tight around her throat and pearls around that, and he renders her hair in cotton-candy loops. It really is a very good job. It rains on the day they put it over her grave.

In November our whole school takes a bus to Plokštinė, an abandoned underground Soviet missile base where the Russians used to keep nukes. It looks like a grassy field, hemmed with birch, with an oversized pitcher's mound in each corner. There are no admission fees, no tourists, just a few signs in English and Lithuanian and a single strand of barbed wire—all that remains of seven layers of alarms, electric fences, razor cable, Dobermans, searchlights, and machine gun emplacements.

We go down a staircase in the center of the field. Electric bulbs dangle from cracked ceilings. The walls are cramped and rusty. I pass a tiny bunkroom and a pair of generators with their guts torn out. Then a dripping black corridor, clotted with puddles. Eventually I reach a railing. The ceiling is belled out: One of the pitcher's mounds must be directly above me. I shine my flashlight ninety feet down. The bottom of the silo is all rust and shadows and echoes.

Here, not so long ago, they kept a thermonuclear ballistic missile as big as a tractor trailer. The iron collar around the rim of the hole has the 360 degrees of a compass painted around its circumference. Easier, I suppose, to aim for a compass heading than for Frankfurt.

The urge to know scrapes against the inability to know. What was Mrs. Sabo's life like? What was my mother's? We peer at the past through murky water; all we can see are shapes and figures. How much is real? And how much is merely threads and tombstones?

On the way home Lithuanian kids jostle in the seats around me, smelling of body odor. A stork flaps across a field in the last of the daylight. The boy beside me tells me to keep my eyes out the window, that to see a white horse at dusk is the best possible kind of luck.

Don't tell me how to grieve. Don't tell me ghosts fade away eventually, like they do in movies, waving goodbye with see-through hands. Lots of things fade away but ghosts like these don't, heartbreak like this doesn't. The axe blade is still as sharp and real inside me as it was six months ago.

I do my homework and feed my dog and say my prayers.

Grandpa Z learns a little more English, I learn a little more Lithuanian, and soon both of us can talk in the past tense. And when I start to feel the Big Sadness cutting me up inside I try to remember Mrs. Sabo and the garden that is the afterworld and I watch the birds fly south in their flocks.

The sturgeon we caught was pale and armored and beautiful, splotched all over with age and lice. He was a big softboned hermit living at the bottom of a deep hole in a river that pours on and on like a green ghost through the fields of Lithuania. Is he an orphan like me? Does he spend all day every day searching for some brother he can recognize? And yet, wasn't he so gentle when I got him close to the boat? Wasn't he just as patient as a horse? Wasn't he just about as noble as anything?

Jesus, Dad used to say, is a golden boat on a long, dark river. That's one thing I can remember him saying.

It's quiet in Lithuania in November, and awful dark. I lie on my grandfather's bed and clutch Mishap and breathe in light and breathe out color. The house groans. I pray for Mom and Dad and Mrs. Sabo and Grandpa Z. I pray for those South American tribespeople on the television and their vanishing language. I pray for the lonely sturgeon, a monster, a lunker, last elder of a dying nation, drowsing in the bluest, deepest chambers of the River Nemunas.

Out the window it starts to snow.

Afterworld

In a tall house in a yard of thistles eleven girls wake on the floor of eleven bedrooms. They yawn, press their foreheads to windowpanes. Up and down the surrounding blocks, terrace houses stand in four- and five-story rows. In some, roofs have collapsed. In others, façades have crumbled away to reveal inner beams, empty rooms, green pools of rainwater. The few windows that still have glass in their frames reflect back rectangles of sky.

Saplings grow from ruptures in the street. Flights of pink-rimmed clouds sail overhead.

A three-year-old named Anita Weiss calls hello down the stairwell. Twice, three times. One story below, another girl replies. Two older girls go from floor to floor collecting everyone. Five-year-old Ilouka Croner. Eight-year-old Bela Cohn. Inga Hoffman and Hanelore Goldschmidt and her older sister Regina. Nearsighted Else Dessau.

Downstairs they find no furniture, no toilets, no doors on

the cupboards, no draperies over the windows. The sinks are unplumbed. Ulcerations of paint blister the walls. House martins loop past cracked windowpanes. The girls sit in what was once a parlor in the strengthening daylight. All wear dresses of mismatched sizes. Most are barefoot. Some yawn; some rub their eyes. Some flex their arms and fingers as if they have been fitted with new limbs.

"What is this place?"

"They said there would be promenades. Gardens."

The youngest peer out into the thistles. The oldest frown and search their memories. Several sense something recently settled there, something ghastly, something that might come alive if they poke at it too much.

Nine-year-old Hanelore Goldschmidt treads down the staircase with her hands cupped in front of her. She scans the faces in the parlor.

"Where's Esther? Is Esther here?"

No one answers. A tiny paw, poking out between Hanelore's fingers, trembles visibly.

Inga Hoffman says, "Is that a mouse?"

Else Dessau says, "Has anyone seen my glasses?"

Regina Goldschmidt says, "They can bite, you know."

Hanelore whispers into her hands.

Regina says, "Keep it away from the little ones."

Several of the girls glance continually toward the doorways. Expecting Frau Cohen with her housedress and apron to stride in and clap her hands and make an announcement. Get a broom. Get a mop. She who rests rusts. Breakfast will be served in twenty minutes. Her skirts smelling of camphor. Four dozen of her cabbage rolls browning in a skillet.

But Frau Cohen does not come through the doorway.

The last to come downstairs is sixteen-year-old Miriam

Ingrid Bergen. She walks to the front door and opens it and stands looking out. In the dawn light a block away through the haphazard trestle of saplings a single doe steps lightly. It pauses; it twitches its long ears toward Miriam. Then it steps behind a tree and vanishes.

No entryway, no front walk. No paths trampled through the thistles. There are only the blank faces of the neighboring houses and lank curtains of ivy dangling from gutters and a single gull floating above the broken street. And the light, which seems to carry thousands of miles before it passes over the rooftops in an obliterating silence.

Miriam turns. "We're dead," she says. "I'm sure of it."

2.

Esther Gramm is born in 1927 in Hamburg, Germany. Her mother's labor is long and harrowing. For several minutes Esther is trapped inside the birth canal without oxygen. Her mother dies of complications; Esther is left with a quarter-inch scar inside her left temporal lobe.

Her father drowns in a canal four years later. Esther is bundled across the city at night: snow over the jetties, vapor rising from the holes in sewer lids. One-horse carriages scuttle along through the falling white.

The Hirschfeld Trust Girls' Orphanage at Number 30 Papendam is a five-story rowhouse in a middle-class Jewish neighborhood. In its dormitories a dozen girls sleep on folding cots. They wear their hair in tandem plaits; they wear matching black stockings and shin-length dresses. They walk to gymnastics class on Tuesday evenings, repair their clothes on Wednesday evenings, weave matzah baskets on Thursday evenings.

Every morning the House Directress, Frau Cohen, listens to the girls read in synchrony from donated readers. *Little Solomon is sweeping the coal bin. Little Isaac is pulling his wagon.*

Esther has been at Number 30 Papendam for a year when she begins having temporal lobe epileptic seizures. She smells an overwhelming odor of celery when none is present. She stands in the parlor downstairs and a sense of impending annihilation swamps her and for a full minute she cannot respond to anything anyone says to her.

Months later, when Esther is six, she is sitting in the washroom in a chair beside the three iron bathtubs, waiting her turn for a bath, when she hears what sounds like a steam engine rumble to life in the distance. Within seconds the train sounds as if it has drawn close enough to explode through the wall. None of the other girls glance up. Frau Cohen carries in a stack of folded nightdresses, her sleeves rolled up, three strands of hair hanging over her eyes. She looks at Esther and tilts her head slightly. Her mouth moves, but no sound comes out.

Esther clamps her palms over her ears. The train roars as if through the throat of a tunnel. Any second it will be upon her; any second she will be crushed. Then the train passes through her head.

Here is what the other girls see: Little Esther slips off the chair in the corner, lands on her side on the tile, and starts convulsing. Her wrists curl inward. Her eyes blink a dozen times a second.

Here is what Esther sees: an unfurnished room. The train is gone, the girls are gone, Hirschfeld House is gone. Violet, snow-refracted light washes through two windows. A man and woman sit cross-legged on the floor. For a moment they look together up through a window into the snow as it blows past apartment houses across the street.

"First we die," the woman says. "Then our bodies are buried. So we die two deaths."

Esther can feel, distantly, that her body is kicking.

"Then," continues the woman, "in another world, folded inside the living world, we wait. We wait until everyone who knew us when we were children has died. And when the last one of them dies, we finally die our third death."

Out the window wind catches the snow and seems to blow it upward, back into the clouds. "That's when we're released to the next world," the woman says. In the Hirschfeld House bathroom, one of the girls screams. Frau Cohen drops the stack of nightdresses. Maybe nine seconds pass. Esther wakes up.

3.

Seventy-five years later, eighty-one-year-old Esther Gramm finds herself flat on her back in her garden in Geneva, Ohio. She is a widow, a grower of prize-winning carrots, and a mildly celebrated illustrator of children's books. She lives alone in a pale blue ranch house on thirteen acres of maples and poplars four miles from Lake Erie. She has lived here for fifty years.

Esther's son and his blond, cross-country-skiing wife live next door in a white colonial on the other side of a wall of willows. Four days ago they flew to Changsha, China, to adopt twin girls. But there have been visa problems, an unexpected bungling of documents. Suddenly everything is in question. They've told their twenty-year-old son, Robert—a college junior home for the summer—that they may have to remain in China for several weeks.

Esther's left hand is clamped in her grandson's right. Her whole body, even the backs of her hands, is damp with sweat.

The windows of her house, visible between the slats of her garden fence, glow lightly against the dusk. Robert presses his fist into his forehead. "Four this week," he says.

"They're real," Esther whispers. She sits up too quickly and her eyesight flees in long streaks. Robert retrieves her eyeglasses, helps her to her feet.

"We're going to the hospital," he says. Clouds of gnats throb against the sky. The first bats whirl out of the trees.

"No." Esther shuts her eyes—they feel strangely untethered. "No hospital."

She leans on him as they cross the lawn. He lays her on her couch; he stabs buttons on his little black telephone.

"Dad?" says Robert. "Dad?" A dull pressure pulses against Esther's temples.

"I saw it again," she whispers. "A tall house in a yard of thistles."

"It was a seizure, Grandmom," Robert says, peering into the screen of his phone. "You were only out for nine seconds. I timed it start to finish. You were in the garden the whole time."

"It felt like hours," Esther mumbles. "It felt like all day."

"Dad," says Robert, talking into the phone now. "She had another one." Robert explains, nods, explains some more. Then he passes the phone to Esther and she listens to her son berate her from eight thousand miles away. He says she must go to the neurology clinic in Cleveland. He says she is being pigheaded, stubborn, impossible. She says she is stronger than he is six days a week.

"Think about Robert." Her son's voice is close, cracking; he sounds as if he might still be next door. But when Esther thinks of the clinic she sees palsied faces riding elevators in chrome wheelchairs; she sees cartoon-character bedscreens behind which rest the shaved heads of children.

"This whole thing is such a fuckup," says her son. "Maybe we should just come home."

"You handle your problems," says Esther. "I'll handle mine."

She hands the phone back. Robert presses END. They eat scrambled eggs in the dimness of the kitchen. Fireflies drift and flash in the amphitheater of her huge backyard. Robert says, "Promise me. If you have one more, we'll go."

Esther looks over at him. Five-foot-two Robert in his blue sweatshirt and army shorts and flip-flops forking in mouthfuls of eggs. Robert has been recording interviews with Esther over the past several weeks for reasons she doesn't fully understand. Something to do with history classes in college. A thesis, he calls it. "Okay," she says. "I promise."

Robert walks home. Esther feels her way down the hall and climbs into bed fully clothed. Her brain swings and bangs inside her skull. These past weeks she has been sensing shapes flowing beneath the objects of her room; she has heard violin music sifting out through the backyard trees. And her senses seem to have grown more acute: She does not want to cook, or weed, or read; she wants only to lean on her elbows in the garden and watch the leaves unfurl, and thicken, and shine. Yesterday she walked the long driveway to the mailbox in a slow drizzle and paused with her hand on the fence and sat down in the gravel and stared up, and let the rain fall into her eyes, and was certain for a long moment that she could sense a silvery, restless world rippling just beneath this one.

Now in her bedroom at 9 p.m., with the lamp extinguished beside her, streams of unbidden memories rise—decades old, deeply buried. She hears the bustle and rush of Hirschfeld House, feet scrambling down the stairwell, dresses flapping on lines in the garden, dance music streaming out of the big, walnut-paneled wireless Radiola V in the parlor. Every Sabbath for eleven years Esther used to take her place at the long refectory table and look from the backs of her hands to the backs of the hands of the other girls, Miriam and Regina and Hanelore and Else arrayed around the table in prayer, and wonder about family, about heredity. Time compresses; Esther blinks into the darkness and wonders for a long moment if she is no longer in Ohio at all, but back inside the rowhouse at Number 30 Papendam, more than half a century ago, a dozen girls on two benches, a dozen young hearts thrumming beneath their sweaters, three blue streetlamps swaying in the wind outside the windows.

4.

With a key Dr. Rosenbaum scratches the soles of six-year-old Esther's feet; with a silver reflector he gazes into her pupils. He listens carefully to her description of the man and the woman and the snow blowing upward.

"Fascinating, these hallucinations," he murmurs. "Do you think she could be imagining her parents?"

Frau Cohen frowns; she does not like fanciful talk. "Is it the falling sickness?"

"Maybe," the doctor says. "More fat in her diet. Fewer sugars. Let's not pack her into the asylum just yet."

Two weeks after the seizure in the bathroom, Esther has another. Again she finds herself watching a man and woman in an unfurnished house. This time they pad down a stairwell into a twilit city. They wind between canyons of terrace houses for what seems like several hours, joining a slow march of others out in the cold. Everyone moves in the same direction. Snow lands on the shoulders of their coats and gathers in the brims of their hats.

Dr. Rosenbaum prescribes a bitter-smelling anticonvulsant called phenobarbital. It comes in a jar the size of Esther's fist. A glass dropper is slotted through the lid. Esther is supposed to swallow six drops three times a day.

A month passes. Then another. Sometimes Esther feels slow and glassy; sometimes she finds it impossible to sit still during lessons. But the drug works: Her moods stabilize; her mind does not derail.

Miriam Ingrid Bergen, a long-waisted seven-year-old with a delicate chin and a penchant for risk, takes Esther under her wing. She shows her where Frau Cohen keeps her tobacco, which bakeries will hand out scraps of dough; she explains which boys in the market are trustworthy and which are not. Together the two of them stand in the Hirschfeld House bathroom and stack their hair in various arrangements and draw ink around the rims of their eyes and laugh into the mirror until their ribs ache.

Esther spends much of the rest of her time drawing. She sketches ancient cities, tattooed giants, banners fluttering from spires. She draws fifty-story bell towers, torch-lined tunnels, bridges made from thread, strange amalgamations of imagination and what feels peculiarly like memory.

She turns seven; she turns eight. One month, it seems, no one in Hamburg is wearing armbands and the next month practically everyone is. Photos in Reich newspapers show soldiers on parade, tanks draped in roses, plantations of flags. In one picture six German fighter-bombers fly in formation, wingtip to wingtip, suspended above a mountain range of clouds. Eight-year-old Esther studies it. Spangles of sun flash from the windshields. Each pilot leans slightly forward. As if glory is a lamp dangling just beyond the blades of the propellors.

Little tin stormtroopers appear in toy shop windows, some

with flutes, some with drums, some on glossy, black stallions. Boys from other neighborhoods march past Hirschfeld House and yell crude songs up at the windows. Frau Cohen is spit on as she waits in a queue to buy cheese.

The sleeping giant is waking up, says the wireless in the living room. *A year of unprecedented victories and triumphs is behind us. Courage, confidence and optimism fill the German people.*

"Citizenships are being revoked," Frau Cohen tells the Hirschfeld girls as they sew a thicker set of drapes for the dormitory windows. "The directors say we need to start preparing for *Auswanderung.*"

Auswanderung: It means emigration. To Esther the word evokes images of butterfly migrations; desert nomads rolling up tents; the long, unpinned chevrons of geese that pass over the house in autumn.

Frau Cohen stays up late writing letters to the Youth Welfare Department, to the German-Israelite Community Office. The Hirschfeld girls are given English lessons, Dutch lessons, comportment lessons. Esther and Miriam hold hands between their cots in the winter darkness and Esther whispers destinations into the space above their beds: Argentina, Antarctica, Australia.

"I hope," Esther says, "we are sent together."

"Only children from the same family," Miriam says, "get sent together."

The radio says, *The Führer's relationship to children never ceases to move and amaze us. They approach him with complete trust, and he meets them with the same trust. He alone is to be thanked for the fact that for German children, a German life has once again become worth living.*

On Esther's ninth birthday Dr. Rosenbaum arrives with nine pencils wrapped in ribbon. "Growing up so tall," he marvels. He replenishes Esther's bottle of anticonvulsant; he asks her a series of questions about her latest illustrations. He looks for a long time at a drawing in which a miniature city sprouts from the head of a pin: tiny rooftops covered with tinier tiles, tiny flags waving from infinitesimal spires.

"Extraordinary," he declares.

At dinner all the girls sit as close as they can to Dr. Rosenbaum's wife, a tiny woman with bright silver hair who smells of cashmere and perfume. She tells the girls about bridges over the Arno, apiaries in the Luxembourg Gardens, sailboats in the Aegean. After the meal the oldest girls serve cake on the Hirschfeld House tea set, and everyone gathers around Frau Rosenbaum in the parlor to examine her picture postcards: Stockholm, London, Miami. Spiderwebs of rain fall past the windows. Violin music whispers out of the big Radiola V. Frau Rosenbaum describes the November light in Venice, how it simultaneously hardens and softens everything.

"In the evenings that light is like liquid," she sighs. "You want to drink it."

Esther closes her eyes; she sees archways, canals, staircases coiling around mile-high towers. She sees a man and a woman crouched in front of a window, cross-hatchings of snow falling beyond the glass.

When she opens her eyes, a crow is sitting on a branch just outside the window. It turns an eye toward her, cocks its head, blinks. Esther walks toward it, sets her palm against a pane. Does she see it? Just there? Something glowing between its feathers? Some other world folded inside this one?

The crow flaps away. The branch bobs.

Frau Rosenbaum murmurs another story; the girls sigh and giggle. Esther looks out into the night and thinks: We wait. We wait until everyone who knew us when we were children has died.

5.

Eighty-one-year-old Esther wakes at 6 a.m. and has to lean against the wall as she walks to the bathroom. Her whole house seems to sway back and forth, as though in the night someone has towed it four miles north and set it adrift upon the swells of Lake Erie.

The sun rises. She makes herself toast but has no appetite for it. Out in the garden a rabbit sits chewing, but Esther cannot muster the effort to scare it away. Just now her stomach feels as if it is pulsing, as if hornets are convening inside it.

A train roars to life in the distance. Esther kneels, then falls onto her side. She seizes.

In something like a dream, Esther watches Miriam Ingrid Bergen lead Hanelore Goldschmidt up the stairwell of a tall, narrow house.

Three flights, four flights. The rooms they pass have nothing in them. At the top of the stairwell Miriam pushes through a trapdoor into an attic. From twin hexagonal windows in the dormers they peer out.

Dangling fire escapes, truncated chimneys, rusted ducting. A narrow canal choked with trees. All the rooftops have weeds sprouting from between tiles; some have caved in entirely. No smoke. No trams, no lorries, no generators, no whanging hammers or clopping horses or shouting children. No surface clatter. No sheets of newsprint flying in the wind.

"Is this Hamburg?" whispers Hanelore.

Miriam doesn't answer. She is looking at a distant building perhaps twenty stories tall: the tallest building she can see. From its roof a steel-lattice radio antenna anchored with guy wires rises still higher; at its very summit a single green beacon flashes.

A flock of small black birds wheels slowly around it.

"Where is everybody?" asks Hanelore.

"I don't know," says Miriam.

They return downstairs. The other girls sit against the walls wordless and afraid and a bit hungry. Sand in their eyes. The smaller ones nodding off again. Phrases flutter between them. "No matches?" "There's no one?" "How can there be no one?" The wind, washing through the cracked windows, carries the smell of seawater. The big, empty house moans. The thistles creak.

Esther wakes up. She has another generalized seizure in her bathroom at noon. And a third in the kitchen around dusk. Each time she sees the girls she lived with as a child. They drink from a nearby canal; they collect crabapples and carry them back to the house in the pulled-up hems of their dresses. They go to sleep shivering on the floor in front of the cold hearth.

After dark Esther finds herself in her bed not entirely sure how she got there. There is a smell in the air like dust, like old paper, like nothing alive.

Leaves swish against the gutters of her house, a sound like lapping water. She cannot remember if she has eaten anything since breakfast. She knows she should call Robert but the energy to sit up and reach for the telephone will not come. Out her window, clouds blow past stars. On their huge undersides she imagines she can see the reflected wash of an antenna beacon as it flashes green, green, green.

6.

Autumn in Hamburg, 1937, and the house martins depart for the Sahara. The storks, Dr. Rosenbaum has told Esther, will travel all the way to South Africa. While all through the country Jewish people are hurrying north, in the opposite direction, toward the ports.

Signs sprout outside the butcher's, outside the theater, outside Schlösser's restaurant, always painted in the same trim calligraphy. *Juden sind hier unerwünscht.* No walks for pleasure. No smiling. No eye contact. These rules are not written down but they might as well be.

Esther is ten when the first emigration letter arrives. "The elders have arranged for Nancy to be emigrated to Warsaw," Frau Cohen announces. Several girls clap; others hold their hands over their mouths. Everyone looks at Nancy, who chews her bottom lip.

Out, away, *Auswanderung.* Warsaw: Esther imagines grand palaces, silver candlesticks, food carts rattling through ballrooms. She draws streetlamps reflected in a river and a four-wheeled carriage pulled by two white horses bedecked in bells. A trim driver with a tasseled whip rides on the box and inside a little girl in long gloves sits behind a veil of silk.

Two dawns later, fourteen-year-old Nancy Schwartzenberger stands in the hall clutching a cardboard suitcase nearly as big as she is. Inside she has crammed her Hebrew reader, several dresses, three pairs of stockings, two loaves of bread, and a china plate left to her by her deceased mother. Her carefully handwritten luggage tag is looped through the handle.

The remaining Hirschfeld girls crowd the top of the second story stairwell, still in their nightdresses, the older ones holding up the youngest so they can see. Down in the parlor Nancy is small in a white cardigan and navy blue dress. She looks as if she cannot make up her mind whether to laugh or to cry.

Frau Cohen walks her to the deportation center and comes back alone. A single letter comes from Nancy in October. *I'm sowing buttons all day. The men I came with are lyeing pavement for motorrways. This work is hard. Its awful crowded. I'd die for a latke. Bles you all.*

Through the ensuing winter rumors swirl through Hirschfeld House like tendrils of some invisible gas. The girls hear that all stores owned by Jewish people will be ransacked; they hear the government is preparing a weapon called the Secret Signal, which turns the brains of every Jewish kid to paste. They hear policemen are slipping into Jewish houses at night and shitting on dining room tables while everyone is asleep.

Each girl becomes a carrier of her own individual measure of hope, fear, and superstition. Else Dessau says the Foreign Exchange Department is allowing steamships crammed with children called *Kindertransport* to travel to England. Before departing, they may go to any department store in the city and select three traveling outfits. Regina Goldschmidt says the police are taking all the handicapped people in Hamburg to a brick house behind the Hamburg-Eppendorf hospital and sitting them in special chairs that shoot their private parts with rays. Epileptics, too, she says, and looks straight at Esther.

Gold and silver are confiscated. Driver's licenses are confiscated. Smoked herring disappears; butter and fruit become memories. Frau Cohen starts rationing paper and Esther has to resort to drawing on the edges of newspapers and in the margins of books. She draws an ogre closing a butterfly net over a platter-sized city; she draws a gargantuan crow crushing rowhouses in its beak.

Surely, Esther tells Miriam, they will be deported soon. Surely they will be welcomed elsewhere. Canada, Argentina, Uruguay. She imagines Nancy Schwartzenberger sitting down after a day's work with a dozen others, steaming dishes passing from one hand to the next. She draws the lights of chandeliers reflected in sparkling tableware.

In November of 1938 Esther and Miriam sit inside the neighborhood druggist's in a leatherette booth with three squares of chocolate between them. It's the first time Frau Cohen has allowed them out of Hirschfeld House in four days. Every customer who enters seems to know something new: The synagogues are going to be burned tomorrow; the Jewish Shipping Company will be aryanized; all the adult males in the neighborhood will be arrested.

An elderly man runs in and claims boys in jackboots and armbands are breaking windows in a shoe shop on Bender-strasse. The drugstore goes quiet. Within ten minutes the remaining customers have slipped out. Esther can feel a famil-iar, slow apprehension coiling itself around her throat.

"We should go," she tells Miriam.

The overweight druggist sits down in a booth across from Esther and Miriam. His face looks as pale and hard as a pebble of quartz. Every now and then he emits an audible whimper.

"Who's he talking to?" Miriam whispers.

Esther tugs at Miriam's sleeve. The druggist stares into nothingness.

"I hear his family has already left," Miriam whispers.

"I don't feel well," Esther says. She takes her bottle of anti-convulsant from her pocket and sets three drops onto the back of her tongue. Outside, a gang of boys pedals past, bunched over their bicycles, one trailing a long crimson flag.

The druggist's telephone, mounted to the wall behind the counter, rings five, six times. The druggist's attention flips from the telephone to the window.

"Why won't he answer the telephone?" whispers Miriam.

"We should go," whispers Esther.

"Something's wrong with him."

"Please, Miriam."

The phone rings. The girls watch. And as they do the druggist takes a razor out of his pocket and cuts his own throat.

7.

Esther is riding with Robert in his father's Nissan on the way to Foodtown when she hears a train explode to life off to her right. By reflex she glances out the passenger window across Route 20, where no cars are coming and no trains have run for decades—a pleasant midmorning light falls onto a weedy roadside lot—and her legs stiffen and the smell in the car suddenly turns sour and the streetlights appear to flare and then wink out.

Esther comes back to her senses inside the neurology center in Cleveland. A plastic EEG recording cap, studded with dozens of wired electrodes, is installed on her head. Robert sleeps in the corner chair with the hood of his sweatshirt pulled up and the strings drawn so tightly that only his nose and mouth are visible.

A nurse in a blue smock tells Esther she has had an absence that lasted almost three hours. "But you're here now," she says, and pats the back of Esther's hand.

When he's awake, Robert plays some sort of videogame on the screen of his phone, or watches quiz shows on the television mounted in the corner. Twice he has long, one-sided telephone conversations with his parents in China. She's okay, Dad. She's right here. They're doing tests.

In the evening a redheaded neurologist sits beside Esther's bed. Robert reads from questions he has written down in block printing on the torn scraps of a grocery bag. The doctor offers even-tempered answers. The lesion inside Esther's hippo-campus, he says, is almost twice as large as the last time they scanned it. They don't know why it's growing but it's surely responsible for the increased severity of her convulsions. They plan to adjust her medications, increase dosages, introduce neuroactive steroids. They will need to observe her for a week. Possibly longer.

Esther hears little of this. Everything feels watery and remote right now; the drugs make her feel as if she looks out at her room through flooded goggles. Time drifts. She listens to Robert's electronic game as it emits its anesthetic beeps. Among the ceiling tiles she watches barefoot girls tear small, pink crabapples from trees; they eat quickly, ravenously; they move about pale and strange in their undergarments with the ladders of their ribs showing; they shamble along broken streets, the smallest of them tripping now and then because her shoes are too large; they are gradually subsumed by fog and an unwavering, internal thudding, whether of Esther's heart or of some intramural hospital machinery, Esther cannot say.

Around midnight Robert leaves Esther and drives the Nissan fifty miles back to Geneva from Cleveland and sits in his parents' big kitchen alone. His college friends are hundreds of miles away and he has not stayed in touch with high school friends from town. He probably should be reading history books, working on his thesis, editing interviews he has already recorded with his grandmother. Instead, he watches half a television movie about two kids who travel back in time and eats a bowl of canned soup. Out in the yard moonlight spills through the trees.

His mother calls from China to say that his grandmother will need things: toothbrush, cholesterol pills, underwear, something to read. "Underwear?" repeats Robert and his mother, sitting on a folding chair in a government-run transition house in Changsha at 2 p.m., says, "Just do it, Robert."

Moths flutter against Esther's porch light. The entry hall feels damp and empty. Robert wipes his shoes; he walks through his grandmother's kitchen for perhaps the thousandth time. But it feels desolate tonight; it feels as if something vital has been stripped out of it.

He packs a blouse, some pants, a pair of slippers. On the table beside her bed is a novel and sticking out of its pages is a sheet of paper the size of an index card. Robert tugs the card free.

On one side is a smudged pencil drawing: a house with weeds growing out of its gutters. Five stories, two gables. Around the foundation more weeds flow outward into a broken, overgrown street.

On the other side of the card are the names and birthdates of twelve girls. It looks old: The paper is yellow, the text gray.

Name, reads the row across the top, then *Date of Birth, Date of Deportation,* and *Destination.* For each name, the dates of deportation and the destinations are the same. *29 July, 1942. Birkenau.*

Robert reads each name, going from top to bottom. *Ellen Scheurenberg. Bela Cohn. Regina Goldschmidt. Hanelore Goldschmidt. Anita Weiss. Zita Dettmann. Inga Hoffman. Gerda Kopf. Else Dessau. Miriam Ingrid Bergen. Esther Gramm.*

8.

In August of 1939, another Hirschfeld girl—Ella Lefkovits— is deported to Romania. She is seven years old. A week later

Mathilde Seidenfeld receives her own summons: She is being sent east with a distant uncle to a place called Theresienstadt. "They say it's a spa town," Mathilde murmurs. On her last unmarked sheets of paper Esther draws avenues lined with steaming pools, marble bathhouses, crystal globes glowing on top of brass poles. She writes *For Mathilde* across the bottom, tucks the drawings into Mathilde's suitcase.

In nightmares Esther burns; she sees flames chew through the draperies of the dormitories; she hears the overweight druggist gulp wetly as he slumps over in his leatherette booth. No letters come from either Ella or Mathilde. By now three new, younger orphans have replaced the deported girls at Number 30 Papendam; two of them are infants. Everyone speaks quietly; up and down Papendam passersby glance toward the sky, as if being hunted from the air.

Germany bombs London; Esther turns thirteen. She swallows her doses of anticonvulsant; she cranks in laundry from the lines in the garden. She listens to the distant sounds of ship whistles and the ringing of the harbor cranes. She speaks to Miriam about faraway places: Katmandu, Bombay, Shanghai. Miriam seldom replies.

In September a newspaper notice demands that all Jewish-owned radio sets must be delivered to collection centers by the twenty-third. Two nights later the twelve Hirschfeld girls gather in the parlor with Frau Cohen, Dr. and Frau Rosenbaum, and Julius, the old custodian, to listen to one last broadcast on the Radiola V. State programming plays an opera from Berlin. The girls perch on the sofas and along the floor with their legs crossed beneath them. The house fills with a grand, staticky voice.

Frau Cohen mends stockings. Dr. Rosenbaum paces. Frau Rosenbaum sits with her back very straight and closes her eyes for the entire performance. Every now and then she inhales deeply, as if the speaker were emitting some rare fragrance.

Afterward the girls remain seated as Julius unplugs the Radiola, loads it onto a dolly, and thumps it down the front steps. Where the radio once stood remains a rectangle of floorboards less faded than the rest.

9.

In the clinic in Cleveland Esther drifts through dizzy, medicated hours. The steroids will prevent edema, the neurologist says; the anticonvulsants will prevent more seizures.

Robert stands over her at what might be noon of her third day there with a sheet of watercolor paper and a fistful of pencils. All his life they have drawn together; as a boy he'd sit in her lap and they'd draw superheroes, spaceships, pirate galleons. He used to spend hours peering into the framed drawings Esther had hung around her house; he'd practically grown up in her lap reading children's stories she had illustrated. Mice tramping upright through a torchlit tunnel. Princesses ferrying lanterns through a forest. Now Robert pivots his grandmother's eating tray across her midsection; he props up her back with a pillow and fits the arms of her glasses over her ears.

It takes Esther a full ten seconds to coax her fingers into picking up a pencil. Robert watches patiently, standing beside her, his head tilted.

With great effort she brings the pencil to paper. In her mind she pictures a white house, eleven girls peering out of eleven windows. She traces a single line across the page. Time passes. She manages another line, then two more: a lopsided rectangle.

When she holds the paper up to the lenses of her glasses, it's a welter of faint crisscrosses. Nothing resolves out of it.

"Grandmom?" asks Robert.

Esther looks at him through tears.

10.

The house cook disappears. Julius the custodian is sent to a labor camp. No letters come from either of them. By now Frau Cohen is spending several hours a day in ration queues, deportation request queues, and paperwork queues. The oldest girls prepare meals; the younger ones wash dishes. Esther draws steamships in the margins of old newspapers: four fat smokestacks, crowds at the railings, porters on the ramps. Any moment the summons will arrive; any moment they'll be sent away, the horns will blow, the migration will begin.

In the fall of 1941, when Esther is fourteen years old, Dr. Rosenbaum misses an appointment with her for the first time. Frau Cohen sends Miriam and Esther to his clinic. The girls walk quickly, fingers interlaced; every few blocks Esther swallows back an upsurge of panic.

At his little ground floor clinic the doctor's bronze nameplate has been pried off the wall. Through a side window the girls stand between hedges and watch a fumigator pump clouds of gas into what had been his examination room. The carpet has been rolled up; the cupboard doors are gone.

"They've emigrated," decides Frau Cohen. "They are well-connected people and it was probably fairly easy for them. They waited as long as they could, and then they fled." She looks Esther in the eye. "Stay busy," she says. "You'll be with us."

Esther thinks: He would have told me. He would not have

left without telling me. She peers into her jar of phenobarbital. Inside is enough liquid to last maybe two weeks. Maybe, she thinks, the medicine was something Dr. Rosenbaum invented to prevent Frau Cohen from sending her to an asylum. Maybe it's merely sugar and water.

Esther tries three different apothecaries. Two won't let her enter. The last asks for her name, address, and identification papers. Esther scurries out of the shop. She rations herself to three drops a day. Then two. Then one.

Unexpectedly, her brain feels quicker, electrified; a night passes in which all she does is draw by candlelight: twenty-thousand cross-hatchings of pencil, dark cities full of rain, pale figures moving down snowy streets, only a few circles of white on the paper to represent streetlights. Draw the darkness, Esther thinks, and it will point out the light which has been in the paper all the while. Inside this world is folded another.

Hour by hour, day by day, her senses sharpen as her moods destabilize. She feels giddy, then anxious; she yells at Else Dessau for taking too long in the bathroom; she yells at Miriam for no reason she can articulate. At times the walls of the dormitory seem to be thinning out; lying in her cot in the middle of the night, Esther believes she can see through the floors above her into the night sky.

And one winter afternoon when the house seems particularly quiet, the toddlers napping, the older girls doing laundry in the garden, more than nine years since her first generalized seizure, Esther hears a steam engine roar to life in the distance. She stops in the hall at the top of the stairs and clenches her eyes.

"No," she whispers.

It roars toward her. Hirschfeld House vanishes; Esther walks through a lightless city at nightfall. Between the buildings are warrens and featureless alleys and stony burrows. Soot rains from the sky. Every doorway she passes is crammed with dirty, silent people. They sip gray broth or squat on their heels or study the lines of their hands. Crows flap from gutters. Leaves fly along the streets and die and rise into the air once more.

Esther wakes at the bottom of the stairs with a bone sticking out of her wrist.

11.

Esther has been at the clinic for six days when she asks Robert to take her home. He winces in the corner chair and folds himself over his knees. His shoes look huge to her; his feet seem to have grown another size in the past week. In the guts of the walls, hospital machinery makes its throbbing hum.

"I need to get out of here," she says.

Robert drags his hands through his hair. His eyes water.

"The doctor says it's best if you stay, Grandmom. Dad and Mom should be home in a week. Maybe two."

Esther works her jaw open and closed. It is increasingly difficult for her to speak. Orderlies clatter past. Somewhere a toilet flushes. How much longer can they keep her here? How much longer can she listen to this monstrous, mechanical, pounding thrum?

She looks over at her grandson, sweet Robert hunched over his knees with his curly hair and Cleveland Browns shirt.

"I need to be outside," she says. "I need to see the sky."

By her eighth day in the clinic Robert is practically crying as soon as she starts in on him. An intense urgency sweeps over Esther at unexpected times; she feels as if she has left a burner on, or a child locked in a car, and everything possible must be done to avoid catastrophe. Twice she is caught by nurses as she limps past their station in her gown in the night, barefoot, trailing an IV tube. At other times the hospital is hardly present; she cannot say how long she will be away, or where she is going.

Robert talks about the redheaded neurologist, how he seems like a good doctor. Robert's parents, he says, have made a breakthrough in China and plan to return home with the twins in fifteen days. "Fifteen days isn't long. And they take better care of you than I can. You have to wait till they release you."

Esther tries to rouse herself into full consciousness. "These drugs make me feel dead. Can't you open a window?"

"They don't open, Grandmom. Remember?"

"They don't grow up," Esther says. "The toddlers stay toddlers. The teenagers stay teenagers."

"What toddlers?"

"The girls."

Robert paces beside her bed. His tennis shoes smell of cut grass and gasoline; he has been working two days a week for a landscaper. The light coming through the window is dark green. Out beyond a parking lot, taillights slug forward along an interstate.

"That's in your head," Robert says. He twirls his father's car keys around his index finger. "The doctor says what you see is only real in your head."

"Real in my head?" whispers Esther. "Isn't everything that's real only real in our heads?"

"He says without the medications you'll have more seizures. You could die."

Esther tries to sit up. "Robert," she says. Out the window the clouds have darkened considerably. "Bobby. Look at me." Her grandson turns. "Do I look like I have a lot of time left?"

Robert bites his lower lip.

"I need to go home."

"You said that, Grandmom."

"What if they're not in my head? What if they're real? Waiting for me?"

"Waiting for you to do what?"

Esther doesn't answer.

Robert's voice quivers. "You're asking me to help you die."

"I'm asking you to help me live."

12.

The police condemn a Jewish nursing home four blocks away. Frau Cohen takes in twenty elderly people. The men cram into the parlor; the women divide themselves between the sewing room and the dormitories.

Two weeks later ten more elderly people appear at the front door. By mid-January, Number 30 Papendam brims with people, anxiety, and lice. Every Wednesday Frau Cohen boils pots of disinfectant. Displaced people are camped out in the cellar, in the custodian's closet, in the classroom, and on the floor of the dining room—a typist, a former librarian, a retired professor, merchants and jewelers. Each walls off a few square feet of floor space with suitcases, some fractured polygon in which to lay out clothes or play cards or dream.

Esther wakes at night with her wrist throbbing beneath its makeshift splint. Coughs ricochet up through the walls; girls scratch themselves in their sleep. Weeks pass without a seizure, then three or four come in a cluster: exhausting episodes, preceded by a minute or two of giddiness during which the train roars toward her and everything seems to speed up and glow, as if the walls of Hirschfeld House might incandesce.

Esther wakes to the aged faces of strangers peering down at her in equal parts concern and horror. As if they look down at something from another planet. Her handwriting goes berserk. When she walks up the stairs Miriam has to take her elbow. "You're not walking straight, Esther. You keep veering to your left." In the mirror she is a fragile, sickly creature with outsized eyes.

At meals everyone watches how much Frau Cohen spoons onto plates. Esther can feel the eyes of the men on her as she eats. In her mind she hears Regina's voice: *They're taking epileptics, too.*

Esther and Miriam spend nights hand-in-hand. A floor below a man reads aloud in Hebrew about the children of Israel. His words seem to reverberate through the tall house. *Thy walking through this great wilderness these forty years the Lord thy God hath been with thee; thou hast lacked nothing . . .*

Beyond the curtains snow taps against the windowglass. Crows blow above the leafless trees. A last few gas-burning trucks roll through the neighborhood flicking their wipers and the canals roil beneath the bridges, and from the station another train rolls steadily east, through the snow, flickering its faint lights.

13.

Robert sneaks her out of the clinic in the middle of a thunderstorm. The nurses gather at a window to watch the lightning, and Robert and Esther make straight for the elevator. They ride six flights down and walk out the sliding front doors. Rain

assaults the parking lot. They sit in the Nissan and run the
heater; the windshield wipers fly back and forth.

He says, "Shouldn't we have filled out papers or something?"

"It's not a jail," Esther says.

Robert whispers to himself as he drives. Esther leans her
head against the headrest. Her left side buzzes with a curi-
ous numbness; the thrill of escaping lingers in her chest. The
far edges of the highway seem to glow; taillights in front of
them ripple in the rain. The little car planes east. Esther closes
her eyes; she sees the blush in Bela Cohn's cheeks from warm
bathwater, all her blood vessels open. She sees the egg-shaped
face of two-year-old Anita Weiss turn up to her, eyes shining.
She sees the forehead of Regina Goldschmidt bunch into fur-
rows, threatening to tell Frau Cohen about some transgression
or another. She sees the quick, busy hands of Hanelore Goldschmidt, and the dark, wild beauty of Miriam Ingrid Bergen.
She sees Hamburg in the months before they left it: the blacked-
out windows, the gloom of Laufgraben and Beneckestrasse, the
sense that the city had become a twilit labyrinth, as if the tri-
secting realities of her life, her drawings, and her seizures had
all fused into one.

Rain pounds the windshield. The air smells like iron.
"Thank you," whispers Esther. "Thank you, Robert."

14.

Rationing. Confinement. Miriam and Esther begin spending
afternoons in the Hirschfeld House attic: a refuge strung with
cobwebs and crammed with ancient donations. Twin hexagonal windows look out over the neighboring rooftops. With
the windows open they can hear the snuffling of the confined

people in all the houses around them, whispered prayers rising through ceilings, rumors drifting along hallways, final hopes settling into walls.

In the back of the attic looms a half-ton cedar wardrobe, thick-paneled, painted white. Esther can stand on the low shelf inside without her head reaching the top. She starts spending whole afternoons up there, clambering over the old tables and lamps to kneel in the huge wardrobe and draw labyrinths with the stub of her last pencil onto the smooth, white interior panels. She draws bridges interlacing above other bridges, column-faced temples, trees growing upside-down in caverns. As if inventing a haven into which she and Miriam might flee.

It's March when Esther descends into the dining room and sees Dr. Rosenbaum talking with Frau Cohen. He's wearing a brown suit and a maroon tie and at first glance Esther decides he must not be real.

But he is. He's frighteningly thin. The hems of his trousers are pulped and one shoe is missing a lace. Half-moons of dirt are grooved under his fingernails. He embraces Esther for a long time. From a pocket he withdraws two pencils, brand-new, bright red. To Esther their very existence seems almost impossible.

She whispers in his ear. "I ran out of medicine."

"Everybody has run out of everything."

"And I've been seeing people crammed into houses. People squatting on sidewalks. Waiting for something."

Dr. Rosenbaum nods. "Like when you were little."

"There are more of them now," Esther says. Whether she means people or seizures Dr. Rosenbaum does not ask.

He was in a labor camp for nearly a year. They only released him, he says, because he is a doctor. He has not seen his wife in all that time. "Minsk," he mumbles. "They say they sent her to Minsk."

Dr. Rosenbaum spends nearly all his time at Number 30

Papendam, examining the sick, plucking nits from the children's heads, or sitting in the garden, oblivious to the cold, collar unbuttoned, coat around his shoulders, his back against a tree, his big hands in his lap like listless machines. At nights he goes to sleep amongst the men, his grizzled head laid across his leather instrument bag, his steel-framed glasses folded atop his chest. Esther sits with him whenever she can. "Minsk," she whispers. "Do you think she's happy there?"

"Happy?" asks Dr. Rosenbaum. He looks down at Esther with a look she cannot understand—it seems part heartache, part wistfulness, part amazement. He pats her head and looks away.

The days ratchet past. Frau Cohen drills her charges in ever-increasing regimentation—reading requirements, calculation speeds, Bible stories. Homework, supper, prayer, sleep. But for Esther time is beginning to disintegrate; twice in April she finds herself a block away and cannot remember how she got there. Sometimes she finds Miriam is holding her hand in the attic, or on a bench outside an unfamiliar house.

"You wandered off, Esther. You wouldn't listen to me. You kept asking me where you were."

She rests her head on Miriam's shoulder; she listens to her friend's slow, reliable breathing. "Remember the pendulum?" she asks.

Years earlier, in what seems now like a former world, Dr. Rosenbaum had taken several of the girls to the cinema for Esther's birthday. The newsreel before the film showed a temple in Paris. Inside, beneath a huge, vaulted dome, a golden ball swung from a two-hundred-foot wire. On the bottom of the ball was a pin, and as it swung on its wire, the pin scraped a design into sand scattered across the floor. Foucault's pendulum marked the turning of the Earth, said the narrator; it always swung; it never stopped.

Now, sitting with her ear against Miriam's rib cage, Esther can see the pendulum swinging above the city: huge, terrible, swinging on and on, ruthless, incessant; it grooves and regrooves its inhuman truth into the air.

15.

In Ohio Robert makes his grandmother meals, telephones his parents twice daily, and sleeps on Esther's sofa. Occasionally he opens his laptop, intending to work on his thesis, and stares at the screen for a while.

Esther seems happier, he thinks, to be at home, among her houseplants and drawings and teakettles. She can get herself dressed; with a cane she can move in a slow triangle from the bathroom to the bedroom to the kitchen. In two weeks his parents will be home; in a month Robert will be back at school.

Two days after returning from the clinic Esther is standing at her bathroom sink when the train roars in the distance. She takes a knee, then lets herself down onto the carpet. In something like a dream she watches Miriam, Hanelore, and five-year-old Ilouka Croner walk ruined, buckled streets. Gulls cruise overhead like ghosts. They pass the rusting skeleton of a crane and listen to a roof leak into a hollow warehouse and wander through factories stripped of machinery. Finally they reach the twenty-story building Miriam has been looking for. When the girls look up they can see a grid of windows narrowing as they rise and the naked struts of the huge radio antenna ascending into the sky. Its beacon flashes green, goes dark, flashes again.

The stairwell is unlocked and unlit. Hanelore leads; Miriam carries Ilouka on her shoulders. Fifteen flights, sixteen flights. At the top floor is a single door with no knob. Hanelore looks back at Miriam, then pushes it open. The entire top story is an expansive square room with no dividing walls. Six windows on each side look down onto a panorama of the city.

The girls step inside breathing heavily. In the center of the big room a chrome broadcast microphone sits in a stand on top of a wooden table. No wires lead from the microphone. There appears to be no other entrance into the space. Just twenty-four windows, several missing their glass. And the table. And the microphone on top.

Miriam lets Ilouka down. The harbor beyond the city is calm and gray beneath a slow drizzle. Along its shoreline strands of weed are strung and a wooden promenade has slumped off its piers and fields of rain fall across the water. A low, wet breeze flies through the room.

No boats winking out there. No buoys sounding their bells. Nothing on the horizon.

Rain falls on the sea. Out there fish travel in numberless schools and whales freight their colossal hearts through the cold dark. Ilouka looks up at Hanelore. "What is that?"

"It's a microphone."

"What's it for?"

"For talking to people."

"What people?"

Hanelore looks at Miriam. Miriam walks barefoot to the table in her ragged dress. She leans over the microphone. She whispers, "Esther?"

16.

"I saw Frau Rosenbaum," Esther tells Dr. Rosenbaum. He is sitting in his usual place against the tree in the garden. It's a bright spring day and several of the people working amongst the seedlings straighten and look over. "I saw her walking through a city. She was singing to herself."

Frau Cohen is washing pots in the corner of the yard. "You should be in arithmetic, Esther," she says.

Esther says, "She sang, *What can grow, grow without rain? What can burn and never end?*"

Dr. Rosenbaum sits up very straight. He looks at Esther with his palms pressed flat against the ground.

"That's enough, Esther," says Frau Cohen. To Dr. Rosenbaum she says, "She doesn't know what she's saying."

"They were in a city but they walked out of the city and through a forest into a valley full of tents. They were all moving toward these tents and the fabric of the tents was flapping in the wind. Frau Rosenbaum sang, *A stone, a stone can grow, grow without rain; Love, love can burn and never end.*"

Emotions are flowing across Dr. Rosenbaum's face like clouds; he is, Esther realizes, clutching her forearm.

"Enough, Esther!" says Frau Cohen.

"Draw it for me," whispers Dr. Rosenbaum.

She draws the scene as she remembers it on the interior of the doors of the white wardrobe with her last pencil. She draws a sprawling, smoking city with a harbor on one side and a forest on the other. At the far edge of the forest she draws hundreds of tents hemmed in by the walls of a valley. Finally she draws Frau Rosenbaum, a tiny figure in a long procession of pilgrims: silver hair, a long coat, her mouth open in song.

After three days Esther calls Dr. Rosenbaum into the attic. He climbs into the wardrobe, knees cracking. With a candle in his fist he studies the drawings; he moves his face closer; he mutters to himself.

Esther sits on the floor on her hands. The old doctor hunkers in the wardrobe, back to her, the candlelight silhouetting him. After a minute she sees him extend a long finger and lightly touch the figure of his wife amidst the inch-high rows of pilgrims.

She thinks: And when the last one of them dies, we finally die our third death.

When Dr. Rosenbaum climbs out of the wardrobe, he looks at Esther for a very long time. In the morning he's gone.

17.

Around noon, every day, Robert escorts Esther to the deck behind her house and sits her down in a patio chair beneath an umbrella. As the hours pass she swings between two versions of herself: one present, even talkative, using a cane to hobble out to the garden, staring into her honeysuckle vines, the flowers fluttering in a strange, hinged way, as if each is stirred by a different wind. She nudges a branch with the tip of her cane; the flowers become butterflies and flap away.

Then there's the other Esther, a darker, hallucinating, nauseous Esther, who arrives in the evening. Crows spiral down out of the helmet of the sky; her accent thickens; phrases of German and Hebrew stir up from recesses of her memory. She is tipped backward in time.

Four days after she leaves the clinic, the vision in Esther's left eye starts to dwindle. When she closes her right one she can watch the backyard diminish gradually: first the trees, then the grass, then the sky, until all that remains are the posts of the garden fence, like bolts of white cloth, or housedresses rippling against the encroaching gray.

Sometimes Robert reads quietly to her from the newspaper.

Sometimes he sketches in a notebook: trees, flowers, things he would not be brave enough to show his friends. And sometimes he sets his little digital recorder in front of her and asks her questions.

"Tell me about Grandpa."

"Grandpa?"

"Dad's dad."

"I was taking tickets at the theater in New Jersey. He kept buying tickets even though he wouldn't go inside to see the show. He was much younger."

Robert laughs. "How much younger?"

"A few years, I guess. But he seemed so much younger." She is quiet awhile. "After the war, it amazed me that the world could still make young people."

Robert drapes quilts over her lap, adjusts the umbrella over her head. Leaves whisper in the trees. Little trapdoors open out in the lawn and close again.

"I'm studying the war in college."

"Last year," Esther says.

"Next year, too," he says. "I'm writing a big paper on it."

"I remember you didn't like the way they taught it."

"At first it was all about armies and treaties and tanks," Robert says. "Churchill, Hitler, Roosevelt. Like it was ancient Egypt or something. Like it happened a really long time ago."

"History," she says.

"But you were alive for it. You remember it. That's what my thesis is about, remember?"

He waits but Esther doesn't say anything more. He picks up his little recorder and presses a button and sets it back down. "Were you scared, Grandmom?"

"Not of the things you might think."

"You mean like dying?"

"Yes, like dying."

"So what things did scare you?"

Esther tugs at her collar. Her glasses are smudged and her mouth is partly open and Robert cannot tell if she has more to say.

18.

In July sixteen more displaced people arrive at Hirschfeld House. Among the new faces are more Esther recognizes: a coach driver, a newspaper hawker, a furniture maker. A tobacco-starved grocer in creaking shoes. None of them seems to know what has happened to Dr. Rosenbaum.

The weather turns hot. The house is unbearably crowded and there is not enough food. Toilets overflow; washrooms bulge and reek. Frau Cohen boils vats of sheets in the garden. Through the open attic windows Miriam and Esther imagine they can smell roasting goose, tomato soup, meals from long ago.

Esther turns fifteen. She feels, all the time, as if she has some important appointment looming, the details of which she can no longer remember. Often she fails to answer questions that are put to her. More than once Regina Goldschmidt, directly in front of Esther, asks Frau Cohen to take Esther to the hospital.

"We can't keep her here any longer," Regina says. "She's getting worse."

Frau Cohen's once thick arms are visibly thinning; her hair sits across her skull limp and gray. She clears her throat. "Regina—"

"We can just tell a policeman," Regina says. "Surely he'll help us."

"Surely he won't!" cries Miriam. "I'll watch her. Let me take care of her."

Frau Cohen runs her palms down her apron; she sends the girls away.

Miriam and Esther move their cots to the attic. On July 26, four hundred and three English aircraft bomb Hamburg at midnight. Miriam and Esther watch from the attic windows. Spotlights spring up from points around the harbor. Hundreds of filaments of red light ascend from hidden gun emplacements. At their apexes the threads bloom into ganglia of red flak, white in their centers.

Esther presses herself to the floor. "We should get downstairs," she whispers.

Miriam does not take her eyes from the window. "You can go."

All through Number 30 Papendam people wake and listen to the sirens and the pounding of the antiaircraft guns; they troop silently to the cellar and huddle together in the darkness.

Esther stays with Miriam. Deliberately, almost lazily, the airplanes descend over the city. Bright streaks of tracer bullets come flashing up from the dark. The airplanes slip lower; they hold formation. At some signal bombs drizzle out of their bellies all at once: In a blink thousands of black spots are pouring through illuminated wedges of sky. The bombers scramble. The bombs fall diagonally.

Esther thinks: Swarms of locusts. Flocks of birds.

From their dormer windows the girls watch incendiaries fall through rooftops twenty blocks away and their casings open into light. White, phosphoric flames flow like water into gutters. Within seconds independent fires have linked up; soon entire houses are in flames. Above them clouds of smoke and ash bloom in harlequin colors: red, green, orange. Whole quarters of sky flare, then are sucked back into darkness. It feels to Esther as if she is staring up into a vast, electric brain. And from the brain little flaming sheets of paper and pillows and books and shingles rain slowly down over the city.

She sees a golden pendulum swing through space. She hears a woman's voice tell an old story: *And the light broke over the world and it broke into a thousand thousand pieces, and these pieces fell into all events and all creatures.*

She wipes her eyes.

"Oh, oh, oh," whispers Miriam. *"Schön, am schönsten."* Beautiful, the most beautiful.

19.

In Ohio seizures flow through Esther. A steady electrochemical pulsing washes up out of her temporal lobe and overtakes the coordinated firing of her consciousness. Her arms stiffen, her head falls back. The seizures no longer seem to impair her consciousness so much as amplify it. Through her right eye she can see Robert turn her on her side and hold her hand; through her left she watches shadows eclipse the trees.

Maybe, she tells Robert, during her clearest moments, a person can experience an illness as a kind of health. Maybe not every disease is a deficit, a taking away. Maybe what's happening to her is an opening, a window, a migration. Maybe that's what Dr. Rosenbaum saw in her; maybe that's what he was thinking as he stared into the white wardrobe that afternoon up in the attic of Number 30 Papendam: that there was something in her worth saving.

Robert nods uneasily. He brings her soup; he brings her triangles of toast. He tells his parents Esther is doing better. He tells them she is as indestructible as ever.

In seizures Esther watches Miriam walk the girls in groups through the abandoned city to the tall building with the radio mast on its roof. The girls look up at the flashing beacon at the very top and then they climb the long flights to the twentieth floor. Their voices come to Esther in the bathroom, in bed, on the deck in full daylight. She sits very quietly; the leaves rustle; she hears the faintest scratch of a girl's voice, riding along beneath the breeze. She hears a little girl say, "But it's not even hooked up."

"I'll go," a third voice says, suddenly amplified. "Papa worked in a furniture store. We lit candles on Fridays, kept the Sabbath. Even after I was sent to Hirschfeld House I thought everybody did the same. It wasn't until I saw the signs and asked Frau Cohen what they meant that I knew we were Jewish."

Or: "Okay. Right. I had an uncle in the United States. When I was thirteen—this was years after my parents were gone—Frau Cohen wrote him a letter asking if he could sponsor a trip. For me. Whether he could find me a place to live, feed me, all that. Get me out of Hamburg. I told her not to write that he'd have to feed me. I told her to tell him I could find my own food. My uncle wrote back right away. *Things are tight here,* he wrote."

A long pause. Esther closes her eyes. She hears the voice say, "He didn't know."

Sometimes she sees the girls above her garden. They trudge up a long, switchbacked staircase, the youngest holding the hands of the oldest; they sit up on the twentieth floor in the big square room, a quarter mile above Esther's yard, taking their turns at the microphone, some of them lying down with their hands laced behind their heads, listening to the harbor wind streak through the broken windows, a hundred feet above the treetops.

Esther whispers their names into the darkness of the backyard. Ellen, Bela, Regina, Hanelore, Anita, Zita, Inga, Gerda, Else, Miriam. Robert is at her elbow. "Tell me about them," he says.

"Anita Weiss had a lisp. She used to catch her tongue between her teeth. Zita could never keep the hair out of her eyes. Regina had a widow's peak. The other girls said she was mean but I think she was always afraid. She didn't trust that anything could be permanent."

"Who was your best friend?"

"Miriam," Esther murmurs. "I loved her. She was older than me. Just a few years younger than you are now."

Robert hands her a mug of tea. A minute passes, or an hour. Why, Esther wonders, do any of us believe our lives lead outward through time? How do we know we aren't continually traveling inward, toward our centers? Because this is how it feels to Esther when she sits on her deck in Geneva, Ohio, in the last spring of her life; it feels as if she is being drawn down some path that leads deeper inside, toward a miniature, shrouded, final kingdom that has waited within her all along.

Robert's parents call from China; they need a certain lawyer's phone number; they need Robert to deliver something to his father's office. They plan to be home by the fifth of July. They want to know if Robert needs them home sooner.

"It's not awful," says Robert. "Being with her. It's sort of amazing, actually." He is quiet awhile; his mother breathes on the other end. "But I don't know how much longer I can do it."

That afternoon he pulls a two-wheeled bike trailer made for children from the depths of his parents' garage. He straps seat cushions inside, mounts it behind his bicycle; in the evening he helps Esther into the trailer and pulls her down their long street.

They go slowly; he avoids traffic and hills. That night they ride for a full hour, through the dusk and into the moonlight, passing farms and occasional subdivisions, down the long, flat, rural roads of northeastern Ohio, maybe one car passing every ten minutes, and Esther feels as if she is being pedaled through a half-world of shimmering trees and fields and water towers and great flexing pools of shadow. In the distance, over Lake Erie, hazy thunderheads stack up in coral-colored towers. Robert pedals hard and with great seriousness, and Esther feels the blood pumping through her.

"Are you comfortable, Grandmom?" Robert asks, turning around, panting.

"More than you know," Esther says.

20.

On July 28 the summons finally arrives for the Hirschfeld girls. The eagle and the cross on an envelope. No stamp. As if delivered from the office of God. Frau Cohen calls the girls from their various chores; they sit facing her while she unfolds her reading glasses.

Around them a thousand houses in Hamburg smolder. Around them prisoners of war load bodies onto wagons and sailors drowse over their guns. In the garden behind the orphanage a former bank manager rakes between rows of cabbages.

They are to travel on foot to a school gymnasium beside the Central Hotel. From there a deportation agent will escort them to the Ludwigslust railway station. There are long, meticulous lists of what it is advisable to bring—nightdresses, mittens, candles, shoe polish, eyeglasses—and what is not advisable—rugs, plants, books, matches. There are directions for how everything should be labeled and conveyed; each girl is given a deportation number.

Where, where, where. Regina Goldschmidt finally gets the question out first. The girls lean closer to hear the reply; several clamp their hands over their hearts. Frau Cohen flips through the papers.

"Warsaw."

Esther tries to catch her breath. She has the sense that if she lets herself blink, she will see another world rippling beneath this one. Warsaw—how many times has she imagined Nancy Schwartzenberger's life there? She tries to remember Frau Rosenbaum's picture postcards. Old town. Wilanów Palace. The Vistula River.

All afternoon the girls pack their things. Esther concentrates—candles, shoe polish, nightdress, arithmetic book. Underwear, birth certificate, thread. She thinks of Nancy Schwartzenberger sewing buttons. How old will Nancy be now? How exciting if they can manage to meet up with her!

Maybe, Esther decides, they will have more space in Warsaw. Maybe there will be apothecaries with white gloves and loaded shelves.

Auswanderung. The paths of the birds.

At the other end of the attic nine-year-old Hanelore Goldschmidt besieges Miriam with questions: Will there be school? What about gymnastics? What kind of animals will they have? Will we be allowed to go to the zoo? Miriam goes downstairs, helps Hanelore choose among her few possessions. Before supper the girls carry their suitcases to the front door and leave them in a row with their tags bristling from the handles, all of it to be brought in wheelbarrows to the station in the morning.

After prayers Esther and Miriam climb the staircase to the attic and push open the trapdoor. They lie down beside the big white wardrobe. The attic beams tick in the heat; spiders draw their webs between rafters.

"Warsaw can't be worse than this," Esther says.

Miriam says nothing.

"Don't you think so?"

Miriam rolls onto her side. "The only thing I've learned so far, Esther," she says, "is that things can always get worse."

Beside her friend in the attic that night Esther slips into dreams and when she comes back into herself it is very late. Not a single light shines out the window. Someone is walking hunched through the furniture around her. The figure stoops in front of the girls' cots for a long moment. Watery breathing. Cracking knees. Miriam sleeps.

"Dr. Rosenbaum?" He looks thinner than ever in the gloom of the attic.

"Very quiet," he whispers.

"What's happening?"

"Shhh."

She thinks: He came to say goodbye. In the morning we're leaving, so he came to say goodbye to me.

"Your dress," he says. "The coat, too."

She pulls on stockings, laces her shoes. Miriam does not stir. Esther follows Dr. Rosenbaum down five flights of stairs, past sleeping children and muttering crones and doomed men at last into the parlor, where he peers with all his attention through a gap in the curtains. Someone snores at the other end of the room. Someone else coughs.

Are they leaving so early? Why not wait until morning?

Every time she tries to ask him something, he hushes her. Out in the street the springs of a truck ring dully as its tires rattle across the cobbles. "The curfew—" Esther says, and Dr. Rosenbaum hisses, "Now," and hurries her out of the house and through the gate. The truck's headlights are not running and Papendam is very dark. The truck's back swings open; inside is a void, a blankness out of which scared faces slowly bloom: The truckbed is stuffed with people.

"Hurry," says Dr. Rosenbaum.

"But Miriam!" cries Esther. "My bag!"

"Go," says Dr. Rosenbaum, and pushes her in.

21.

Eleven murdered girls wake up on the floor of a tall, unremarkable rowhouse. Esther wakes in her bed in Ohio, her grandson asleep down the hall on the couch. Frau Cohen wakes at Number 30 Papendam in 1942, washes her face, and pulls on her cleanest housedress. She laces her shoes, pauses on the threshold of the kitchen, and sends up her requests to God. Please watch over us as we begin our journey. Please don't let me falter.

Within the wet enclosure of a single mind a person can fly from one decade to the next, one country to another, past to present, memory to imagination. Why Esther and not Miriam? Why not any of the others? Why did Dr. Rosenbaum choose her? Getting Esther out of Hamburg cost him everything: certainly all his money, perhaps his life. Was Esther the one good thing he could do, the one thing he could smuggle out?

She wakes in a cottage in the woods. The ceiling is low and the furniture is roughhewn. Old pickaxes and sawblades and crampons are fixed haphazardly to the walls—the effect is of a rusting, historical suffocation. The cupboards are dens of superstition: filled with a putrescent reek, jars of dark elixirs, unlabeled pain remedies, molasses, crystals, something marked "belladonna," something marked "trumpet of death." Out the tiny windows hundreds of birch trunks gleam bone white against the dawn. A home to forest people involved in some dark, gnomish magic.

In front of the cottage Dr. Rosenbaum is asleep on a log bench without a blanket to cover him. She fears he is dead but when she says his name he opens his eyes.

"What happened?"

"You seized. We brought you here."

"I don't remember."

Birds flit here and there, crying thinly. The sky is colorless.

"I should be with *them*," Esther whispers.

"You're tired," Dr. Rosenbaum says. "This has been an ordeal." As if this were it, as if now it were over. Esther hears herself whisper to Miriam, years before, in the darkness of the dormitory: *I hope we are sent together.*

Dr. Rosenbaum smiles at her. "It's best to stay inside." She spends the day washing in and out of nightmares. Dr. Rosenbaum boils a pot of turnips; he sits with her and holds her hand. In the evening he hands her a letter handwritten in English, a sheaf of British pounds, and an address in London.

"When the truck comes back," he says, "I'll return to Hamburg."

Esther's vision swims with fear. "No. Please. Miriam. And the others."

Dr. Rosenbaum squeezes her hand between his two big, cold palms. "Where they are going, you do not want to go."

Esther tries to compose a sensible protest.

231

"Go live your life, Esther." An hour later he's gone. She is picked up that night by a man with six other children riding in a trailer beneath a sheet of canvas; they ride together through the dawn. A boy whispers that they have entered Denmark; another argues they are going to Belgium. One of them has wet himself and soon their rocking, lightless compartment reeks of urine. At midmorning the man hides them in a windowless, dirt-floored, seven-by-seven cellar.

They spend the next thirty-six hours there, a girl's hip pressed into Esther's shoulder, a young boy sniffling against her other side, the yelps of faraway dogs and the long silences of nightfall and the rumbles of airplanes passing far above. Rumors ripple between the children: They are being sent to Ireland, or England, or South America; a boy repeats, "We are going somewhere better," over and over, as if saying it will make it so. Twice someone unlocks the door and pitches in a loaf of hard, dark bread and locks the door again.

In that place Esther's face is crammed up against a board and in the board is a large, dark knot. All through the daylight hours she stares into that knot and sweats into her nicest dress until there is no longer any water in her to sweat out. Over and over the words pass through Esther's mind: *I should be with them.* She watches the Hirschfeld girls climb the stairs of a glowing palace in Warsaw. The doors open; the girls step into a white foyer. They stare up into the thousand glittering diamonds of a chandelier. Someone in uniform comes down a long staircase to greet them. The doors slowly close. The light fades.

The cellar smells of sweat, hunger, terror, and human waste. The others know no more and no less. Whenever there is enough light Esther stares into the knot of wood until its grains squirm with miniscule figures, carriages and trams, streetlamps and little coachmen dressed in velvet carrying whips, weathered houses and naked trees, and the more she stares into it she realizes it contains a dark city, alive, microscopic, teeming with people and rain and grime.

Twice Esther has grand mal seizures down there in the darkness. Her legs rattle against the slatted walls as the others try to hold her still, someone's hand clamped over her mouth, someone else holding her on her side. She sees Miriam Ingrid Bergen riding a train, peering out a window, one of the younger girls in her lap. She sees a family waiting out in the darkness.

After the second day the children are smuggled to London onboard a fishing boat with guns newly welded to its bow. In Anglia, Esther shows a longshoreman her money and the letter from Dr. Rosenbaum. She is taken to a clinic where a man in a doctor's coat gives her a set of secondhand clothes, a bottle of phenobarbital, and emigration papers for the United States.

22.

Inga Hoffman says, "There was a Jewish shoe store on Benderstrasse. The night they were breaking all the windows we watched a boy smash through the door and crawl inside. His father waited outside and when the boy came out with four pairs of shoes he looked down at the boy and scolded him. I thought he was scolding him for stealing but he was scolding him because one of the pairs he had taken had two right shoes. He sent the boy back in to correct the problem." She tries a laugh but it comes across closer to a gasp.

Little Zita Dettmann says, "Not everyone was mean to us.

Two ladies left a crate of pastries on the front steps. Do you remember that? I put one in my mouth right away. Inside was strawberry jam. Strawberry jam!"

An even smaller voice sings, *One little goat, one little goat, which my father bought for two zuzim . . .*

Gerda Kopf says, "You hear stuff like your whole life passes in front of your eyes. But it's not true. A life is really big, it contains a billion things, as many needles as there are on a pine tree. There's no music, but there is a sound, like a far-off screech. Or smoke rising. Or like a woman inhaling a little, like she's about to sing."

A pause. A shuffling. Esther sits in the backyard and rain thrums on the umbrella Robert has braced over her. A sweetness rises in the air, rich, intertwining—hollyhock, rain on grass. Esther hears Regina Goldschmidt's voice wash through the trees. "The lady at the end of the block had no home. Everyone called her Mrs. Glasses. She slept on the sidewalk for years. The other girls would say: Why doesn't she just leave? I knew why. Mrs. Glasses had nobody. She had given up. I brought her a hairbrush because her hair was disgusting. And then I got to thinking she was cold and so I gave her my red scarf, too. My brown one was nicer anyway. Then I brought her the afghan with the colored circles on it from the cupboard in Frau Cohen's room. I set it down beside Mrs. Glasses while she was sleeping. Her hands were scaly, I remember, and I was glad she didn't wake up. Two days later the police took her away for stealing and I didn't say anything. I never saw Mrs. Glasses again. None of us did. That's my memory. That's what I remember."

The rain slows. The leaves drip. The garden steams.

23.

The Jewish Rescue Authority places Esther with a childless couple in New Jersey coincidentally named the Rosenbaums. They are first-generation Romanian immigrants and they live on a two-bedroom houseboat. At the tiny table in what the Rosenbaums call their galley they feed Esther meals that seem obscenely large: slabs of eggplant, hunks of chicken, steaming bowls of green bean soup. Three times a day the three of them sit down to eat at that table, in that floating house that smells of bilgewater and foot cream and baklava.

Esther writes Miriam every day. Mr. Rosenbaum bundles the letters in groups of six and mails them from the post office in Toms River. Where they go, who they reach, what hands dispose of them, Esther will never know.

Stories of the camps trickle into the newspapers; they are all Mrs. Rosenbaum can talk about. Why? is the question Esther continually asks herself. Why did Dr. Rosenbaum save her, why was she pulled out, why not Hanelore, Regina, Else? Why not Miriam?

She swallows a steady stream of anticonvulsants. She sells tickets at the movie theater. She tries to believe that the world can be a reasonable place. But most days the silence of her cramped, chilly room on the Rosenbaums' boat overwhelms her: lit an eerie blue from a pier light outside, no voices of children, no music, only distant foghorns and ropes chiming mournfully against masts, everything rocking back and forth.

Memory becomes her enemy. Esther works on maintaining her attention only in the present; there is always the now— an endlessly adjusting smell of the wind, the shining of the stars, the deep five-call chirrup chirrup of the cicadas in the park. There is the now that is today falling into the now that is tonight: dusk on the rim of the Atlantic, the flicker of the movie screen, a submergence of memory, a tanker cleaving imperceptibly across the horizon.

It is never warm enough. She buys spring dresses and quilted jackets and walks to the theater on a hot day but feels some deep chill within her.

Esther is twenty-six and fluent in English when she meets the boy who will become her husband. He is small and gregarious and perpetually on the brink of loud and catching laughter. He meets her at the movie theater; he is a hospital orderly but he wants to be a bicyclist; he dreams of opening a bicycle shop; he sits her down on park benches and tells her about his plans. They'll go somewhere far away, they'll sell bikes, they'll repair them, they'll have a family.

The contents of his plans are not nearly as important to Esther as their sound—the deep sureness of them. And his voice! He has a soft voice, a voice like a piece of silk you might remove from a drawer only very occasionally, something you'd want to run your hands over again and again.

That she can be alive with this boy—share vanilla ice cream; stroll through markets, buy cabbages big as cannonballs—sometimes fills Esther with a paralyzing, breathtaking shame. Why should she get to see this? While the other girls could not? She feels as if pieces of her are barely held together—if she lets up for a moment, she will fly apart.

And yet isn't there a blessedness, too? Isn't she beginning to breathe again, the way an animal might breathe after running from a predator for a long time, and finally slowing, and looking up, and watching the leaves wave overhead in their multitudes? She was alive, she was still alive. She could lay her head on this boy's chest and listen to the tumble of his heartbeat. She could stare at the crystal doorknob of her tiny ticket taker's booth for an entire afternoon, a pad of drawing paper in her lap, waiting for the evening sunlight to come through the left-hand window at the right angle. When it finally does it sprays prisms of color across the wall.

She and the boyfriend move to Ohio. They get married; they get a loan; they start his bicycle shop. Everything is round: rims, tires, sprockets, chain loops. Everything smells of chain grease; everyone pays in cash.

The arch of a handlebar, sweeping back to the grips. Thirty spoked wheels hanging from hooks; freewheels and hubs; chain stays and cranks; the concentric spirals of painted chain guards. A rack of bells: chrome, brass, aluminum. Suspended from a beam are hundreds of rims. Round-headed screws gleaming in pails. Bearings in jars, bearings in buckets. Sheaves of spokes tied with strips of cloth.

Esther works the cash register or opens her sketchpad on the glass counter and draws while her husband fiddles with a series of portable radios, a spectrum of American stations: country, jazz, folk, swing.

They have a son. After school he draws beside his mother at the counter, the two of them working on matching sheets of paper, and when he gets older he works beside his father, running the links of a salvaged bicycle chain back and forth through a basin of oil, watching the rust fall away, feeling the rivets ride cleanly in their bushings, lubricant beading in the little golden hairs on his wrists.

Out, away, *Auswanderung*. Esther builds for herself as modest and normal and steady a life as she can manage. She is not allowed to drive a car, her medication continues to give her upset stomachs, and occasionally she is seized with wild, clutching feelings of dread. At times her wrist throbs; she feels indistinct, and wonders if she might have died in that cellar with the knothole, and considers the possibility that every-thing that has come after has been a dream. She reaches for her husband's shape in the night; she clings to him.

It's Mrs. Rosenbaum, still living on her houseboat in New Jersey, who sends her the deportation manifest. Esther is thirty-five years old when it arrives; it waits in the mailbox between a utility bill and an advertising flyer. Inside the first envelope is a second, and Esther waits two days to open it. By then she has decided that she knows what it will say.

She thinks: The others will be there but maybe Miriam will not. How could Miriam die? Miriam was never a person with illusions; she had always had the strength of her own pragma-tism. Maybe only the deluded had been slaughtered. But of course everyone was slaughtered.

Forty cards. Several of them have hundreds of names on them.

It is easy enough to find July 29, 1942. Twelve birthdates, twelve girls. Miriam's name among them. Esther's, too.

24.

Robert's voice grows fainter, as if Esther is receding behind him, as if he is still pulling her behind his bicycle and the trailer has uncoupled and the boy has pedaled off without noticing. Finally all Esther can hear as she sits on her deck on the last day of her life is Miriam's voice. The backyard is gray at every hour; Robert is little more than a warm presence.

"At the edge of the city we found a forest," Miriam's voice says, "and we'll have to go all the way through the forest. And then at the end we'll climb a hill and when we reach the top, down below is mist, Esther, a thick ribbon of it, hiding the view. The vapors fall and condense and whirl around themselves.

But sometimes they part for a moment, and down there in that valley I saw a thousand tents, Esther, ten thousand maybe, each with a lamp burning inside it, all of them rustling and flapping in a breeze. A whole city of golden tents glowing down there beneath the mist."

There is a pause. Then: "We're going there, Esther. You and me. All of us."

<h2 style="text-align:center">25.</h2>

At dusk on the fourth of July the woods echo with the explosions of neighbors' fireworks. Robert nails a Catherine wheel to a tree and it sprays rainbows out into the night.

Esther sits on the deck with a blanket around her legs and a dreamy, lost expression on her face. Whenever Robert asks if she is uncomfortable it takes her a little while to reply that she is fine. At this very moment his parents are thirty-thousand feet above the Pacific, two little girls asleep in the seats between them.

The wheel spews a last paroxysm of sparks. The darkness reasserts itself. Robert clicks on a flashlight and rummages through his box for another firework. Fireflies float and flash in the trees.

"What about one more, Grandmom? We've got tons of these."

Esther doesn't reply. Robert says, "Okay, let's do a big one." He sets his lighter to a wick and the wick burns down and a rocket fizzes into the sky.

Esther's gaze casts up through a thousand leaves, a sea of them shifting against a flower of noiseless, golden sparks. Which part of them is her, and which part is the rest of the world? She tips backward onto the lawn. The sparks fall through the sky. A locomotive stampedes through her head.

When Esther wakes, it's night. She can feel the sanded planks of a floor beneath her knees, a windowsill beneath her fingernails. Out the window, clouds blow past stars. The more Esther looks, the more stars she sees.

Somewhere below her a little girl's voice is calling hello. Esther feels her way to the doorway. It is pitch dark in the hall. An old fear returns, rising in her chest, climbing her throat. She finds a stairwell; there is a wobbling banister. One flight, two flights. There's a bit more light on the first floor, starlight washing through curtainless windows.

No furniture. No doors on the cupboards. Again she hears a voice, calling from somewhere outside. Esther finds the front door. Beyond is a harbor wind, and a sky swarming with infinitesimal lights.

Standing in the belt-high thistles are eleven girls, their faces smears of white in the darkness. Miriam is easy to spot: the tallest of them. Barefoot. Regal in her tattered dress. She takes Esther by the hand and helps her climb down out of the doorway. "We've been waiting," Miriam says, and smiles a sweet-faced smile. Esther breathes. The wind settles. The twelve of them stand in the thistles looking back for a moment at the empty house crouched there in the night. Then they all start walking down the street.

26.

Robert is a senior in college; he's home for Thanksgiving. Five days, seven inches of snow, twenty degrees. It's the first snowfall of the year and everything is familiar and new all at once:

the leafless hardwoods ringing his parents' house; the mingling smells of slush, gasoline, and firewood in the garage; the confused, wondrous looks on the faces of his two four-year-old sisters as they look out the living room windows into snow for the first time.

His father slices carrots in the kitchen. His mother wrestles the girls into matching pink snowsuits. Out the windows everything is either gray or white. The radio murmurs another storm warning; the twins stand very still as their mother pushes mittens over their hands.

Robert leads them out through the garage. A last few snowflakes slip down from the clouds. The girls plod through Robert's tracks in tandem, heads down, into the big, white amphitheater of the backyard. They stand together amidst the falling white. Then the girls' exuberance surges; they run out in front of Robert; they laugh, they fall down, and roll over, and squeal. Robert lopes after them, hands in his pockets.

After a few minutes the girls trudge between the naked willows at the left edge of the yard and disappear into what was once Esther's property. Now it's vacant, a realty sign covered with snow at the end of her driveway.

Every tree, every post of the garden fence, is a candle to a memory, and each of those memories, as it rises out of the snow, is linked to a dozen more. Over there is the birdfeeder Robert broke his wrist trying to hang; over there Esther helped him bury his parakeet named Marbles. He used to throw a football onto the section of the roof above that garage window and wait for it to come rolling off the gutter. He shot a squirrel out of that locust tree and carried its body on the blade of a shovel to the compost pile. He made tie-dyed T-shirts one summer day with his grandmother in the same spot where his sisters' little boot prints now crisscross the snow.

The girls are throwing snow up into the air and watching it glitter as it sifts down around them. One yells, "You are, you are!" and takes a few running steps and then falls down onto her hands and knees. Robert helps her up. Already the heat from her face has melted the snow on it. "You're okay," he says.

Every hour, Robert thinks, all over the globe, an infinite number of memories disappear, whole glowing atlases dragged into graves. But during that same hour children are moving about, surveying territory that seems to them entirely new. They push back the darkness; they scatter memories behind them like bread crumbs. The world is remade.

In the five days Robert will be home his sisters will learn to say "rocks," "heavy," and "snowman." They'll learn the different smells of snow and the slick feel of a plastic sled as their brother drags them down the driveway.

We return to the places we're from; we trample faded corners and pencil in new lines. "You've grown up so fast," Robert's mother tells him at breakfast, at dinner. "Look at you." But she's wrong, thinks Robert. You bury your childhood here and there. It waits for you, all your life, to come back and dig it up.

Now the girls are clawing sticks out of the snow and tracing shapes with them. Above them the clouds shift and—abruptly—sunlight avalanches across the yard. The shadows of trees lunge across the lawn. The snow seems to incandesce. Robert has forgotten that sunlight can look so pure, pouring out of the sky, splashing across the snow. It brings tears to his eyes.

Jing-Wei, the taller of the girls, lifts a long, black branch out of the snow and tries to hand it to him. "For Rob-ert," she says, and blinks up at him.

Acknowledgments

Thanks to the American Academy in Rome and the Idaho Commission on the Arts for financial help while I worked on this book. I'm also indebted to Wendy Weil, Nan Graham, and Susan Moldow for their continued confidence in my work. Lots of folks helped with particular stories, especially Rachel Sussman, Rob Spillman, Ben George, and Laura Furman with "Village 113"; Cheston Knapp with "The River Nemunas"; Matt Weiland and Helen Gordon with "Procreate, Generate"; and Jordan Bass with "Afterworld" and "Memory Wall." My mother, Marilyn Doerr, offered useful feedback on all six stories; watching her care for her mother taught me about patience, love, and the fragility of memory.

This book is for Shauna: wife, editor, counselor, best friend.

About the Author

Anthony Doerr is the author of three books, *The Shell Collector, About Grace,* and *Four Seasons in Rome.* Doerr's short fiction has won three O. Henry Prizes, a National Magazine Award, and a Pushcart Prize, and has been anthologized in *The Best American Short Stories, The Anchor Book of New American Short Stories,* and *The Scribner Anthology of Contemporary Fiction.* He has won the Barnes & Noble Discover Prize, the Rome Prize, and the New York Public Library's Young Lions Fiction Award. In 2007, *Granta* placed Doerr on its list of twenty-one Best Young American novelists. Doerr teaches in the MFA program at Warren Wilson College, and he lives in Boise, Idaho, with his wife and two sons.